AF767285

Praise for Lynn Cahoon and Her Irresistible Cozy Mysteries

AN AMATEUR SLEUTH'S GUIDE TO MURDER
"The prolific Lynn Cahoon starts another winning cozy series!"
—*Criminal Element*

"Cahoon launches a promising new series with endearing characters and a charming locale."
—*Kirkus Reviews*

"Plan a cozy day by the fire with a cup of tea, snuggle in, and enjoy. The day will be over before you know it. And there may even be time to make Lynn's Yummy Murderous Mac and Cheese for dinner."
—Nancy Coco, author of the Candy-Coated Mysteries

"If you love cozy mysteries, you will love *An Amateur Sleuth's Guide to Murder*—a delightful mixture of a practical guidebook and a clever fictional mystery."
—Valerie Burns, author of the Mystery Bookshop Mysteries

FIVE FURRY FAMILIARS
"A fun read for those who enjoy tales of witches and magic."
—*Kirkus Reviews*

THREE TAINTED TEAS

"A kitchen witch reluctantly takes over as planner for a cursed wedding . . . This witchy tale is a hoot."

—*Kirkus Reviews*

ONE POISON PIE

"*One Poison Pie* deliciously blends charm and magic with a dash of mystery and a sprinkle of romance. Mia Malone is a zesty protagonist who relies on her wits to solve the crime, and the enchanting cast of characters that populate Magic Springs are a delight."

—Daryl Wood Gerber, Agatha winner and nationally bestselling author of the Cookbook Nook and Fairy Garden Mysteries

"A witchy cooking cozy for fans of the supernatural and good eating."

—*Kirkus Reviews*

A FIELD GUIDE TO HOMICIDE

"The best entry in this character-driven series mixes a well-plotted mystery with a romance that rings true to life."

—*Kirkus Reviews*

"Informative as well as entertaining, *A Field Guide to Homicide* is the perfect book for cozy mystery lovers who entertain thoughts of writing novels

themselves . . . This is, without a doubt, one of the best Cat Latimer novels to date."
—*Criminal Element*

"Cat is a great heroine with a lot of spirit that readers will enjoy solving the mystery (with)."
—*Parkersburg News & Sentinel*

SCONED TO DEATH

"The most intriguing aspect of this story is the writers' retreat itself. Although the writers themselves are not suspect, they add freshness and new relationships to the series. Fans of Lucy Arlington's 'Novel Idea' mysteries may want to enter the writing world from another angle."
—*Library Journal*

OF MURDER AND MEN

"A Colorado widow discovers that everything she knew about her husband's death is wrong . . . Interesting plot and quirky characters."
—*Kirkus Reviews*

A STORY TO KILL

"Well-crafted . . . Cat and crew prove to be engaging characters and Cahoon does a stellar job of keeping them—and the reader—guessing."
—*Mystery Scene*

"Lynn Cahoon has hit the golden trifecta—Murder, intrigue, and a really hot handyman. Better get your flashlight handy, *A Story to Kill* will keep you reading all night."
—Laura Bradford, author of the Amish Mysteries

TOURIST TRAP MYSTERIES

"Lynn Cahoon's popular Tourist Trap series is set all around the charming coastal town of South Cove, California, but the heroine Jill Gardner owns a delightful bookstore/coffee shop so a lot of the scenes take place there. This is one of my go-to cozy mystery series, bookish or not, and I'm always eager to get my hands on the next book!"
—*Hope By the Book*

"Murder, dirty politics, pirate lore, and a hot police detective: *Guidebook to Murder* has it all! A cozy lover's dream come true."
—Susan McBride, author of the Debutante Dropout Mysteries

"This was a good read and I love the author's style, which was warm and friendly . . . I can't wait to read the next book in this wonderfully appealing series."
—*Dru's Book Musings*

"I am happy to admit that some of my expectations were met while other aspects of the story exceeded my own imagination . . . This mystery novel was light, fun, and kept me thoroughly engaged. I only wish it was longer."

—*The Young Folks*

"*If the Shoe Kills* is entertaining and I would be happy to visit Jill and the residents of South Cove again."

—*MysteryPlease.com*

"In *If the Shoe Kills,* author Lynn Cahoon gave me exactly what I wanted. She crafted a well told small town murder that kept me guessing who the murderer was until the end. I will definitely have to take a trip back to South Cove and maybe even visit tales of Jill Gardner's past in the previous two Tourist Trap Mystery books. I do love a holiday mystery! And with this book, so will you."

—*ArtBooksCoffee.com*

"I would recommend *If the Shoe Kills* if you are looking for a well written cozy mystery."

—*Mysteries, Etc.*

"This novella is short and easily read in an hour or two with interesting angst and dynamics between mothers and daughters and mothers and sons . . . I enjoyed the first-person narrative."

—*Kings River Life Magazine* on *Mother's Day Mayhem*

Books by Lynn Cahoon

The Bainbridge Island Mystery Series
An Amateur Sleuth's Guide to Murder * Confessions of an Amateur Sleuth

The Tourist Trap Mystery Series
Guidebook to Murder * Mission to Murder * If the Shoe Kills * Dressed to Kill * Killer Run * Murder on Wheels * Tea Cups and Carnage * Hospitality and Homicide * Killer Party * Memories and Murder * Murder in Waiting * Picture Perfect Frame * Wedding Bell Blues * A Vacation to Die For * Songs of Wine and Murder * Olive You to Death * Vows of Murder * Merry Murder Season

Novellas
Rockets' Dead Glare * A Deadly Brew * Santa Puppy * Corned Beef and Casualties * Mother's Day Mayhem * A Very Mummy Holiday * Murder in a Tourist Town

The Kitchen Witch Mystery Series
One Poison Pie * Two Wicked Desserts * Three Tainted Teas * Four Charming Spells * Five Furry Familiars * Six Stunning Sirens * Seven Secret Spellcasters * Eight Enchanting Elixirs

Novellas
Chili Cauldron Curse * Murder 101 * Have a Holly, Haunted Holiday * Two Christmas Mittens

The Cat Latimer Mystery Series
A Story to Kill * Fatality by Firelight * Of Murder and Men * Slay in Character * Sconed to Death * A Field Guide to Homicide * A Killer Christmas Wish * Caught Dead to Write * Murder on a Snowy Evening * Formal Fatality

Novellas
Body in the Book Drop

The Farm to Fork Mystery Series
Who Moved My Goat Cheese? * Killer Green Tomatoes * One Potato, Two Potato, Dead * Deep Fried Revenge * Killer Comfort Food * A Fatal Family Feast

Novellas
Have a Deadly New Year * Penned In * A Pumpkin Spice Killing * A Basketful of Murder

The Survivors' Book Club Mystery Series
Tuesday Night Survivors' Club * Secrets in the Stacks * Death in the Romance Aisle * Reading Between the Lies * Dying to Read * Sleuthing with the Stars

Eight Enchanting Elixirs

LYNN CAHOON

Kensington Publishing Corp.
kensingtonbooks.com

This book is a work of fiction. Names, characters, businesses, organizations, places, events, and incidents either are the product of the author's imagination or are used fictitiously. Any resemblance to actual persons, living or dead, events, or locales is entirely coincidental.

To the extent that the image or images on the cover of this book depict a person or persons, such person or persons are merely models, and are not intended to portray any character or characters featured in the book.

KENSINGTON BOOKS are published by

Kensington Publishing Corp.
900 Third Avenue
New York, NY 10022

Copyright © 2026 by Lynn Cahoon

All rights reserved. No part of this book may be reproduced in any form or by any means without the prior written consent of the Publisher, excepting brief quotes used in reviews.

Without limiting the author's and publisher's exclusive rights, any unauthorized use of this publication to train generative artificial intelligence (AI) technologies is expressly prohibited.

If you purchased this book without a cover you should be aware that this book is stolen property. It was reported as "unsold and destroyed" to the Publisher and neither the Author nor the Publisher has received any payment for this "stripped book."

All Kensington titles, imprints, and distributed lines are available at special quantity discounts for bulk purchases for sales promotion, premiums, fund-raising, educational, or institutional use. Special book excerpts or customized printings can also be created to fit specific needs. For details, write or phone the office of the Kensington Sales Manager: Attn.: Sales Department. Kensington Publishing Corp., 900 Third Avenue, New York, NY 10022. Phone: 1-800-221-2647.

KENSINGTON and the KENSINGTON COZIES teapot logo Reg US Pat. & TM Off.

First Printing: August 2026
ISBN: 978-1-4967-5285-7

ISBN: 978-1-4967-5286-4 (ebook)

10 9 8 7 6 5 4 3 2 1

Printed in the United States of America

The authorized representative in the EU for product safety and compliance
is eucomply OU, Parnu mnt 139b-14, Apt 123
Tallinn, Berlin 11317, hello@eucompliancepartner.com

To our furry friends, who like Mia's familiars, keep us in touch with our higher power by teaching us pure love.

Eight Enchanting Elixirs

CHAPTER 1

What is the making of a man? His body or his soul?

Mia closed her eyes, trying to block out the argument going on in the next room with her grandmother Mary Alice Carpenter and Dorian Alexander. She refilled the coffee carafe and grabbed more cookies from the pantry. In a few hours, Finn and Abigail would be in here, getting ready for deliveries. From what she'd heard, Christina might hang around too.

All because a golem with Dorian's mind and soul had walked into Christina's engagement party with a smile and a wish—for Mary Alice to marry him, instead of Robert, her betrothed. The problem was, too many people in Magic Springs knew that Dorian had been killed in town a few years ago. The coven members might accept his return without question, but there needed to be a cover story for the more human townsfolk. Maybe Dorian could have a twin brother and go by Derek. Or Doug. Or even Dean.

She'd talk to Mark Baldwin, the town police chief, who was now aware of the magical parts of the town and considered magic-adjacent through his wife and daughter, who both had some power. Power that, according to coven canon, they shouldn't have. This sharing of power was getting more common.

The world was just getting weirder and weirder.

She headed back into the waiting room and called out, "I've got more coffee."

"That's very nice of you, dear. You've blossomed in the last few years into such a remarkable woman." Dorian looked down at Mr. Darcy, who was curled on his lap. "Your cat is quite taken by the changes you've made. Especially with your suitor."

"Mr. Darcy should stay out of my love life. As should you," Mia said as she set down the tray. "So, what have we decided, if anything?"

"He can't stay at my house, so you'll have to find a room for him here." Grans refilled her coffee cup.

"I can get a room at the Lodge." Dorian leaned back, focusing on Mr. Darcy, rubbing the top of his head.

"You will not. You've already put the coven in enough danger of discovery with your shenanigans when you showed up for Christina's engagement party. You need to keep out of the public eye for the rest of your stay. My word, Dorian, don't you ever stop?" Grans rolled her eyes as she concentrated on her ex-boyfriend. "Even dead, you're a pain in the butt."

"One, I'm not dead. Well, maybe my original body is, but I'm fine with this new one you created. You did a very detailed job making this body, Mary Alice." The smile he gave her grandmother made Mia blush. "And two, I understand your concern. I don't agree with it, but I understand. I'd love to stay here at the academy because it feels like home anyway. If that's okay with my hostess."

An old John Denver song about home and country roads played from the speaker system.

Dorian frowned as he listened. "Have the house ghosts been more active since I've been gone?"

"It's not the ghosts. That's Gloria. My kitchen witch familiar? At least that's what I thought she was. Recently we found out she's one of the elders. Did you have contact with her when you were in the spirit world?" Mia shook her head. Gloria was the academy's resident kitchen witch spirit, tethered to a doll, probably here to either watch out for Mia or train her in some way. Grans wasn't certain yet.

"Nice of you to frame it that way rather than when I was a cat." Dorian rubbed Mr. Darcy's ears. "But no, my time-sharing Mr. Darcy's body felt more like waking up from a long sleep and then being different. I didn't communicate with the ghosts. I saw them, but I think that was more of Mr. Darcy's power than my own. I'm telling you, I don't think I died."

"Well, you did." Grans let out a long breath, then turned to look at Mia. "I hate to ask, but is it okay that he stays here?"

"Sure, but we need to change his backstory. Finn lives here, and I can't explain the whole you-made-a-golem-for-your-ex-boyfriend-who-was-sharing-my-cat's-body-for-several-years-after-he-was-killed story." Mia broke a cookie in half. "I think that's just a bridge too far. She knows she has witch blood in her veins, but I think right now, she sees that more as a cool party trick than the power she may or may not develop through her training. Call it my sixth sense."

"I chatted with Finn last night when we came back from the party. She's very bright. And I believe she'll train into an exceptional witch." Dorian tapped his finger on his lips, pondering the issue. "But you're right about the need to change my name. What about Damien Alexander? I can be a cousin, or a slightly more attractive younger brother."

"As long as you don't invite your kids to visit, I think that might work with the people in town." Grans stood. "I need to go home. I have to call Robert and deal with this debacle."

"I'd rather not see or talk about my children. They were a disappointment in how they handled my demise." Dorian gently took her hand. "Mary Alice, just promise me you'll think about my proposal. We would make an amazing partnership and I still love you."

Grans stared into his eyes and just when Mia thought her grandmother was going to succumb to Dorian/Damien's charm, she jerked her hand away. "It's not a good time for me to be getting married anyway. I will postpone the engagement with Robert. He'll be hurt, but I'm sure he'll see my side in this chaos. But don't think that means you've won me over. I still haven't changed my mind."

And with that, Grans stood and headed to the door. Mia stayed at the table, watching her. So much had gone on in the last month, having Dorian back was just par for the course. She waited for Grans to leave, then turned to ask, "Where do you want to set up a bedroom? I have a guest room in the apartment, or we can update a room on the second floor."

"Let's do the second floor for now. When are you moving in with Trent? With a dragon to consider, I'm sure you're already thinking about the next step in your relationship." He pointed toward the hallway to where Finn's room was located. "Make sure she's okay with me staying here. I don't want to scare her."

"The house ghosts like her," Mia said, then added, "and the library."

He smiled as he turned back. "What's not to like? She's very much one of your tribe already. I always wondered about your ability to collect people. Maybe it's one of your gifts from the Goddess to help you in the fight."

"If there's a fight, I'm not going to be leading it. All I want is to run my catering company and be part of the community. I don't want to become some magical Joan of Arc, fighting for the rights of the downtrodden."

"Sometimes what we want is superseded by what is the right thing to do. Don't build your box until you know all the things you want to let in and those things you want to keep out." Dorian tapped his finger. "I wonder if I've been called back for something more than just my love for your grandmother. Has she been doing all of your training?"

"Yes. The coven says I need to keep training so I can test out for level four next year. But I'm not sure I want to level up. Even just being level three hasn't been much of a blessing so far," Mia admitted.

"I'm going to look over Mary Alice's training plan. And I'll have furniture sent over to set up living quarters on the second floor. I may need to do some remodeling, if you don't mind. All at my own expense, of course." He tapped the table with the palm of his hand. "It's time to get things moving. Where will I find the keys to the second floor? I need to get busy on my space. I may need a bed upstairs in your apartment for a few nights, if that's okay."

"The alternative is to have you sleeping on this couch or renting a room at the Lodge, so I think we'll make do with the guest bedroom in the apartment." She stood and checked the security camera by the door. "Abigail, Finn, and Christina just arrived to start their day. I'll let them know that Damien is staying with us on the second floor for a while."

"You even said that with a straight face." He chuckled as he pointed to her office. "Is the key to the classrooms in there?"

"Hanging on a red ribbon. My lab's key is on a purple ribbon and the other rooms that Grans and Christina have appropriated for storage have a yellow ribbon. So any room the red ribbon key will open is up for grabs. I don't think any of the remaining rooms have secret exits to the outside, but with the academy, you never know. Just let me know and we'll rekey the rooms you choose. I'll keep one of the keys, just in case, and you get to pick your ribbon color."

"I'd love blue. Like your grandmother's eyes." He disappeared into the office as the front door opened and the three women came inside.

Abigail's eyes widened as she saw Mia downstairs. "Oh, I figured you were at work already or I would have invited you to the house for breakfast. We just finished talking about our next week's schedule. We have several additional deliveries, as well as two holiday parties, one that will be held here. I was planning on emailing you the monthly calendar in case you have room in your schedule to help us out."

"That will work. I'm heading to work as soon as I change. I had a meeting with Grans and Damien, Dorian's brother, this morning. He's going to be staying here at the academy for a while. He'll be living on the second floor," Mia added, directing the information to Finn. "He shouldn't bother you."

Finn shrugged, her purple hair, longer now, flipping with the movement. "No worries. He seems nice. We talked last night after the party. I stepped out of my room for some snacks after my game and he was drinking tea. He has a huge crush on your grandmother. It's so sweet."

Mia relaxed a little with Finn's words. Finn already seemed comfortable around Dorian, now Damien. Mia needed to start thinking of him with that name, so it shouldn't be an issue having him in the academy. "Well, if anything happens that feels weird—I don't expect anything, but just in case—let me know."

Finn rolled her eyes. "Between you and Abigail, you're both so sensitive to my feelings. I love being here, but you two need to relax a bit. I can deal with more than you think I can."

Mia laughed and looked at her watch. "I guess I need to stop babying you then and get to work. I have a nine o'clock staff meeting at the Lodge. I'll see you all tonight. Call me if there are any issues."

The last statement she'd addressed directly to Abigail, who responded with a nod. She knew the undercurrent of the question. She would watch out for Damien and make sure he stayed put.

Sometimes being between two worlds made her life a little crazy.

She headed upstairs to change into her work clothes and head to her normal job. And she felt good about it. There, all she had to deal with were human issues, like holiday parties and a boss who liked everything documented in triplicate.

At least this boss didn't want to fire her, unlike the last one.

Mia had just finished her last meeting when her personal cell phone rang. Trent Majors, Abigail's son and Mia's boyfriend, was calling. "I'm so happy to hear your voice. This day has just been weird," Mia said.

"Sorry, then, it's about to get weirder. So, Cerby's at-home training program has been approved and Sonja McMann is here to train him. Sarah's bringing over Tempest, Elisa Marie's puppy, to see if he's a hellhound too. If so, Sonja says she can train both of them here." Trent explained the updated process. Sonja McMann was a member of the werewolf tribe that lived in the deep forest just north of Magic Springs in the Sawtooth Mountain Range. When there were bigfoot sightings in northern Idaho, it was usually one of the McManns who had been out running with the moon.

"That's great. I didn't want you to have to send Cerby back to the training camp. You know he hated being away from you." Mia rolled her shoulders and opened her calendar for the week. "When is she starting?"

"Now. And bonus, she's staying here at the house. Mom tried to get her to stay with her, but Sonja says for this to work, she has to be here with both dogs. So Mark's going to be mad at me because if Tempest is a hellhound sent by the Goddess, Sarah and the baby have to stay here with us. Dad's going to take charge of the store because I can't leave the house for six weeks." He paused. "I'm sorry, I'm stuck here."

"Maybe I could come over." Mia didn't like these rules at all.

"Sorry, but you, Mark, and every other person is banned until the training is complete. Mom's going to send over meals and groceries." His voice dropped. "I'm sorry for disappearing on you like this, but it's better for Cerby."

"I know. I'm just going to miss you." She made a note on her calendar six weeks into the future. "You're going to miss Thanksgiving, but at least you'll be off house arrest by Christmas. I have a new house guest too."

Mia told him about Dorian staying at the academy and his name change, as well as his new living arrangements.

"I'm glad someone will be there for you guys." Trent paused, then asked, "Do you think we're overreacting? Maybe Cerby doesn't need hellhound training."

"Do you want him freaking out and changing in public?" Grans had been clear and very detailed when she'd told Mia why even a Maltese like Cerby needed training. "This is better, and it's only six weeks. We'll talk every night."

He promised to call later and hung up. A few minutes later, she got a call from Mark Baldwin, complaining that his wife, child, and new puppy might have to be living at Trent's for the duration of the training.

"I don't know what I can tell you, Mark. I'm not happy about it either. Maybe you'll get lucky and Tempest is just a dog," she suggested, but then he went off again.

Fifteen minutes later, she got him off the phone and tried to return to her scheduling project. As soon as she settled in, her phone rang again.

It was Grans.

"Grans, I'm trying to finish something up so I can head home. Is it something we can talk about later?"

"No, Mia. It's not. The National Office has sent over another testing expert. You're going to be tested again at the end of the week." Grans sounded stressed.

"I thought I had a year before I had to retest for Level Four. Why did they move up the test?" Mia sighed and closed out her computer. Obviously she wasn't going to get anything else done today. She might as well head home.

"The test isn't to move up. It's your original test. They're making you retake it because people have been complaining about the results."

"That's just stupid. I didn't cheat. You know that. What good does retesting do?" Mia pulled on her coat and grabbed her keys out of her bag. It had been a horrible day. Grans and Dorian fighting. Trent's news. And now she had to retest to prove she could be a witch?

What else could go wrong. "What happens if I don't retest?"

"Don't even joke about that," Grans said. "Anyway, I need you home. They've taken the protection of your sealing off. They see this as a total redo. With the power you have, everyone's going to be watching. I tried to get the coven to keep the protection seal on, but Cleo said it's impossible. Once you go back in for a retest, the spell comes off automatically. You're in danger. Again."

"Great. Trent's stuck in his house and I'll be quarantined to mine. This isn't good on a relationship." Mia locked her office and headed out to the parking lot. At least her boss would understand when she told her the real reason she couldn't work at the Lodge this week. If Blake was human, Mia would have to make up some contagious disease.

"I'm more worried about your life than your happily ever after dreams," Grans said before hanging up.

Chapter 2

As she walked to her car, Mia called Blake Sandburg, her boss at the Lodge, to explain her inability to be at the office until this testing fiasco was dealt with.

After Mia finished telling her about the new examiner coming into town, Blake let out a big sigh. "The coven does what it wants to and the rest of us are just pawns. I still need you to be available by phone at all times. I'm sure you can video chat with your staff in the planning processes. We have holiday parties scheduled throughout the month. I'll tell everyone you have the measles."

"They're going to believe that?" Mia had been vaccinated against all of the normal human childhood diseases as a kid and the witchy ailments, like dragon breath, this year. Grans hadn't insisted that Mia's mother do the extra immunizations because at that time, everyone thought her mom would be the next kitchen witch.

Except, Mia thought, Gloria. She'd known long before her mother had broken the news to Grans that she was abdicating. Mia wondered if her mom thought she might turn away from the craft as well. Especially when Mia had her own life and goals to work in food service.

She tuned back into Blake's reciting of all the parties in the next month, even though Mia knew the schedule because she'd been the one to develop it. "Blake, I'll do all I can from home. I just can't step in and fix something on-site. I'll need you or one of the other department heads to deal with any emergencies that needs someone in person to fix."

"Okay, I guess we'll just have to deal with it, won't we? You're lucky I understand how fickle being part of the coven can be when you're trying to be as normal as possible. Most members either work for a coven-owned business or are self-employed."

Mia could hear Blake typing as they talked. She was already in her car and pulling up to the academy. As she got closer, she could feel the protective wards surrounding her. She hadn't noticed her angst until she arrived home and it started to ease. "One more thing, my retesting is Friday, so I'll be unavailable by phone that day."

A loud sigh came over the phone's speaker.

"Fine, I'll cancel my weekend plans for the spa treatments in Sun Valley. I should have guessed that something like this would happen. I never get time to just relax," Blake said before ending the call.

As Mia tucked her phone into her tote and headed to the academy building, she heard chirping in the tree behind her. She looked back and saw Buddy watching her.

"Hey, I thought you all were stuck at home." Mia walked over and reached out to rub the baby dragon on the nose. He leaned into the affection, then held out a bouquet of flowers with a note attached. Several of the blooms had been crushed, but it was the thought that counted, right?

Trent must already know about the retesting. She opened the card and read his message aloud. "You did it once, you can do it again. Teach them a lesson and test out higher. Level four, here you come!"

Buddy chirped his agreement with the message. She could swear the purple dragon was smiling.

"Tell Trent thank you. And be careful flying home. No letting yourself be seen by any humans." She gave him a hug. She was going to miss Buddy and Cerby almost as much as Trent.

He chattered something, as she felt his wing curve around her body, gently patting her back. He was going to miss her too. Mia's eyes teared up. How could she have fallen in love with a dragon as quickly as she had? Buddy was part of the family now.

Wow, had her life changed since she left Boise and moved to Magic Springs.

She heard footsteps behind her, and when Buddy released her, she turned to see Abigail standing and watching them.

She felt the wind as Buddy headed to the sky, but as she turned to look, he'd already turned invisible. "Bye, Buddy."

Abigail put her arm around Mia and they walked together back to the front door. "Six weeks will fly by, and next week we'll have this silly retesting done and you'll be too busy to even think about Trent and the zoo being stuck at the house."

"I'm that predictable, am I?" Mia wiped away the tears that had fallen during Abigail's pep talk. "It's stupid, but when Buddy showed up with flowers, the emotions just bubbled up to the top and out my eyes. I hate crying."

"Most strong women do, but you get those emotions out. How did Blake take your forced confinement?"

Mia shrugged. "Better than I'd expected. Frank would have tried to fire me. At least I don't have to worry about that. And with Dorian, no, Damien, here, it's probably a good idea."

"Just a heads-up, he has a construction crew on the second floor, so the place is a madhouse." Abigail pointed out the truck and construction van Mia had missed driving in due to her distraction with seeing Buddy. "Maybe it's best that we don't have a dragon or a hellhound wandering around the property this week."

Mia heard Gloria's giggle and, from the look on her face, so did Abigail. "We still have a golem and a library filled with ghosts. I'm not sure they'd even notice Cerby or Buddy."

"I don't think Damien likes being thought of that way." Abigail looked up the stairs where Mr. Darcy sat, watching them come through the door. "And your cat is being awfully protective of your new houseguest. He's following him everywhere."

"It has to be weird for him to have Dorian as a guest in his body for so long, then to meet him in real life. Most cats just have to deal with eating dinner and finding a sunny spot to nap. My guy has familiar duties as well as his cat nature. And he's suddenly alone in his body. Mr. Darcy has a lot going on." Mia smiled at him and he waved his right paw at her. "But he seems to be doing well with it all."

"Okay, well, I'm going back to the kitchen. We don't need you, but if you want to come in and help or just hang out, you're welcome." She glanced at the office. "Have you heard when Christina and Levi are going home?"

"We haven't talked since the party. Why? Has Levi said anything?" Christina Adams was Isaac's little sister. Mia had been engaged to Isaac and when they broke up, she'd gotten emotional custody of the teenager. Mia thought she got the best out of the deal. Now, Christina was an adult. She'd finished her degree and been offered a catering director position in Portland, Oregon. Levi, who was Abigail's son and Trent's brother, had bent down on one knee and proposed, as well as moved to the Pacific Northwest with her. They were starting a new life. Except they were still in Magic Springs after their eventful engagement party.

To make matters more complicated than finding the right apartment or shopping area, Christina had just found out she had magical blood. She didn't necessarily have powers, but she came from a magical family. Now, she was studying the same books that Mia had been studying to take over her kitchen witch role and to take the stupid test. Mia hadn't wanted to test high; she just wanted the coven to leave her alone. If Christina decided to test after she finished her initial training, she'd know if she had any natural power.

Something was bothering Mia about Christina and her move. Maybe because she wouldn't be running around like a headless chicken this week, she could focus on what was really going on with her best friend. Was it jitters from the upcoming wedding? Or something more?

Her phone rang, pulling her out of her pondering. Since the caller ID showed the Lodge, she assumed it was Blake. "Sorry, I have to take this."

"Go ahead, I just wanted to warn you about the mess." Abigail headed to the kitchen as Mia started up the stairs. Mr. Darcy followed her to the third-floor landing and waited for her to open the door. Had she fed him this morning?

"This is Mia," she answered the phone before it could go to a fourth ring.

"I am so mad at you. How in the world did you get measles? Don't tell me didn't get your vaccinations. It wasn't an option for me, but maybe I'm older than you." James Holder, the Lodge's head chef, kitchen manager, and one of Mia's friends, chastised her.

Mia wanted to chuckle. She had gotten her normal vaccines as a normal kid, but then she'd moved to Magic Springs, where other illnesses surrounded the magical kids. She'd just gone through a series of vaccinations from the local witch doctor. No, that sounded wrong. The coven doctor. "No, I got my immunizations. I don't think I have measles, but my doctor wanted to be extra careful until the tests come back, just in case. I don't want to make a lodge guest sick by coming in."

"Oh, well, that sounds more reasonable. Blake made it seem like you had the plague. There's so much going on out there. You never know what's going to hit you." He paused, then with the next breath, asked, "Are you okay? Do you need anything? What can I send you over? Chicken soup?"

"Abigail's here and mothering me already." Mia hated to lie, but James didn't know about her heritage. Besides, how could she explain something like this? "How's work? Anything I need to know?"

"You left a few minutes ago. Nothing has happened yet. You're getting freaked out about something that may never happen," James replied.

"You just wait. The first night is always itchy. May you pay for your insolence in tons more reports for our boss lady," Mia joked as she opened the apartment. She needed to make a list of things to get done here at the academy or she would go crazy. The good thing was, she always had a long list of things to do. The one thing she wasn't adding was studying for her test. If she scored lower, maybe all this attention would go away.

"Blake brought us all together a few minutes ago to talk about your inconvenient absence. Her words, not mine. Anyway, she had to have a meeting, never mind that I'm busy keeping the food coming out." A crash sounded on the other side of the line. "I've got to go. My new line cook is all thumbs. Tell Finn to expect as many hours as she can give me."

As she said goodbye, she thanked the Goddess for the opportunity to keep Finn out of the house more. Maybe Damien would find a new home sooner rather than later. Sounds of hammers and saws drifted up from the second floor. Or maybe not. He sounded like he was making some major changes to the old classrooms. She shut the door and glanced at Mr. Darcy. "You're loving having Dorian back, aren't you?"

In answer, he flicked his tail, then jumped on the couch for a nap. He blinked his eyes at her once, then curled up on a pillow.

At least someone's world had been changed for the better with all the craziness around here. Her cat was purring.

Mia looked over her planner for the week. The test was Friday, which meant that the witch protection spell might not be reapplied before Monday. She hadn't mentioned that to Blake. She would have just complained more, but it wouldn't be a shock to her. And who knew, maybe the coven would be timely because this was overkill on their part. Mia wondered who had complained to the National Office about her scores. It wasn't like she'd worked on making anyone in the coven leadership her friend. In fact, she'd done the opposite and not joined the rank and file because she wanted to be independent. From the stories Trent and Abigail told, membership made that hard. The coven did what it wanted to do with your life. Including giving you leadership jobs you didn't want and deciding who you should marry and procreate with to strengthen the bloodlines.

She was making those decisions on her own, thank you.

As if her mind had summoned him, Trent's name showed up on her caller ID. "Hey, just checking on you. Buddy said you looked a little lonely."

She smiled at the phone as she sent her last reminder email to her staff. "Is 'lonely' one chortle or two?"

"I'm sure Sonja has a dragon language book you can borrow. Oh, tell Mark it's bad news. Tempest is a hellhound. His family is stuck here with me for six weeks."

"Five weeks, six days, but who's counting." Mia texted Mark to let him know. Sarah had probably already broken the news to him, but Mia added a standing invitation to dinner. He probably had dinners sitting in the kitchen freezer with a how-to-heat list organized by days, as well as instructions on when and where to buy more packaged salads. But he might like the company. "How are my three favorite guys?"

"Two guys, one female dragon. I thought I told you. Mom says that sometimes it's not clear what the dragon's sex is until they go through puberty." He sighed. "I'm not looking forward to that."

"Buddy's a girl? When did you find out? We need to change her name. Buddy sounds wrong."

"I've had that conversation with Cerby and he insists it's Buddy. His friend. No name change needed." A female voice called his name. "Anyway, it's dinnertime here. I need to go. We all eat together, but thank the Goddess for Sarah. Neither Sonja nor I are talented in the cooking department. I love you."

Mia started to answer but realized Trent had hung up. She made sure everything looked clear on her calendar, then decided to wander downstairs. Damien—she was trying hard to think of him with that name—stood on the landing, talking to a man Mia didn't know.

"Oh, Mia. This is Nathan Boyle. He's my contractor for the remodel. Nathan, this is the academy's owner, Mia Malone." Damien waved her over into the conversation.

"It's an honor to meet you, miss. I'm so thankful to get a look at the inside of this historic building. I'm so happy that you saved it from being razed a few years ago. The workmanship on this building is amazing. It's not going to take long to remodel those rooms. I have some ideas on how to enhance some of the original features, if you don't mind. Like a chalkboard in the living room would have many purposes. You could even turn it into a kids' room later."

"Oh, that would be amazing." Mia looked over at Damien. "I thought maybe you were just doing some painting and door changes."

Nathan started to laugh. "This is a lot more. I'll get the designs finished tonight and I can show you in the morning. If that's okay."

"That will be fine. I'm doing a staycation for the week, so I'll be here. Twenty-four seven." Mia ignored the questioning look Damien was giving her. "I'm heading downstairs to see who's around for dinner. Damien, are you going to be eating at home?"

"No, I'm sorry. I made other plans. I could change them." Damien waved at Nathan, who headed downstairs. "I'll see you in the morning, Nathan."

"I'll be here at seven, unless that's too early, Miss Malone." Nathan turned at the bottom of the stairs to get her attention. "I don't want to interrupt your vacation."

"Seven's fine." Mia watched him leave and then turned back to Damien. "Don't change your plans. I'll go see if Finn or Abigail are here. I'm sure Christina's already back at the Adams's condo with Levi."

He followed her down the stairs. "I don't think anyone's here. Not sure where they all are—I have enough trouble keeping up with your grandmother—but I heard that Finn's working a second job. That girl has a lot of energy and determination. I wasn't like that in college. It took the love of a good woman to calm me down."

"Are you referring to my grandmother or your first wife?" Mia could feel that the first floor was empty. Everyone had already left. Mia watched Damien pause at the front door. "Because if it's Grans who settled you down, it didn't happen until you were in your late sixties."

"I was a late bloomer." He smiled. "Don't wait up. Abigail made sure I have the main door key as well as the one to your apartment. If I'm really late, I'll sleep on the couch down here."

"Come on up. Finn sleeps on this floor, and I'd rather have you in my guest room than where she can wander into you. Who knows what happens when you sleep in that body?"

"My body, the golem, is just like any other human body, except I can't procreate. Something I'm not excited about doing again anyway. Not with how my kids turned out." He held up his hand. "Have a nice evening."

After Mia grabbed a frozen dinner, bread, and a couple of different cookie doughs from the catering kitchen, she left a note on the counter of what she took, then headed upstairs.

She hadn't been alone in the academy for a long time. Trent usually hung out here at night, and sometimes Christina and Levi joined them. They played board games or watched a movie, and always talked. She liked the feel of a houseful of people, and she could tell that the academy did too. What would happen when she moved in with Trent?

Who would keep this place filled and happy?

The wind howled mournfully outside.

Chapter 3

Grans's car showed up on the security monitor as Mia took out the last batch of cookies. Mia hurried downstairs to let her in and noticed Muffy and two suitcases on the step beside her. "Grans, what are you doing?"

"Tanking my engagement, according to Robert. I told him that I couldn't leave you alone in this house for the week. You could be targeted. Then he asked me where Dorian was sleeping, and I told him the truth. You would have thought I'd said in my bed." She picked up the suitcases and came inside. "Come along, Muffy. Although now that I think of it, that's not a bad idea. Text Dorian and tell him to sleep at my house. The key's under the mat."

"Grans, that's the first place a thief would look." Mia shut the door, checking that there wasn't more luggage sitting outside, or that the car doors were still open.

"I have the key spelled, dear. No one can see it unless I want them to. Besides, the house would never let someone inside. Not after what happened." She shivered at the memory. "I'll take the elevator. Please take Muffy up with you on the stairs. He needs the exercise."

Muffy growled at the comment, but then followed Mia up the stairs. The fluffy, mixed-breed dog had put on a little weight in the last few years and Grans wasn't happy about it. "I hear you're staying a while?"

Muffy stopped at the second-floor landing and sniffed a few times.

"Yes, we've had visitors." Mia really needed to get people around her or she'd become a crazy cat lady, talking to all the animals.

Gloria started laughing, and "Crocodile Rock" blasted in the stairwell.

Mia shook her head as she and Muffy headed upstairs. "No way. If I'm getting a pet besides Buddy, it's going to have fur, not scales."

"Who are you talking to?" Grans asked as she set down her luggage. She opened the door and sniffed the smells coming from the kitchen. "Perfect, I'm right on time for dinner. Good evening, Gloria. I take it you're providing the music?"

"She has a funny sense of humor," Mia added, closing the door. "I'll take your suitcases to your room."

"I'll text Dorian. You'd be too nice." Grans sat at the table. "Those cookies smell amazing. Shortbread?"

"Yes, we froze a few batches to see if it would work. Care to be a guinea pig?"

"Cookies are cookies, especially when I'm stressed.

I don't understand why Robert is being such a pill about this whole thing." She waved me off as she texted Dorian using one hand. The other had a cookie in it. Mia thought it was going to be that kind of night.

After she'd set Grans's suitcases in her room, she was surprised to see Christina's Land Rover come into the parking lot. Christina had her own key, so Mia wasn't going to run down to help, but then she saw Christina's two suitcases. The Goddess must have heard that Mia was lonely.

She opened the door just as Christina, tears flowing down her face, pulled out her key. "What on earth?"

"Levi is the worst. I can't believe I ever said I'd marry him. We can't even get along after an amazing engagement party." She fell into Mia's arms, then, after getting a hold of her crying jag, stood up. "No talking about him. No trying to get me to see his side. I'm starving and need carbs."

"You've come to the right place. Grans is already here." Mia grabbed one of the suitcases. "Stairs or elevator?"

"Elevator. I can't believe how loud the construction guys are during the day. I can hear them over the blender." She wiped her face. "Damien's staying here?"

"Not anymore. He's staying at Grans's tonight. And probably until this testing thing gets sorted out. Robert is not amused," Mia added.

"Okay, so no guy talk at all. We'll add in anything about Trent and Sonja. Good thing Sarah is there or Sonja might just jump him one night while she's there. According to Levi—crap, I said his name. Anyway, according to Trent's brother, Sonja had a thing for Trent in high school. Like Cheryl had for Le—I mean, Trent's brother."

"Almost good catch. Trent's a free agent. If he cheats, I'll just have to cut him up for dragon food. If Cerby lets me get close." Mia handed Christina the other suitcase. "I'll see you upstairs."

As she took the stairs, she sent a message to the Goddess. "Really, I was fine. Just one night alone wouldn't have killed me."

A warmth spread through Mia, and she knew she'd been answered. The Goddess wanted her to know she was safe and had friends. Even if it meant both Levi and Robert had started a fight between the couples. It was never the woman's fault, right?

Mia was sure everything would work out the way it needed to, but sometimes life was messy. And she was just a bit addicted to that kind of a life. Maybe she had a lesson to learn tonight too. Being alone wasn't a bad thing.

She opened the door to find Christina and Grans already chatting and decided that being surrounded by friends and family was better. A lot better.

The next morning, Grans sat at the kitchen table drinking coffee and reading her emails. As Mia's trainer, she'd received the official letter from the National Testing Bureau. She turned her laptop toward Mia so she could read it. "I should have forwarded this to you, but then Robert came over, and now I'm waiting for an apology from him. I should do what Christina is doing and not use his name. Former fiancé? Or untrusting failure?"

"How about we just say *him*?" Mia focused on the email. Grans was right. The protection provided by the coven to local witches disappeared as soon as the email was opened. She felt the last of the spell slip away as she finished reading. That was kind of crappy of them. What if she was out of town? She pushed away the annoyance with coven policy. Like Blake said, the coven did what it wanted. She kept reading. "Wait, this says the tester will be arriving on Tuesday. So she or he should be coming in today. Maybe we can get them to test me early?"

"You don't want that. Besides, the tester can't change it. She's already set aside Friday for the link up to the National Testing Site. The test is run on, well, what you'd call a computer. It's not, but let's go with the analogy. The computer only has enough bandwidth for a certain number of testers during the session. If you keep reading, you'll see in the fine print they think the last test's results were affected by an overscheduled testing computer."

"It says the tester computer is named Dave?" She looked up. "Like in the space movie?"

"The tester is a he, not an *it*. Some witches are specialists in the testing arena. Dave is one of those specialists. He's really nice, but he doesn't go out much. His head is a little bigger than normal, so people tend to stare. They all live in a compound in Texas. It's near the beach, so they can get out and enjoy their days off."

Grans checked her planner. "I'm at your disposal until Monday morning or whenever your new scores come in. Is it bad I'm hoping for a level four?"

Mia smiled as she turned the laptop back to her grandmother. "You and Trent. I'm hoping for a level two."

"Never hide your talents under a bushel. It does nothing for you or anyone else." Grans pointed at Christina shuffling down the hallway. "It lives!"

"Not funny. One too many glasses or bottles of wine. What can I say? And why are you singing the old Sunday school song?" Christina poured herself coffee, glanced at her phone, then tossed it away.

"What song?"

"About letting your talents shine? I can do the hand gestures too." She glared at the phone. "Trent's brother has been calling and texting all morning. He wants to talk."

Mia noticed that Christina still wore her engagement ring, a good sign she hadn't given up on a life with Levi. "Shall we do hash browns and eggs for breakfast?"

"Anything that will soak up some of this hangover would be great." Christina started to stand. "I hope Abigail doesn't need me to work today."

"We'll have you better by then. No worries." She glanced at her grandmother, who silently nodded. She'd mix some magic potion into Christina's food. The problem with hangover magic was that it didn't work on the potion maker. Just their customers or patients. She started peeling potatoes. Maybe having a week off just to veg wasn't such a bad idea. This issue with Levi and Christina would give her time to figure out where her friend's head was on the magic thing.

And it'd distract her from missing Trent.

Mr. Darcy mewed at the window. She set down the potatoes and went over to look out. Buddy hovered outside the third-story window with a note in her paw, or claw, or whatever it was called. Mia opened the pane and reached out. Buddy dropped the envelope into her hands, chortled, then took off. She turned invisible as she left.

Mia closed the window, took the note over to the sink, and set it down.

"Open it. One of us should have a happy love life." Christina had taken over peeling the potatoes and Grans was chopping onions and peppers. "Especially when your love notes are sent via dragon special delivery."

Mia picked up the note again. "If you insist. 'Dear Mia, don't freak out.' Uh-oh, this isn't starting out well." She read more to herself, then set down the note. "We better hurry with breakfast and add more potatoes to that pile. Abigail's on her way over and my test has been scheduled for today at ten. She told Trent that she and Grans need to drive me over to headquarters, just in case."

"We have deliveries today," Christina said as she took out two more potatoes. "I guess it's just me and Finn in the van."

"Abigail's bringing Levi to help. I guess the don't-freak-out part of the message applies to you as well."

Mia put the letter on her kitchen desk, planning on reading it again tonight. If she wasn't worn to the bone from the test. The security monitor beeped, and she saw Abigail's SUV pull in. "I hope Damien plans on being here for his workers today because the house is going to be empty."

"We Are Family" played out of the walls.

"Who needs a speaker system when we have you, Gloria." Mia gently touched the doll's broom and went out to open the apartment door for Abigail and Levi. "We are a big group. Oh, and I have to talk to Nathan Boyle about renovation plans before I leave for coven headquarters."

"And change. Jeans aren't appropriate. Wear a suited skirt or a pantsuit." Grans eyed the clothes Mia had chosen for the first full day of her staycation.

"I wore jeans the first time," Mia grumbled but was saved from Grans's retort when Abigail and Levi came in. He looked like a lost puppy and stared at Christina.

"Good morning, girls." Abigail came into the kitchen with a large tote bag she put on the floor. "Christina, you look lovely."

"I look like hell warmed over." Christina threw a dagger stare at Levi. "But you look ready to fight dragons."

"Dear, we don't fight dragons. Or we haven't in centuries. They are too rare to lose even one of them. People, on the other hand . . ." Abigail walked over to the stove. "What's going on with the hash browns? I'm starving."

Levi disappeared downstairs to check on Finn after

breakfast, and take her a plate that Abigail had set up for her. Christina cleaned up the kitchen as the other three headed to the living room.

"I have a few things for your protection at the testing. I think they will hit you with a higher-level test this time, so don't worry if you don't think you know the answer. Use your intuition and just take the first answer that comes to you." Abigail started pulling things out of her bag.

"Good thing I don't have test anxiety like some of my friends. One of my high school friends took the LSAT a few years ago and called me crying afterward. Of course, it didn't help that her boyfriend picked a fight with her the morning before she took the test. I don't think he wanted her to go to law school." Mia picked up the cotton shirt that Abigail had set out. "This is pretty."

"Wear it under your suit jacket. Most families have garments that they've tested in for centuries. This is from my family. The boys wore Thomas's family garments when they tested. I always hoped I'd have a girl to hand this down to."

Grans pointed to her necklace. "Don't take off your protection locket for any reason. Not even if this Suzanne Parker asks you to. In fact, wear it under your shirt so she won't see it."

"I made you a lunch to give you energy while you're testing. There's just a little magic in the food, nothing that would sway the tests one way or the other. I followed the coven's directions to the letter." Abigail pressed her lips together. "Usually, it's the trainer who gets the notice of the test date and time, and it's typically a month out. Not the night before. This Parker woman is playing games with us. She's got a reputation. She's a close descendant of the Salem witches, so she has a better-than-thou attitude. I believe she only tested out at a one when she tested, so you're messing with her head."

"I'm not in it for the fight. They can drop me to level one if they want. I don't want to join the coven or be part of leadership. It all feels like high school and the Honor Society group. I got in fair and square, but they never told me about the meetings. Then they kicked me out for missing too many." Mia sighed. "I just want to run my business and deal with the kitchen witch responsibilities."

"Dear, I think we're way past that now." Grans pushed her toward her bedroom. "Go get changed. We need to go."

Suzanne Parker wasn't a fun, happy tester. Mia's first tester had been calm and encouraging. This woman barked questions at her and wrote in her notebook after every answer.

Mia looked around the room at coven headquarters. It was the same room where she'd tested before, but now, instead of the calm, comfortable table and chairs, she was sitting on a black wooden chair, her hands folded in her lap. She wiggled her butt on the wooden seat. It wasn't comfortable after just a few minutes. What would it feel like after eight or more hours?

"Mia Malone, the egg, is it the beginning or just the end?" Suzanne barked the question at her.

She was standing somewhere behind Mia, but Mia had been told not to look behind her. She wondered what was back there.

"Miss Malone? An answer, please?" Suzanne prodded.

Mia thought about the question. "Both. It depends on who's perspective you're in. If you're the developing chick inside the egg, it's the beginning. If you're the hen who laid the egg, it's the end of her struggle."

"What is the world made of?"

This one Mia knew the answer to immediately. "Earth, wind, water, and fire. We all come from these four elements."

"What is your strength as a witch?" No pause or response after the question. At least Hugh had given her an idea of how she was doing. Today she would pass or fail but not know the answer until after she finished.

"I feed people, body and soul." Mia wasn't sure that was her only strength, but she loved cooking, and that love had to be part of her witch powers. Didn't it?

She didn't have long to think about the idea before another question was shot at her.

"Name the ingredients in a healing potion."

"For what illness or injury?" Mia asked. Instead of getting an answer, Mia was asked another question.

"Do the stars rule our actions?"

She recognized this type of question. It was an essay, and she treated it as such, pondering between the short answer of yes or no and finally giving her own opinion that had been supported by the previous parts of her answer.

"Name the ingredients in a truth serum."

The questions went on and on. They took a break just as Mia's bladder felt like it was going to explode and Cleo brought in fresh hot coffee to the room. After the coffee and Cleo were gone, Suzanne Parker started again with a new round of questions.

"What fairy tale explained the theory of love?"

Hours later, Mia was sweating and had almost fallen out of her chair twice. Suzanne walked around the chair so she could study Mia's face.

Mia took a deep breath and prepared for the next question.

"The test is over. Results will be announced in the usual process. You can leave." Suzanne stared at her. "I doubt you'll pass this testing."

The test had taken twice as long as the original testing, and when Mia left the exam room, Cleo handed her a brownie in a little box. "You earned this today. I just sent off your answers, and your results will be transmitted to your trainer—Mary Alice, correct? I hear there was a mix-up on the testing announcement and everything went to Abigail instead."

Mia wanted to give a snarky reply, but she could see it wasn't Cleo's fault. And she was so tired. "Yes. Is anyone here to pick me up?"

Levi came through the door. "It is I, your trusted squire and driver, ready to take you home. The gang—well, most of it—is waiting at the academy. We're having a watch party for the results. My parents want to make sure I asked about the results. They'll be posted at midnight on the coven's website as usual, correct?" This question he aimed at Cleo, who blushed and nodded. He took Mia's arm and bag. "I'll take this one off your hands. I bet she falls asleep in the car before we get home."

"Take care of her. Dark forces are around this week," Cleo said as they headed out the door.

The warning was chilling, but at this point Mia just wanted to be home.

As he walked her into the car, he kept his arm around her. "You look like shit. Sorry the test was so hard on you this time. Coven leadership is nasty. No wonder Trent refused to be part of the mentoring program. He would have been set up for life. They pay crazy money, but you have to be like them. Cold and unfeeling."

Clouds formed over them on a perfectly clear day. They looked up and saw lightning bouncing from one cloud to the next.

"I'll shut up and we'll get you home." He helped her into the passenger side of his Jeep. Typically, it took her ten minutes to get home from council headquarters, but Levi did it in half that time. He didn't even park, just drove straight to the front door. Abigail was waiting for them as Levi helped Mia get out of the car.

Sitting on the couch, Mia felt strength coming back into her body. When she'd left the test, she'd felt like a wet noodle, drained of any energy, even with Abigail's lunch. Now, she started to feel like herself. Grans put a cup of tea in her hands.

"Drink all this before you even try to talk." Grans's voice shook a little, and Mia looked up into her eyes. "I've been monitoring your vitals, and the witch almost killed you there at the end. I'm ready to do the same to her. I'm filing a formal complaint with the coven.

You're a kitchen witch. You weren't training in battle magic."

Abigail rubbed Grans's shoulders. "I think she's more than just a kitchen witch, Mary Alice. Mia, don't worry about anything today. Just drink that tea."

Mia followed orders, but instead of getting energized from the tea, she immediately fell asleep.

As she started to wake up, she heard voices around her. Blinking, she saw she was still downstairs and a group encircled her. Damien, Grans, Abigail, Christina, and Levi sat around the coffee table, making a circle with her and Mr. Darcy on the couch. Muffy lay on the floor by Grans's chair, watching Mia.

She slowly blinked and sat up, stretching as she did. The darkness outside the windows told Mia she'd been asleep for a while. She checked her watch. It was late. The results should be arriving any time. "Can I get some water?"

Levi handed her a bottle from a cooler he'd set up next to him. "We can't leave the circle until you're back to normal. I'm hoping that's soon because I need to use the restroom soon."

"Gross," Christina said, but she smiled. She was sitting between Levi and Abigail, so either they'd patched up their fight or Abigail was trying to make that happen by putting them in close proximity to each other. "How are you feeling, besides thirsty?"

"Good." Mia quickly took inventory of her body from her head to her toes, like she'd learned in yoga. "Better than good. Whatever was in that tea worked."

"That was just a sedative to give your body time to

recover. Whatever you're feeling, that's all you." She glanced at the laptop. "Thirty seconds to the announcement. You're right on time."

Mia sipped her water as she watched the center of the circle. This time, a woman who looked like she'd stepped out of a *Bridgerton* TV show appeared in her living room.

"Mia Malone, you have passed your test with flying colors." The historically dressed woman smiled at her. "Your next test will be scheduled in six months. Congratulations on reaching level five. You've been working hard and this testing proves it. Make sure you talk to your coven leadership about what type of role you desire to serve in our organization. We see big things coming your way. Thanks for all your hard work, and welcome to your next step as a coven member. Participation. A bank deposit will show up monthly based on your test level."

With an arm flourish and a twirl, the witch filled the room with sparkling stars and disappeared. The stars lingered.

"This isn't happening." Mia groaned and leaned back into the couch. "I don't want to be level five. I was hoping I wouldn't even hit level four."

"Wishes and horses," Grans said, then repeated, "wishes and horses."

Chapter 4

"Congratulations, my dear. I don't think there has been a level five on a first testing for years." Damien came over and pulled Mia off the couch to give her a hug.

"Second testing. It's my second testing. I was supposed to be a level three or four at the most. But five?"

"The harder the test, the more likely a strong witch will score higher," Abigail explained. "I worried that Parker's zeal would affect the results."

A loud knock sounded at the front door.

"Who's that?" Mia turned toward the door. Muffy started barking and Mr. Darcy arched up and started hissing.

"Calm down, everyone, it's probably Thomas thinking I can't drive home on my own." Abigail hurried over to the door. "Did you hear?"

Instead of Thomas, Suzanne Parker stood at the door. "How did you cheat this time? I was there, watching every step. Do you have a friend in the testing department? I knew the coven was way too casual about this. I will find out and you will be banished from the community."

"I didn't cheat." Mia stood and walked between the group and the door. Muffy was on her right side and Mr. Darcy on her left. In the darkness, Mia spotted Buddy flying in for the argument as well. She perched on a tree on the other side of the parking lot. Mia could see fire in the dragon's eyes. "I think you need to leave and take your false accusations with you."

"I just wanted to tell you that I'm watching you. And I'm not leaving Magic Springs until I bring you down." Suzanne Parker glanced back at Buddy, who was watching her.

"Then you might as well buy a house here and move in. It's a lovely community, even for people who don't deserve it, like you." Damien picked up Muffy and tried to calm the dog.

"You! You're an abomination and should be burned. No one gets to cheat death." She glared at him. "Mark my words, you'll disappear sooner rather than later."

"You're threatening us?" Abigail pointed toward the door. "You need to leave, now. We don't act this way in Magic Springs. I'll have your job for this."

"I don't care. She's not a level five and I'll make sure she never receives a dime of the allotment." Suzanne Parker turned to walk away. "And your dragon's going to a zoo when I get back to Nationals. Exotic pets aren't allowed near humans. You should know better."

A chortle came out of the tree, but Mia didn't think Buddy sounded happy. She stepped outside, hopeful that the coven had reapplied her protection, and watched the woman drive off in a rental. She looked up at Buddy. "Go tell Trent I'm fine and we don't need him here. We're safe."

Buddy chortled again but followed her instructions after a brief hesitation and glance toward the road where Parker had disappeared. At least Mia hoped Buddy went straight home and didn't trail Suzanne Parker in her silver rental to the hotel to eat her. Dragons got rid of the evidence of a killing. Trent had told her that early on when Buddy first showed up in Magic Springs. Mia dialed and quickly explained things to Trent as she came back inside, locking the door behind her.

"Buddy's home," Trent said. "Mad as a wet hen but here. She keeps talking about someone threatening you."

"Suzanne Parker, my tester. She's taking this level five thing personally. And they're sending me money? What do I have to do for them to get a monthly check? Don't get me wrong, it would be helpful, but if I'm selling my soul to the devil, I'd like to know the terms before I spend the money."

He chuckled. "I'm not sure. I was never a level five. I don't know anyone at that level. They don't talk to me anymore."

"Not since you turned down your mentorship program?" Mia asked, wondering why Trent hadn't talked about the last straw that made him turn over his "official" power to Levi.

"Levi has a big mouth," Trent suggested.

"I think his mouth is exactly the right size. You've been keeping secrets from me. How am I supposed to make good decisions if I only have one side of the situation?" Mia wasn't angry at Trent, but her words sounded like it. Probably the Parker factor.

He grunted, either agreeing with her statement or just clearing his throat. "Anyway, watch out for Suzanne Parker. Stay home until she leaves town. This will all blow over."

"Maybe." Mia had a bad feeling about Suzanne Parker. "How's training going?"

"Cerby blew a hole through the side of the house and Tempest has turned the baby into a statue a few times. She seems to think it's funny. Em howls when Tempest performs magic for her or to her, depending on the way you see it. And no one seems to be potty-trained, not even the baby."

Mia started laughing. "So, you're telling me it could be worse? Suzanne Parker could turn me into a statue and pee on me?"

"Exactly." He sounded more relaxed now.

"Go to bed. I've got a house full of people I need to debrief with. I love you." Mia walked back to the living room, where everyone seemed to be talking at once.

"I love you too. I'm not sure I'm worthy of a level five, though."

Before she could answer, he hung up.

"How's Trent?" Abigail asked. "Did Buddy get home?"

"Yes, Buddy's home, and I don't think she had time to blow up Parker's car on the way. She wanted to tell

Trent everything." Mia rolled her head back and forth. "Now, the female thing makes more sense with Buddy. She's a protector and I'm one of her charges."

"She does love you," Grans added. "Dorian, I'll see you in the morning. We need to talk about this threat. If Suzanne Parker tells the National Office that you broke your contract, you'll be out of that body and on to the next world before you know it. You know they hate reincarnation of any type."

"I'll deal with that," Damien said, his voice cold. "You and Muffy should head to bed. Do you want me to take him out one last time?"

"That would be sweet. Mia, would you make sure Muffy gets into the apartment tonight?" Grans headed to the elevator. "I swear, life doesn't have to be this hard."

Abigail watched as elevator doors closed. "And yet it is. We need a meeting with all of us, well, besides Trent and Sarah. Maybe we can put them on speaker-phone. We need a plan to deal with Suzanne Parker. You don't want to take the next test for setting a level. It's barbaric."

"I'm not even going to think about what another test might be like. I'm worn out from this one. As soon as Muffy is back inside, we're heading to bed. Christina, are you staying here?"

The girl blushed so hard the roots of her blond hair glowed red. "No, I'm going back to the condo with Levi. Abigail, do you want us to drop you off?"

"I can drive, dear, no matter what my husband

thinks. I'll see everyone in the morning. Finn's heading off to the Lodge to work because Mia's Morsels is closed tomorrow. We'll do a brunch meeting in Mia's apartment." Abigail put on a coat and grabbed her keys out of her purse. "But I wouldn't mind you walking me out."

Mia walked to the door with the others. Mr. Darcy sat on the stairs, waiting for her.

As they said their goodbyes, Damien came up and handed her Muffy. "All taken care of. I'll see you in the morning." Then he kissed her on the cheek. "Congrats on level five. You deserve it. I knew the first time I met you that you were going to be something special."

"You're too kind." Mia leaned against the doorframe. "Dorian, can I ask you a question?"

"It must be serious if you're using my real name. Yes, of course." He adjusted his driving gloves.

"Is there really going to be a war?" Grans and the others had been talking about the signs for months now. Like how Trent and Em were granted hellhounds by the Goddess. And how the family power was being shared between the upcoming generation, at least here in Magic Springs. If Nationals found out, Trent and the others would be banned, or worse. Mia didn't want to think about it.

Dorian started. Apparently that wasn't the question he'd expected from her. Finally he answered. "It feels the same as before. The first war, we were fighting a common enemy. Now, I'm afraid the fight will be an inside job. We could be hurting one another without even knowing it."

* * *

Mia's phone rang at six the next morning. Swearing, she reached out from under the covers and found the phone. "What?"

"Turn on the news," Trent said.

As Mia did, she thought about Trent's tone. Something was wrong, and even in her sleepy state, she could feel his pain. "What's going on?"

"Just listen."

Mia sat up and turned up the volume.

"Just to recap, a local tourist has been found dead on the mountain. Sources say that the woman, one Suzanne Parker, apparently died of exposure. Her body was found on a cross-country trail, not far from the trailhead parking lot. Her rental car was located in the parking lot. Magic Springs Police have closed that section of the ski resort as they complete their search of the area. Police Chief Mark Baldwin wouldn't comment except to say that it was an open investigation. We'll let you know when the area reopens for skiers."

Mia turned off the television as the female anchor went on to talk about what to wear on this chilly morning. She turned back to the phone. "Tell me there's another Suzanne Parker visiting Magic Springs this week."

"You missed the description. Dark hair, pale skin, and working for the National Creative Arts department out of Boston," Trent said. "It's your tester. I took a picture of her photo on my phone, which the newspeople got from when she checked into the Lodge on Monday." He paused. "I just sent it to you. I wish I wasn't stuck in the house while this is going on. Why would someone kill a coven testing specialist? It's like attacking the people who transcribe reports in the CIA. They don't know anything."

Mia checked the picture. "That's her. I didn't know she liked to ski, but then again, I didn't know much about her except she was mean to the bone and seemed to hate me. She loved making me squirm on an answer. I could see it in her eyes when I paused to think. Then, when I answered the question, she'd frown. Finally I just stopped pausing. I would either pass or fail, but she wasn't going to intimidate me."

"That's one of the reasons you went up to level five. Confidence in the answer sometimes counts more than if it was right or wrong. Mom's heading your way for a meeting of the minds. I wish I could be there."

His words made her feel better. She knew no matter what, things were going to be okay. And if the coven refused to put back on her protection while the testing was sorted out and she had to quarantine herself, she'd just go over to Trent's. As long as she didn't go in and out, Sonja couldn't say anything. Well, she could, but Mia wasn't going to listen. She was a level five, after all. Her newly found level should be good for something, right? "I'd be surprised if they weren't already in the kitchen, plotting the next step. Our families can be a little intense."

"That is the understatement of the year. Sarah has breakfast ready and she'll want to hear the news. Call me when you can. I miss you."

As she hung up, her bedroom door opened and

Mr. Darcy pushed his way through. He sat looking at her and then meowed.

"Everyone is here and no one has taken the time to feed you? What are they thinking?" Mia jumped out of bed and went into the adjoining bathroom to get ready. Mr. Darcy followed her, making sure she wasn't planning on going back to sleep. And when she was ready, he held his tail high and ran out of the room.

"Tell Abigail there better be coffee," Mia called after her cat.

When she got to the kitchen, she'd been right. Everyone was there, including Thomas, Abigail's husband. He was on his tablet, doing things for the store. He glanced at his watch when she came in.

"Don't complain. No one knocked on my door to wake me." Mia took the coffee Abigail handed her and sat on the only empty chair. "So, you all saw the news? Thoughts?"

"Maybe it was an accident like the news said. She could have gone out on a late-night stroll or ski and couldn't make it back." Christina was eating a doughnut.

Mia saw the faces on the others in the room. "You don't think it's a skiing accident."

Thomas spoke first. "After we had the incident where Albert died while visiting Magic Springs before his last assignment, the National Office made a rule that if you were out on assignment, you could do no vacationing or recreational activities, even if you took a leave day. Once you got on the plane to your official destination, you were on the clock. No exceptions. Suzanne Parker wouldn't have broken protocol like that. She was a stickler for the rules." Thomas stood, putting his tablet in his briefcase. "I have to go to the store and sign for a delivery. It's early and the driver is almost in town. Abigail, please let me know if you need my assistance with anything dealing with this matter."

"Oh, do you have to go?" Abigail stood to kiss her husband.

He rubbed a spot of flour off her face. "If your son had just sent the little hellhound back to the McMann camp for his training, I wouldn't be needed at the store. I can't just close it down, now, can I?"

"Cerby didn't do well at the sleep away camp," Mia said, standing up for Trent's choice. She didn't like him being stuck there, but she wasn't going to let anyone criticize his decision. Not even his father.

"No hellhound does well at sleepaway camp. They are called Velcro dogs for a reason. He should just have told the little guy he had to go. Everything would have worked out." He kissed Abigail. "Just like it will in this situation. See you all soon."

After he left, Levi sighed. "Dad means well, but he's old school in this way. I don't think he realizes that as a hellhound, Cerby's more than just a familiar. He's a part of the family. Anyway, what are we going to do about Suzanne Parker's death? I guess our first question is, where was Mia last night, or rather this morning, around two?"

"Levi!" Abigail turned on her son. "First you talk bad about your dad, then you accuse Mia of killing that woman?"

"One, I didn't talk bad about him; I was trying to explain his utter lack of giving a darn about the problem. And two, we need to rule out Mia because she's the most likely suspect. Although she passed to level five, so maybe killing her tester isn't motivation. Never mind." Levi reached over and grabbed a doughnut.

"Okay, thanks for the trip down nowhere lane. But to answer your question, I was asleep in bed alone. If Mark wants, he can see the security tapes that show my car in the lot all night. What else do we know about Suzanne Parker?" Mia pulled out a notebook. "She was sent because someone here complained. That person couldn't have been happy when I not only passed again but went up two levels. Who would be that upset?"

"Whoever is next in line to go into coven leadership." Abigail stared at the monitor. "And we might be able to find out who that is right now. Brandon Maxwell and Sabrina Clayborn have come to call."

The group all stared at the security monitor that showed the two people with the highest-ranking coven leadership positions in Magic Springs get out of a black SUV.

"Let's take this meeting downstairs. Dorian, you stay here." Grans stood and finished her coffee. "They must have heard of your arrival. Let's just not give them a good look at you, especially because we're trying to pass you off as Damien. Do you even have a brother?"

"He lives in Latin America, helping the locals, but yes, I do have a brother." He refilled his cup. "Mia, does this monitor show the downstairs room as well?

I'd like to keep an eye on all of you. Christina and Levi, stay up here with me. We don't want people looking at the two of you, either."

"So many secrets." Abigail shook her head. "This would have been easier if your brother had kept the heritage. He would have been at a high-enough ranking to keep these two out of Mia's house."

"Mom always liked Trent best," Levi called after them as they left the apartment.

Chapter 5

Mia could hear Brandon and Sabrina arguing through the front door, but they hadn't knocked yet. She swung the door open, surprising them. "Good morning, how can I help you today?"

Brandon shot Sabrina a look that stopped whatever she'd been going to say next. Then he turned and smiled at Mia. "We came by to congratulate you on leveling up so quickly. It's such a testament to your grandmother's teaching. I don't think I've ever heard of a kitchen witch going above level four."

"Because typically kitchen witches aren't part of the coven leadership." Sabrina glared at him. Then she turned to smile at Mia. "Of course, we'd never make that mistake with you if you just accept our offer and join the coven. We need exciting new blood like you in our group. And let me add my congratulations. I worked on leveling up for years before I just gave up. Maybe I should try again? You could help me study."

"Maybe." Mia left it at that. She wanted to leave the discussion open so one of these two would tell her what she needed to know. Like how Parker was killed. "Do you want to come in? Or was that all you needed?"

"Oh, we'd love to come in and have some coffee." Sabrina pushed her way through the front door, then froze as she saw Abigail and Grans sitting at the table, notebooks in front of them.

"We're just talking about the business. Grans has some amazing ideas on expanding our line to include bath salts and light charms. Nothing too crazy; just some hot cocoa that also lulls you to sleep. You know, light kitchen witch magic." Mia wanted to slap both of them and show them what a kitchen witch could do, but she felt Grans's calming influence behind her, as well as the laughter Abigail was holding back.

"Oh, that would be lovely." Sabrina took Brandon's arm and together, they stepped into the academy. "I can't believe all the remodeling you've done in here. It looks more like a grand home than an old school."

"Yes, it's quite remarkable." Brandon seemed to catch his stride as they moved into the living room to join Abigail and Grans at the table.

"I'll go get more cups. We have Christmas Bell and Stocking cookies on the table. Feel free to take one or more." Abigail stood and headed to the kitchen, but she wasn't gone long. When she came back, she poured the coffee and handed a cup to both. "Isn't it amazing?"

Brandon stopped looking around, then realized Abigail was talking about Mia, not the remodel. "Oh, yes, we're all so proud. It's been years since an Idaho-born witch tested out at this level."

"Technically Mia's not an Idaho-born witch," Grans remarked as she broke open a cookie.

"What are you talking about, Grans? I was born in Boise." Mia wondered what game her grandmother was playing with the coven leadership.

"No, you were born in Ontario, Oregon. Your dad had gone on a job interview that didn't pan out, but he didn't want to leave your mom alone, so she rode along. What she thought was back pain turned into a two-week-early birth. I had to drive to pick your mom and you up because your dad had to be at work the next Monday. It was quite the mess. But you were worth it."

"I've never heard that story before." Mia sipped her coffee. "But Brandon and Sabrina didn't come over this morning to talk about my less-than-illustrious birth. What's going on with Suzanne Parker's death? Have you heard anything?"

The look on their faces told Mia they hadn't thought she would bring it up.

Brandon shook his head. "Sorry, no. The only thing I've heard is what's been on television. The police, of course, wouldn't know she was part of our organization. I'm sure the National Office has been notified, though. So sad for her to die in such a lovely spot. I cross-country ski often and that trail is stunning."

"I thought the National Office banned their employees from taking in the scenery or vacation spots when they were on a case," Abigail said as she took another cookie.

"Oh, well, yes, but you know witches. You can't tell us what to do. We're always going off on some broomstick or other." He laughed at his joke, but no one else did. "Broomstick? Like a tangent?"

"They are not the same thing at all." Sabrina rolled her eyes and turned to Mia. "The reason we're here is to ask you again to reconsider joining the coven. We need people like you and with your power. The payments for being a level five are only the beginning. You'll also receive payment for your participation in monthly events, as well as a salary if you take on a leadership role. And, of course, all your travel expenses would be covered. You'd have your own credit card that the National Office pays in full each month. And those are only the financial benefits. You'd be invited to specialized training in any field of study you want to take on. All we ask is that you sign your name on our coven rolls. We'll do the ceremony here, of course, and pay you for the use of the academy and the food."

"That's a tempting offer, but as I told you at Halloween, I'm still thinking about my membership. It's been crazy at work with the holidays, and I just need some time to make this decision. Having to retest on such short notice was stressful." Mia looked up from her coffee. "Do we know who complained to the National Office about my original test? I bet they feel stupid now."

"Complaints about another witch don't go through our local leadership," Brandon lied smoothly. Mia could tell it was a lie because Sabrina's jaw almost hit the table.

He stood and smiled, jerking Sabrina to stand with him. "Well, we don't want to take up any more of your time, especially when we barged in so early. Thank you for the coffee and for considering our request. I'm sure we'll see you around town."

After they left, Mia locked the door and went back to the table. "Thoughts?"

"Sabrina knows who complained, or she knows that Brandon does. He got her out of here before she could contradict him." Grans glanced at her watch. "I've got some potions to work on. Can I use your lab?"

"Of course. Do you think I should go to work?" Mia looked at Abigail and Grans.

"Stay home today. If nothing else happens, you can go in tomorrow. I need to refresh your protection spell. It took a beating during your testing." Grans met Abigail's gaze, and Mia saw a thought pass between them. She wasn't going to ask.

"Sounds good. I'm going up to fill in the others and plan my day. I need to check in with the Lodge, anyway. I've got a holiday party on Friday that I need to make sure is still on schedule." She stretched as she stood. "Then I might read a book that doesn't have anything to do with learning anything. A beach read in December."

"Everything has to do with learning. It just depends on what you need to learn," her grandmother said as she headed to the elevator.

As Abigail and Mia headed up to the apartment, Mia stopped Abigail on the stairs at the second-floor landing. "She's okay, right? Just her arthritis?"

"From what she's told me, Robert's giving her a hard time about Dorian being back in her life. She loved him, and it about killed her when she lost him. She made the golem so he'd leave Mr. Darcy and live a full life somewhere else. And yet he's back, digging in that old wound. I don't know what she's going to do. Her heart is ripped in two." Abigail rubbed Mia's back. "But you're not the only one who's there for your grandmother. She has a lot of friends, including me. We'll get her through this."

As they finished the climb to the apartment, Mia almost believed Abigail's words were true.

The apartment was quiet just a few minutes later. Grans was in the potions lab. Damien was on the same floor, working with his remodel crew. Mia had met with Nathan Boyle, and he'd presented a plan not only to update Damien's rooms into an apartment but also to change several of the second-floor rooms to more of a multipurpose use.

Mia told him what she wanted to do with a cooking school and gave him an idea of what she thought it might look like. He had promised to bring her plans in a few weeks.

Depending on what the allowance from the coven added up to, the funds might help her fix the place up and put away money so she could just run Mia's Morsels. She needed to take it back from Abigail before she became too comfortable with running the company.

Mia had just curled up with a book and some hot cocoa when something hit the wall in the living room. Technically it hit the wall on the other side, in the library.

The ghosts had something to tell her.

She set down the novel with a sigh, slipping the bookmark back inside, then grabbed the keys to the library off the key rack by the door. Finn liked using the library, but Mia still kept it locked. Finn could come and get the key any time, but at least when she did, Mia knew she was in there. She could make sure the girl got out.

She just had a feeling. And until that feeling left, she was going to keep control of the keys.

Mia walked out of the apartment, making sure her door was unlocked, then headed to the library next door. She unlocked the door, and sunshine made her blink. The library was filled with a glow that couldn't be from the gloomy day outside. The glow radiated a happy mood.

"What's got you feeling the feels?" Mia asked as she walked around. She found two piles of books on the table. One had a note on top that said FINN. The pile was filled with new romantasy books as well as some old favorite fairy tales that they used to train new witches.

The other pile was divided into two subjects. Two books were on the building of the academy. Mia held one up. "I suspect you've heard all the remodeling downstairs."

The other book was a history of the village witch. The book was old and looked like an old grimoire. When she touched it, she felt a bit of a buzz. Not a shock, but more of a welcome. "Thank you. This is going to help me understand who I am."

Gloria started up the music again. "We Are Family" seemed to be one of her favorite tracks this week.

So much for just chilling today.

She wasn't upset, really. Now that she knew the book existed, she was anxious to see what it said about her heritage.

As Mia went back into the apartment, the security monitor showed that the doorbell was ringing downstairs. Using the intercom to alert who was there that she was coming, she set down the books on the table and headed downstairs.

One of Damien's construction guys, probably. Mia's apartment and the industrial kitchen were the only two rooms that had a security monitor to notify her of unexpected guests. Maybe she needed to get one installed in her potions room on the second floor. Just in case.

Downstairs, Mia opened the door to find a shivering Mark Baldwin. He wore a heavy coat. She hurried him inside. "How long have you been out here?"

He stamped the snow off his boots, then took off his coat. Rubbing his hands together, he shrugged. "I was on the phone with Sarah because we didn't get to talk this morning due to finding your friend outside turned into a popsicle. Then I called you, called your grandmother, and called Abigail, but no one answered their phones. Sarah said you all had a meeting this morning about your new level. Does this mean you're flying East to become a big shot? Sarah said she's never met a level five before."

"She has. Me. Tell her I'm just the same person I was last week." Mia headed to the first-floor kitchen. Abigail always made a pot of coffee first thing in the morning. Hopefully, some was still left. "Let's get you some coffee. Did you eat lunch? I could make some soup too. I haven't eaten yet."

"Soup would be good." He followed Mia into the kitchen. "I didn't realize how hard it would be to not have Sarah around. She does everything and makes it look easy. I'm going to have to do something amazing for her when she gets back."

"It's nice to feel appreciated." Mia set coffee on the table where they had meetings and then went to the walk-in to get soup. "Clam chowder okay?"

"Sounds like heaven." He sipped the coffee. "Is it bad manners to ask you questions about your trainer when you're feeding me?"

"Tester, not trainer. Grans was—is—my trainer. This Parker woman was horrible. She's the model for the picture in the dictionary under 'witch.' She had a burr under her saddle from the moment I walked into the testing facility. The test was supposed to be Friday, but she came in early and moved it up, which, from the little I know about policy and procedure around these things, isn't done. Nor is it easy to do. She pulled some huge strings to get the date moved. Of course, none of this is what you wanted to know." Mia turned away from the soup pot on the stove and grabbed a bottle of water out of the fridge. She sat down with a huff. "What did you want to know?"

He had out his notebook but hadn't written anything down. "So, you were angry that you had to retest?"

"Surprised more than angry. I haven't even joined their stupid country club and they're giving me crap about what level I tested out on? It's their test, not mine. I couldn't have cheated if I wanted to. I don't know the process." She got up and stirred the soup, turning down the heat before returning to the table. "I'm talking myself into being your best suspect, aren't I?"

"Kind of, but I love the honesty." He sipped his coffee, but Mia could see a smile behind the cup. When he set down the cup and picked up his pen, he said, "Can you talk a little bit about this whole testing process? I know there's a lot you can't tell me, but I just need the dumbed-down version. What happens to a 'normal' witch going through this process? And I can't believe I even asked that question."

"I'm right there with you. The first time I met a McMann and realized werewolves were a real thing made me question what was in the water up here. I was sure I'd been dosed with a hallucinogen. But after a while you get used to it. Let me tell you what I know without giving away all the secret handshakes." Mia held up a finger. "But let me get the soup first. It should be done by now."

"I can help. Are there really secret handshakes?" Mark stood and followed her to the cabinet, where she gave him silverware and napkins and took out soup bowls.

"I was kidding about that, but who knows? Like I've said several times, I haven't joined the coven, so they don't tell me everything. Mainly they tell me the stuff that they think will get me to join. Like the money I'd make as a level five coven rep. They're freaking paying me a monthly allotment now, just for testing out. It's a dream job, at least for some people."

Mia ladled the soup into bowls and set them on the table. Mark took out another bottle of water, and they started eating. As they enjoyed lunch, Mia explained the training process for a "normal" witch. "As I understand it, they usually do their testing either after they finish high school or during their college years. My mother put off the testing until after law school, then, after she tested, didn't join the coven. Grans was fine with that, but she still expected Mom to take on the kitchen witch role someday. When she finally broke the news that she didn't want to be the next kitchen witch, Grans started training me. I was years behind."

Mark had written some notes as Mia talked, but then he set down the pen and focused on the meal. "The soup is amazing, thank you. Sarah will be glad to hear I've eaten. But I have one question. It's not about the case, so you don't have to answer it."

"Okay, and thank you. I've been working on this recipe for years now. The egg dumplings make it perfect, if not strictly traditional, in my opinion." She finished her last bite. "Go ahead and ask. I'm pretty much an open book."

"You seem unsure if you want to live in the witch world. Why didn't you just turn down the kitchen witch role?" He stood and pointed at the stove. "Mind if I get more soup?"

"Go ahead." Mia sat thinking as she waited for him to return with a second piping-hot bowl of soup. The smell made her happy. Wasn't it weird that a food smell could bring up emotions? Comfort, happiness, joy. This was why she loved cooking and feeding others. She knew this was her calling. Not sitting in some office in Boston dealing with witch business, no matter what the pay would be. Money was important, but this level of satisfaction, which she'd never felt before, was worth all the struggles.

When he got settled, she answered his question.

"I want to be a kitchen witch. To learn the history and lore of the village witches. To help people when no one else can. And, yes, to make food that makes others happy. This is my job on Earth. If I was fully mortal, without the magic, I'd be right where I am now. Fixing up an old building to make it a culinary resource for the community. With the kitchen witch role, maybe I can do more than just make people happy with my food." She laughed as she took her bowl to the sink. "Although right now, one or more people are mad about the level of my power and it's gotten someone killed. I'm not so happy about that."

Chapter 6

The next morning, Mia sent a message to Blake telling her she'd be in tomorrow to manage the weekend parties. The response was curt. Mia inferred that Blake had begun to think that Mia had decided she was too good for the job. After a couple of paragraphs ranting about the coven, Blake ended the email with the words "Have a good day off."

Mia blinked at the one line of positivity. Was it snide? Or was Blake actually wishing her well? She decided she'd take it at face value but watch Blake tomorrow for retribution for being off for three days.

Life was never boring around there.

Her cell rang and she saw the name: Trent. She answered the call with, "I'm so glad to hear from you. I miss you horribly."

"Nice to know, but I'm sure I'm not the one you miss." Sarah Baldwin was on the other end of the line. "I took a chance to give you a call because the baby is down for a nap and our evil overlord is studying her lesson plan for today before she calls us out to the backyard for our daily torture. Your guy is doing well, dealing with all these females in the house."

"Sarah, it is nice to hear from you, and it has been a while since I've seen you." Mia tried to backtrack on her first greeting.

"At least you didn't tell me what you were wearing." Sarah giggled.

Mia snorted. "I'm in yoga pants and a Boise State sweatshirt. How about you?"

"Jeans and a polo that Em just threw up on. Typical mom uniform." Sarah answered with the truth.

"Em?"

"Elisa Marie. We've been calling her Em for the last few months. I have no idea why, except I used the initials on my lists, and now she kind of likes it. Kids make their own world, right? Anyway, I won't keep you. The dragon lady's coming for me soon. I wanted to thank you for feeding Mark yesterday. I worry about him not eating."

"He came to interrogate me about the recent death and my role in it. Offering food was only polite." Mia smiled. "Besides, it was my lunch time too. He might have planned the visit that way."

"I wouldn't put it past him. Anyway, thank you. I'll keep Trent out of trouble here for you. Sonja is really pulling out all the tricks to try to get him alone. In fact, the house is too quiet right now. I'll go break up her evil plans."

Mia laughed and was about to tell Sarah that Trent

could take care of himself, but she'd already hung up. Sarah took her promises seriously.

She went into the living room and picked up the novel she'd been trying to finish for a few weeks. She'd given Damien the books on the academy structure last night, before he'd left to go to Grans's house to sleep. Grans was working in the potion lab again this morning. Mia wasn't sure what she was mixing up, but now she had at least a few hours this morning to read.

She was going to take advantage of it. Like Sarah did when Em—Mia loved that nickname—took a nap. With Trent on her mind thanks to Sarah's call, she snapped a picture of the book sitting on the couch and sent it to him with a caption, "My Day."

A text came back quickly. **Lucky. I hear it's a good book.**

He sent nothing else.

Whatever. She set the phone on the coffee table and curled up with the book. Sometime later, she noticed that Mr. Darcy had curled up with her. She rubbed his soft ears before returning to reading. Her life didn't have enough quiet times like this.

When the apartment door opened, Grans came in, her hair wild and slipping out of the clip she'd put it in that morning. Her shirt was stained with some kind of purple goop and she had a pen behind one ear. "You look comfortable. Nothing to do today?"

"Lots to do today, but the last two hours have been peaceful for me. Trouble in the lab?" Mia put in a bookmark and stretched as she stood, getting a dirty look from Mr. Darcy.

"The lab's fine. The protection spell took care of that. Do you want to start lunch while I take a shower? This inquisition spell is starting to make me queasy." She looked at Muffy, who'd just got up from his nap. "I suppose you need to go outside?"

The little white dog wagged his tail and barked.

"I'll get him. He's been sleeping all morning and I didn't even realize he was in the apartment." Mia whisked him up under her arm. "I can get some steps in. Tacos for lunch?"

"Sounds lovely if you can make some Spanish rice to go with it. I'm starving. I didn't eat much at dinner last night. Dorian can drive me crazy at times." Grans paused in the hallway to her room. "Thank you for taking him in. I appreciate you getting involved in all this."

"He and Mr. Darcy are buddies. I guess I don't have a choice but to call him my friend too." Mia watched as a glop of whatever Grans had been working on moved its way down her shirt. "Throw your clothes into the wash. I'll make sure they get in the dryer after lunch. I'm going to work on a design for a workout room on the second floor. Who knows how long I'm going to be here, and if Trent moves in, he'll need one like the one he has in his house."

"That's thoughtful. See you in a few." Grans had already turned and was out of sight.

Mia would pull Nathan aside and ask him about what it might cost to put this vision into reality. She could talk to Trent tonight about what he wanted in a home gym. It would be an excuse to call him.

Muffy ran out the door and frolicked in the front yard. As he turned to come back in, he paused and waited for a car to arrive. When Damien stepped out of his car and came up to the door, Muffy attacked him, begging to be picked up.

"He loves you," Mia said as Damien brought the little dog inside. "You can always tell a person's character by the way the animals in your life respond to them."

He kissed the dog on the head and then set him down on the floor. "He just likes me because I smell like Mr. Darcy. Even after all this time, I can still feel your cat in the back of my mind at times. It's not bad; it's like chatting with an old friend."

"I'm glad the two of you connected. After Christina moved out, I realized how lonely he might be here in the academy without you." Mia didn't mention how lonely she had felt.

"It was an adjustment for me as well. I'm sure you also had some issues adjusting. Now you have Finn here. You're the type to always have people around. You draw people to you."

Mia chuckled. "My ex-fiancé and I had an ongoing fight about that. I was always working, or out with friends, or doing something to the house. I was never there just for him. So he found a replacement. Don't get me wrong, she's perfect for him. Very shallow and all about appearances."

Damien watched her as they walked up the stairs.

"Sorry, that was a little petty. I'm not sure what's going on with me. I seem to be emotional." Mia rubbed her face, making sure there wasn't a tear on her cheek.

As they reached the second floor, Damien put his hand on her shoulder. "I'm surprised you're not curled up in a corner sobbing right now. Someone questioned your magic, called you a liar, and made you retest. The woman who tested you was a sadist, and your main support, Trent, is locked up in a house with a female werewolf who's acting like she's in heat. Not to mention your grandmother's ex-boyfriend, who used to be dead and existed as a spirit in your cat, is moving into your home. Did I miss anything?"

"My boss is mean?" Mia took a long breath. "Oh, and Mark Baldwin says I might be a perfect suspect for said mean tester's death. Par for the course."

"Just take care of yourself. Everything will work out for the best and I'll be out of here in no time." He rubbed Muffy's head. "Go make your grandmother lunch. You're always happier when you're cooking something."

She smiled, remembering how she'd said the same thing to Mark just last night. Damien was right; it was time for the pity party to be over. She might even finish that book this afternoon.

She started up the stairs, then stopped and asked, "Is Nathan supposed to be here today? I'd like to get his ideas on a project I'm thinking about."

"Not today, but I'll let him know you're looking for him. He's a good guy. Getting another project will help them get through the winter. Not a lot of building's going on with all this snow." He said his goodbyes and went down the hall to where his new apartment would be after the classrooms were modified. He'd chosen the two at the end of the hall under the library so if Mia wanted to rent it out, the new occupant would have some privacy from the classrooms she wanted to set up for a future cooking school.

Too many plans, not enough money.

Except for the allowance from the coven. She felt conflicted. Having the money would be nice, but it seemed like a trap. A way for the coven, local or not, to get its claws into her. She was sure they weren't offering a free lunch, but she still didn't know what the fine print on this contract said. She didn't trust anyone who said there weren't strings.

Damien was right about one thing. She needed to cook.

Mia walked to the kitchen and ran into Grans.

"Hey, Grans?" Mia paused. "How does Muffy feel about Robert?"

The answer might just sway her decision on which horse to pick in this race, although she already had an idea.

"Oh, they've never gotten along all that well. He's not used to pets. His familiar is a raven."

Christina called at three and asked if they could go to dinner in Twin Falls. Mia set down the book and stood up, moving Mr. Darcy off her lap. She only had three more chapters, but friends came first. Especially ones who didn't live with her at the academy anymore.

"Of course; what time do you want to leave?" She glanced in the mirror to check her hair.

"Can you be ready in fifteen? That way we can do

some shopping and walk the mall before we eat," Christina responded.

"Sure, girls' trip?" Mia asked, which seemed more polite than asking if Levi was tagging along.

"Levi's heading to his folks' for dinner. Will your grandmother be okay alone?"

Grans had told Mia she had dinner plans with Robert to make some decisions.

"She has plans. I'll see you downstairs in fifteen."

Mr. Darcy followed her to her bedroom and watched as she got ready. "I'll feed you now and let Damien know you're going to be alone tonight. I don't know what time he's leaving, but I suspect he'll stay around until Grans comes back from dinner."

Mr. Darcy yawned like he didn't care what the humans were doing, but Mia felt his relief. "Oh, and Muffy will be here."

His tail flicked as he walked away. Apparently that hadn't been the answer he wanted.

She was downstairs in twenty minutes after feeding both Mr. Darcy and Muffy and explaining to Grans what was happening. She might have made it sooner if Damien hadn't been so chatty about the books the library had provided.

Christina was sitting on the couch, waiting for her.

"Sorry. I'll grab a coat and we can leave. Had to check in with Grans and Damien." Mia grabbed her coat and watched Christina stand and slip on her pink designer puffer jacket. She wore fuzzy Ugg boots and her hair was pulled back with a pink hair band. "You look adorable."

"I'm in need of some major retail therapy. Levi doesn't get it. He wants to talk out all our emotions. I guess in this situation I learned from my mother. Buying is more fun than talking all the time." Christina unlocked the Land Rover. "Besides, you need some new clothes. Those boots are a mess."

"I love my boots. I'll take them in and get them resoled after winter's over. You know, talking isn't a bad thing. Especially with the guy you're going to marry in less than a year." Mia snuggled into the warmed leather seats. She loved Christina's car. Her beater car was on its last legs and barely had a working defrost setting, but it had snow tires and would get her through until she had the money for a better one. Not one as nice as Christina's, but better.

"I know, but this magic thing is just normal for him. He doesn't understand why I'm freaked out about it. My mom instilled in me a fear of magic. She told me many times that it was bad, probably her way of trying to keep me from exploring my birth parents' talents. Now I know why she had such a fit during my Goth stage. I just wanted to wear black for a while because she kept buying me pink."

"You love pink." Mia looked out the window as they pulled onto the highway down the mountain. Now was the time of day deer would be out, looking for snacks.

"Not as a sixteen-year-old who wanted to be anything but her mother." Christina turned down the music. "Even though I knew I was adopted, I was scared to death that I'd turn into a mini mom. You were the one female role model I had that made me think I could be my own person and still be loved, or whatever it was my brother called love. Trent is so much better for you. He listens when you talk. You should see the way he looks at you when he thinks no one's watching. It's fire and ice."

"Fire, I understand. Ice?"

"Solid, and desperately in love," Christina explained. "Anyway, I want to know what you think about me training and eventually testing for a level. Am I too old? Should I just let the magic be part of my history?"

"You could do both. Exploring who you are on the magic level gives you options later. If you want to expand that part of your life, you can. If, like Sarah, you want to step back for a few years, you can as well. Except she's been coming back into the fray ever since the Goddess gave her and Mark, Em—that's what they're calling the baby now. Cute, huh? I think Em getting a hellhound is a warning that we are going to need protection in the next few years. But what do I know? At least if you train, you can fly in the mist with me, and we can ignore what's going on."

Christina was quiet for a few miles; then she spoke. "Mom wants me to walk away from Magic Springs and all the magic stuff. She says it's like my Goth stage, just another way to not grow up. Of course, my first reaction is to go deeper, just to spite her, but this decision is too big to make just because I'm rebelling. With me marrying Levi, and into the Majors family, magic is always going to be there. If there's a war coming, I don't want to be the frail human wife who Levi has to protect from harm. Not that I want to be a warrior. I just don't want to be a burden."

Proud of her friend's growth over the years, Mia smiled at her. "You've grown up into this amazing woman. Do you have tissues? I'm so proud of you, I think I'm going to cry."

"Shut up." Christina laughed but handed Mia a box she had stashed just in case. "So you think my logic is sound?"

"I do. What's the harm in learning something? If you step away later, that's your call. Right now, you can't make the call because you don't know what making it means. I'm not sure what your magic gift is, but I'd bet it's related to your ability to make people feel welcome. Your hospitality career fits right into your strongest magical skill. Like my cooking. I'm a kitchen witch and a healer. I take care of others, which is why I was drawn to buying the biggest building in Magic Springs for my upstart catering company. If I'd been using human logic, I would have found a small, cute old house and just made the garage into a commercial kitchen. Instead, I have a three-story monstrosity filled with humans, creatures, and ghosts. I was worried I'd be lonely with you moving out, but people came right in and took your space."

"Hopefully not my space as your BFF?" They were down off the mountain now and driving into the flatter area where the Snake River had carved a deep canyon so many eons ago. Evel Knievel had once tried to jump it. Christina increased her speed as she drove toward the freeway and town.

Some enterprising humans had built the Perrine Bridge spanning the 1500 feet across the river. Mia always felt queasy as she went over it. The power of the water called to her senses. A pedestrian bridge lined the side of the vehicle area, but Mia couldn't even imagine trying to walk the distance.

The river was like the dividing line between the magic in the mountains and the agricultural community on the other side. Maybe the world would have been better off if the bridge had never been built.

Chapter 7

At the mall, the friends walked through several stores. Christina tried on outfits, then purchased several pieces. Mia found herself looking for underwear and a new pair of casual flats that would replace her current pair. Instead of throwing the old shoes away, she'd move them down to the first floor so she would have footwear if she needed to take out Muffy or Cerby. Dogs didn't wait for you to run up two flights of stairs to get ready before going out. That was how accidents happened.

As they shopped, they talked about little things. The apartment in Portland. Levi's new job. The box of books Abigail, who had taken on the role of Christina's teacher, had sent. "I was a fairy-tale junkie as a kid. Poor Isaac had to read 'Cinderella' and 'Snow White' anytime the folks were out for the night, which was a lot."

"I'm sure he got over it." Mia smiled as she looked through a rack of tops.

Christina glanced at Mia. "You seem like you're okay about what happened between you and Isaac. I would kill Levi if I found him with another woman."

"I'm beginning to think I wasn't as much in love with him as I thought I was. With Trent, it's different. I haven't seen him in almost a week and he's living with three women—four, counting Buddy—and I miss him, but I also trust him." As she said those words, she realized it was true. They had a bond and a little time or distance wasn't going to break that.

Christina thought about what Mia said before answering. "I think you're better off without Isaac. I love my brother, but he's self-centered. Poor Jessica's always running around to get him the right suit or dress shirt. And if she doesn't get a reservation for the exact time he wanted to eat? She hears about it. She's more of a slave than a wife."

Mia laughed. "He never got that royal treatment from me, and neither does Trent. He's lucky if I remember we're going out. My mind has been on a million things in the last few years. He keeps coming back, so I think we're good. Don't worry about me. Let's talk about the wedding and the move. I'm worried about you. With this new magic factor thrown in, is it too much?"

Christina stopped to admire a pile of cashmere sweaters. As she ran her hand over the fluff, she shook her head. "I don't think so. I needed to understand why I was choosing to add more on to a busy year, but we put that to rest. I am not just doing this to upset my mother. That's a plus. The thing is, I've been thinking a lot. I'm not sure us moving right now is a good thing."

Mia looked up from admiring the sweaters she couldn't afford. They were pretty and soft to the touch. "What do you mean?"

"If there's a conflict, maybe Levi and I need to be here. Not in Portland." She looked around, but no one was close. "Is there any way we can nail down a time frame?"

"For a magical conflict we aren't sure is coming?" Mia shook her head. Unusual signs had appeared, including her rapid advancement in the levels and the arrival of two hellhounds in Magic Springs within a year, not to mention Buddy. Having a dragon flying around town wasn't normal. But she wouldn't be fighting age for at least a year. The pups were still in training, as were Finn and Christina. Maybe this was the preparation phase. Or maybe she was just overthinking. The coven might adjust to the new magic in the world versus their limited one-family-member-per-generation rule. But then, why had Suzanne Parker had such a fit about her testing? She paused her ruminating. "I've thought it all out, but I can't tell you one way or the other. I just don't know."

"Well, that's disappointing." Christina pointed at the sweaters. "I'm tired of buying pretty things while you just get basics, so what color do you want?"

"What are you talking about?"

"I'm buying you and me matching sweaters for the holiday parties. When I get back, Levi and I are going over to talk to Abigail and Thomas about training and the cloud over our heads. If she thinks we should stay, we're staying. I'll talk my job into letting me work from home and fly out to the Portland office every once in a while. They don't need me on-site except when we're training staff. Right now, I have to redo their training program from the ground up, which will take months. I can do that from the condo in Magic Springs. And if we're living there, Mom can't come to visit at the drop of a hat." Christina found a powder-blue sweater in her size. "Now, pick a sweater as your adviser fee."

"Think of more questions to ask. I'd really love a new coat too, but we can wait until after Christmas, when the sales are running. These are going to drop at least twenty-five percent in a few months." Mia chose a bright red sweater that would scream Christmas without having bells or trees on the front and would go with her black wool pants. Perfect for her upcoming work holiday parties.

After they'd paid and tucked all the packages into the back of Christina's SUV, they drove to a local steak house nestled in the canyon wall by the golf course. Mia loved this place, and it was her go-to fancy outing with Trent. The hostess sat them at a window table, and Christina excused herself, leaving Mia alone.

She knew what she wanted to eat, so she sipped the wine that the waiter had already brought and scanned the restaurant for anyone she knew.

As a waiter moved away from a table, she saw Trent sitting with Sonja, his hand on hers in the candlelight. The image flickered as she tried to focus. She pulled out her phone, but the call wouldn't go through. As Christina sat down, Mia whispered, "Call Trent for me."

"Your phone is right there." Christina looked at her like she'd lost her mind.

Mia didn't look at her. "Just please call Trent."

Christina did but shook her head. "The canyon must be messing with the phone. It's not ringing through."

Mia needed to break the spell. She knew the room reeked of magic, and if she didn't break it, they might be stuck here for who knows how long. "Call Sarah Baldwin. Do you have her cell number?"

"I do have her number. Are you going to tell me what's going on? You're scaring me," Christina said as she called Sarah. "Hold on a second, it's ringing. Hi, Sarah. Mia wants to talk to you."

Mia took the phone Christina handed her. "Are Trent and Sonja there with you?"

"Yes, of course. Em just fell asleep, so we're all cooking dinner in the kitchen. What's wrong?" Sarah must have heard the emotion in Mia's question. "Do you need help?"

"Can you ask Buddy to fly to the Feathered Moon in Twin and wait for us by the car? I think we might need an escort home. She has some time. We haven't ordered yet." Mia took a breath as the man who had been Trent seconds before transformed back into his true self. She didn't know the couple who the spell caster had used to focus the spell, but she smelled the cinnamon as the spell burst open and disappeared. "We're going to eat dinner and should be ready to drive home in about an hour."

"You're sure that's all you need?" Sarah's intuition was telling her there was more to the story.

"I'll fill Trent in once we're back in the academy. I'd

rather not talk about it now." Mia thanked Sarah and handed the phone back to Christina. "Did you feel or see anything?"

"The room wiggled a little just now. Like a bad television set." Christina glanced around the dining room. "And I just smelled cinnamon rolls when you talked to Sarah. What happened?"

"Someone's been listening in on our conversation and trying to mess with my mind. We'll talk about it in the car. Buddy's coming to escort us home after we eat." Mia signaled to their waiter and opened the menu. "Figure out what you want. We have an hour. Maybe I shouldn't have left the academy today."

After a worried glance, Christina focused on the menu, and they got their order in. As they waited, Mia put aside the wine. She wasn't sure when it had arrived at the table. In fact, she didn't remember ordering it at all. Christina didn't have wine. Just her.

"You're thinking so hard it's hurting my brain," Christina said as she ate her salad.

"I'm sorry. I've never been attacked like this before. Someone wants me off my game. Is it so I don't investigate Parker's death, or is it because of my current level? I need to talk to Grans, and probably Damien. It's a good thing he came back." Mia stopped and held up her hand. "I mean, it's a good thing that Dorian's brother decided to visit us. He has several lifetimes of information we can draw from."

"He is knowledgeable. And cute. I'm surprised your grandmother isn't all over him. He's a catch." Christina's eyes twinkled, and Mia knew she was acting for whoever might be listening.

Mia laughed. "My grandmother has specific tastes in men, and she wants them to be pet friendly. Some in the coven aren't, which is weird, since we all have familiars."

"Isn't Gloria a doll?" Christina frowned as she lowered her voice.

Mia sighed when her plate of seafood fettuccine arrived and the waiter grated Parmesan cheese on top. "Actually I'm beginning to think she's not a familiar after all. I think she's an elder."

Maybe the book she'd been given by the library had information about Gloria, if that was even her name. What if her name was Allegra, or something else, and she'd just started calling her Gloria? No, that wasn't right. Mia didn't know how the doll first appeared in her bedroom, but she'd been Gloria from day one. She had to have been given the name from the witch residing inside.

Was she a spirit? An elder? Was she even inside the doll at all? Maybe she just used it to communicate. Too many questions for a Thursday night. Especially when she had a party to manage tomorrow.

"What are your plans tomorrow night?" she asked Christina, who had ordered trout.

"Levi and I are going to Boise for one of Mom's parties. Isaac got us a room at the Owyhee." She rolled her eyes as she tore a roll in half. "Mom bought me a dress in New York when she and Jessica went a few weeks ago. I hope it fits. I've been eating like crazy. For some reason I'm always starving lately. It must be the cold weather. My body's ready to hibernate."

"How long has that been going on?" Mia watched as

Christina finished the last bite on her plate. Mia asked the waiter for a to-go box and the check.

"Since I started planning this wedding. I've been stressed. Sue me." Christina put her credit card on the table. "Don't argue. I know you haven't gotten any of that level five money yet. Besides, I asked you to come and soothe my edges."

"And you bought me a sweater." Mia held up her hands as the waiter put her leftovers in the to-go container. "And lunch for tomorrow. Unless James feeds me. Then it will be dinner."

They stood and headed out the door. Mia felt the pop as soon as they reached Buddy's protection area. Having a dragon around came in handy as long as she kept herself out of sight.

Buddy appeared in the tree by Christina's parking spot. Clutching an envelope in her claws, she chuffed at Mia.

"Another love note? You two should get a room." Christina got in the car as Mia walked over to accept the envelope.

"Thanks, Buddy, for coming to get us. I might need you tomorrow on my way home. Should I just call Trent?"

Buddy nodded and turned invisible again.

A kid walking with his mother to their car stopped and pointed. "Mom, there's a dragon in the tree. A purple dragon."

"Oh? Is it Barney?" The woman smiled at Mia as they passed. "Television is great, but sometimes his imagination goes wild. He sees dragons everywhere."

"He'll grow up to be a creative. Maybe an artist."

Mia smiled down at the boy, not wanting to confirm or deny the dragon just a few feet from her. The mother couldn't see Buddy, but the kid had.

"That will drive his dad crazy. He's a lawyer and soon-to-be politician. I don't think he wants his son talking about seeing dragons. It's hard to be a parent." The woman waved and climbed into the car.

Mia did the same and then smiled at the pair of yellow eyes she still saw in the tree. "Let's get going. I'll tell you what you missed as soon as we cross the bridge."

"Do you still hold your breath over bridges? Isaac thought that was so weird." Christina pulled the SUV out of the parking lot.

"Your brother's weird, not me," Mia replied, but she knew that people's thresholds for weirdness were determined by what they knew to be true. Isaac knew the world was round and inhabited entirely by humans and the animals that he could see in a zoo. Just like how that kid's dad would tell him purple dragons weren't real—except one was, and his son had seen her tonight.

They were almost in the mountains when Mia finally felt comfortable enough to tell Christina about the spell she'd been drawn into at the restaurant. "I know we were being listened in on because of that vision. I'd said I wasn't threatened by the idea of Trent and Sonja, so someone decided to put my feelings to the test. Someone from the coven and, if I have to guess, probably the same person who requested my retest. Brandon knows who that was, so sometime tomorrow I'll stop by his house for a chat. Maybe he'll let something slip."

"He's really sneaky. There's no way I'd go to his

house alone without backup. He might have a sex dungeon." Christina slowed the vehicle down to take a curve.

"You read too many romances." Mia closed her eyes for a minute. Pulling out of the vision had cost her some energy, especially because she had to verify that what she was watching had nothing to do with her boyfriend. But maybe the vision was a clue. Maybe the fact that Sonja was here this week wasn't a coincidence. Abigail could check that for her.

"Brandon's a dark romance character, but I don't think he's hero material. Not even a morally gray hero." Christina laughed as Mia's eyes popped open and she stared at her. "What? Don't you categorize people you meet into fictional characters? I have to say, Trent is a perfect Prince Charming."

Mia was beginning to think this whole week had been planned to get her off-kilter. And maybe it wasn't just about the testing. "Thanks for driving tonight."

"Thanks for calling in air support. Why is it I'm more freaked out about my possible magical talent than having a dragon for a protector?" She glanced up at the skies as they emerged from a wooded area onto the road that would take them to town.

"I always knew you were smart." Mia glanced at her phone. She'd told Trent she'd call him in the car, but she thought this conversation would be better once she was alone in the apartment. She texted him, letting him know that they were in town and she'd send Buddy home soon.

The response came back quickly.

Maybe you should keep her there for a few days. Mom and Dad are at the academy waiting for you. Call me when you're able.

As Christina pulled her SUV into the parking lot, she pointed out Levi's Jeep in the line of cars parked in front. "Did Trent tell you what was going on?"

"No, but it looks like we have a meeting of our secret club to go to when we get inside. I'm so glad we got some girl time in, I'm worried now I might be locked in the tower for a few years." Mia tucked her phone away.

"Okay, Rapunzel, stop with the dramatics." Christina parked and turned off the engine. "Let's go see what's happened now."

As Mia got out of the car, Buddy landed in her favorite tree on the other side of the parking lot. Mia grabbed her packages, then walked over to chat with her. "Can you go check on Trent and Cerby? I know he wants you here, but I'd like to know they are okay there too. Especially with Sarah and Em there."

When Mia mentioned the baby, Buddy's eyes lit up and the tree bounced a little. She chirped out her answer and took off.

Christina shook her head as Mia returned. "I didn't realize that oak trees could bounce. Buddy is heading to Trent's?"

"For a check-in, then she'll be back here. I hope Trent feeds her before she comes back. Too many stray cats hang around here."

Christina looked stricken. "You don't think . . ."

Mia shook her head. "There are a lot of things I

don't know about dragons, so I'm just concerned. Besides, the way she chattered about Em, I think she has a soft spot for defenseless animals."

"I'm not even going to keep thinking about that." Christina held open the door. "I hope that sweater works out for you. If not, let me know and I'll get you a different one."

"It will be fine." Mia set her packages on the table in the foyer and looked at the assembled group. "Are we starting a meeting of the Magic Springs Magical Outcasts Society for Justice now? Or are we waiting for more members?"

Her grandmother sat next to Damien, with Abigail and Thomas on the other couch, facing them. Levi came up to hug Christina and they sat with the group. Mia took the last seat.

Grans sighed. "It's not funny, Mia. Mark stopped by and said someone sent him a video of you following Suzanne Parker in your car Tuesday night. He thinks you killed her."

Chapter 8

"Mark Baldwin does not think I killed Suzanne Parker. He's just getting confirmation that I was here, with most of you, that night, waiting for my test scores. And if I hadn't been here, the announcement would have found me and announced in the car or wherever I was. Sarah had to have told him that much." Mia sank into a chair. She felt beat, but being back in the academy, under the protection wards, was giving her more strength. "I need to tell you what happened when we were at dinner."

As she started talking about the glamour she'd seen at the restaurant, the room got quiet. Levi stood and went to the fridge and grabbed a beer for both Mia and Christina. After she'd finished with the fact that Trent had sent Buddy to follow them home, Thomas stood and paced.

"We haven't seen magic like this against another witch for ages." He'd paused as he'd formulated his statement, meeting Damien's gaze. "Can you remember the last time, at least locally?"

Damien shook his head. "My books are being delivered next week. As soon as they are, I'll dig into that question, and find out who cast the spell back then. But if I were to guess? It has to be almost a hundred years since we've had proof of this type of tampering."

"I'll spend some time in the archives tomorrow," Grans offered. "I'm concerned that this isn't just about your magical level."

"I have that feeling too. Abigail, can you find out when Sonja was assigned to train Cerby and Tempest? I feel like I was set up to be alone here more than I have been this week. One, to ruin any alibi, but there may be another reason. The vision I had was based on something Christina and I were talking about at the mall. I'm either being followed or a listening spell has been cast on me."

Christina raised her hand. "Or on me. I was supposed to be back in Portland this week. Levi, I think I'm moving back into my old room for a bit. How do you feel about not leaving Magic Springs just yet?"

"I don't think we should leave. Whoever is doing this is skilled at breaking up the group. But I feel weird staying in your family's cabin alone." Levi leaned into Christina. "And I can't go to Trent's."

"You can come home," Abigail said. "You know your old room is always available for you and Christina."

"Okay, maybe the Adams's cabin won't be that weird. Just don't tell your mom I'm there alone. She'll come by to count the silver," Levi said.

"You're awful but not wrong." Christina laughed as she leaned into him. "I just can't leave Mia here alone."

"I have Finn and Grans most nights and Damien during the day." She looked around the room. "I'm rarely alone here."

"But when you are alone, you're in danger," Abigail pointed out. "If you're going back to work, we should have someone with you at all times."

"Really? How is that going to work? I have an event tomorrow and Saturday night. Then I go back full time on Monday. Does one of you want to give up your life to be my shadow?"

Christina held up her hand. "I can. My company has an exchange program with other hotels where we can visit and observe other locations for two months. I'll put in the paperwork tomorrow and should be up and running by Monday."

"I'll call the captain and tell them that my mother is sick and needs her baby boy." Levi grinned at Abigail. "She's on her deathbed, but I hope to bring her back."

"What happens if I visit Portland when this all settles?" Abigail asked.

Levi shrugged. "I pulled you from the jaws of death and nursed you back to health. Too bad I'm in a committed relationship or this story would get me dates for years." He kissed Christina on the cheek.

"Don't push it; you may not be in a committed relationship if you keep this up." Christina swatted at him. Then she yawned, stretching her arms. "I'm glad I still have stuff here. I don't think I could drive back from the condo tonight."

Mia had been quiet while people were chatting. She

looked at her grandmother. "Who else was here when you talked to Mark?"

"Just me. He knocked on the door, then waited for me to get downstairs. He's such a nice young man."

"I don't want to offend you, but . . ." Mia didn't get to finish her statement. Or had it been a question?

"You're wondering if it really was Mark here." Thomas sprinted to the front door, holding out his hands to check to see if any additional wards were in his way. He brought in a box that had been sitting out there for hours. "Whoever is doing this glamoured the FedEx guy. I bet his mind's been wiped too."

He set down the box on the table and scanned it with his mind. When he was done, he turned to Abigail. "Your spices have arrived."

"I was wondering when they would show up." Abigail pointed toward the box. "Leave them there, I'll retrieve them on my way into the kitchen in the morning. I think we should break for the night. Levi? I'd make breakfast if you came home."

"Tempting, but I like my privacy. Even from my parents." He stood and pulled Christina to her feet. "I'm going to take Sleeping Beauty up to her room. Then I'll head out."

"Call me when you're back in the condo," Abigail said. "I'll worry."

"Darling, we've been empty nesters for years. Someday you're going to have to trust that our sons can make it in the world without interference from their mother. Besides, that's Christina's job now." Thomas pulled Abigail out of the chair and into his arms. "Society, we'll see you in the morning. I'll drop this one off on my way to work."

"I'm not going to a day care, Thomas," Abigail replied, kissing Grans on the cheek as she moved toward the door.

"Maybe with all that's going on it wouldn't be a bad idea. Who knew that you taking on a job cooking could be deadly?" Thomas shook hands with Damien, then slapped his son on the back. "Listen to your mother. Call."

"I'm not just a cook, I'm a manager." Abigail slipped on her coat as Thomas left the academy to warm up the car. "Men. Sometimes they're infuriating."

"You would know, you have three boys," Mia said as she watched people leave. Damien followed Thomas out after walking Grans to the elevator. Levi and Christina were already on their way upstairs, which left her and Muffy watching Abigail waiting for Thomas to pull the car closer.

Muffy whined, and Mia put on her jacket and snapped a leash on Muffy's collar. "I don't think you're going to like it out there, but let's get this over with."

Abigail followed them out. "You know if you need Trent, he'd stop the training and come here."

Mia watched Muffy scout the grass for the perfect spot. "I know. I miss him, but I believe we need Cerby trained more than I need him here. Besides, I have things to do, including figuring out why someone wants me to react to all their games. Was tonight meant to make me leave town? Break up the Society? Or was it just a game to hurt me? And they had to know I'd talk to Mark."

"Unless they aren't local. I don't think Sarah's magical genealogy is known outside of town. And no one from the outside would know that your grandmother used to babysit Mark. Maybe they thought a visit from the local police chief would scare you." Abigail waved as Thomas pulled up the car and reached over to open the door. She gave Mia a hug. "You're one of us now, no matter how you got here. Same with Christina and Finn, and your grandmother and Damien. We're a family, no matter what anyone else calls us."

Mia watched them drive away, then heard Muffy barking from the door. Time to go inside before they froze. She waved at Buddy, who was perched in the tree with one eye open.

It was time to make a list of who might want Suzanne Parker dead, besides herself.

The next morning, she was sitting in the kitchen drinking coffee when Grans and Christina came out of their respective bedrooms. She stepped away from the coffeepot when Christina stared at her with her eyes half open. "Get some go-go juice, sunshine. If you're my shadow, we're leaving in thirty minutes."

"I went into catering because most events are held at decent hours, like in the evenings." Christina poured herself coffee and sat next to Mia. "What are you working on?"

"A time line since my last testing. Abigail and I have a theory that the culprit may be from out of town. Whoever sent me the vision of Trent and Sonja last night didn't know that Sarah was in the house with them.

They missed blocking her phone. And they didn't realize that Mark and Sarah were friends of mine. Fake Mark didn't have the information real Mark did." Mia tapped her pen on the paper. "It sounds more convoluted than it really is. Basically, the spell caster didn't know the details. We need to be wary of anything we see because it might not be true."

"I'm working on a truth elixir. It's a complicated potion, but it should give the drinker the ability to see through the glamours. You'll know when it's happening, and hopefully you'll be able to see the person casting it. You have to be close to cast that level of illusion. Dorian and I chatted on the phone for a while last night. He's going to help me make the potions after he gets the workmen started on the remodel. I'll do the library archive lookup later, once the potion is brewing, so he can watch for me while I'm in the library."

"One, you need to call him Damien. What if someone from the coven sees him? And hears you call him by his real name?" That was the problem with lies; they could never be sustained. Especially when you were dealing with honest people.

"And two?" Grans didn't look up from the book of potions she was reading.

"What?" Mia needed one more cup of coffee. Work would keep her busy so she couldn't think about the murder and the things she didn't know.

"You said, one. That tells me you have at least two points." This time, her grandmother looked up.

"Oh, yeah. Two, your plan is really good. Ask the library ghosts if they know of any other books with relevant information." It had worked the one time Mia went to the archives for the coven. She'd just written down what specifically she'd been looking for. "Oh, and see what we can find out about Suzanne Parker. If nothing else, it might give Mark some information on next of kin."

"I'm sure the coven has already notified her relatives. When a witch dies, an alert goes off at Nationals and a memo is sent to the coven. Now we just need to see who comes to claim the body. If Mark is spelled to forget the murder ever happened, it's a clear sign a witch was behind the murder—not a case for the humans to worry about."

"Well, that's nice to know. How many times have they wiped Mark's memory?" This was one discussion Sarah could choose to have with her husband. Mia was not telling him that the coven decided what cases he could or couldn't work on.

"Who knows the exact number," Grans said too quickly, which meant she probably knew the exact number and thought the coven was overreaching. "Oh, don't look at me like that. Most of the time it's just harmless high school pranks. No need to go to jail over a spell gone wrong that turned all the snow bunnies in Magic Springs pink."

"I thought that happened in Arco, near the nuclear site. And it was neon orange, if I remember." Mia decided not to push it. They had too much to deal with without the shenanigans the coven pulled on local law enforcement.

"It happened there too. The kids told the local law enforcement that it was a protest against nuclear proliferation." Grans grabbed two protein bars as they watched

Damien's car come into the parking lot on the security monitor. "I better get started on that potion."

"Say hi for us," Mia called after her.

"Was your grandmother blushing?" Christina asked after the apartment front door closed. "She was a little dressed up to be making potions, right?"

"I guess she made her choice. It must be hard for Robert to be left for a golem." Mia watched Damien get out of his car. His long dress coat made him look like a lawyer. In fact, she thought her dad had the same coat. She needed to call her parents. It had slipped off her list lately, mostly because they would want her to come home to Boise for Christmas, and bring Grans and Trent.

Grans wasn't a problem, even if she had to bring Damien too. But Trent? He had family here, and asking him to give up Christmas with the Majorses for the less-than-exciting meal with her parents filled Mia with dread. Not to mention the questions. *Was it serious? Were they looking at a date?* She'd hate to tell them that the wedding would have to wait until after they potty-trained the hellhound and the dragon matured a little. And they wondered why she never brought a boyfriend home. Mom would understand, but from what Mia knew, Dad was fully human.

She sighed. Her life didn't used to be this complicated. She turned to Christina. "Thirty minutes."

Thirty turned into fifty before they were in the car. Christina drove, which saved Mia from having to defrost her beater. The car always had a bit of a gas smell when she drove it, like it would burst into flames at any moment. Trent said it was her imagination, but Mia didn't think so. One day, she'd be in the car and turn over the engine and that would be all.

She didn't like thinking of bad things. Instead, she asked Christina about the wedding planning and the girl was still talking as they drove into the parking lot for the Lodge. The one thing that always distracted Christina was asking about the upcoming wedding.

As they walked into the Lodge, Mia aimed toward the registration desk. She smiled at the young man who stood there, waiting. "Hi, Matt. This is Christina Adams, if you don't know her already. She's going to be here shadowing for a while, so if you see her go into the employee-only areas, don't freak out, okay?"

Blake came around the corner. "Your friend is shadowing you? What happened to the Portland job? Couldn't cut it in the big city?"

Mia started to say something, but Christina stepped in between them and laid her hand on Mia's arm. "I didn't realize you were following my career so closely, Ms. Sandburg. I'm honored at your interest. But no, they didn't fire me, they're looking at a more extensive role for me. I'll be taking on all of their smaller facilities, like your cute little Lodge. Standardization is the key to quality and cost effectiveness, don't you think?"

Blake mumbled some sort of agreement. Then her eyes narrowed. "Why are you here?"

"Like Mia said, I'm shadowing. I'm sure as soon as you check your email, you'll see that my presence has been approved by your supervisors." Christina stopped talking. Mia felt like she was watching a game of chicken. Each woman waited for the other to blink.

Blake lost the game and walked away. "Whatever."

Mia turned back to Matt. “I was also wondering if I could see the bill for a Suzanne Parker. Can you send her information to my work email?”

“When did she check in?” Matt hurried to write down the name, glad to be out of the battle zone.

Mia gave him the details as she knew them, then paused. “That start date might be wrong, so push it out a few days if you don’t find it on that Monday. Thanks.”

As she and Christina walked to the back of the great room and toward Mia’s office, she said, “You handled Blake well. Another lesson from your mom?”

“She does have a way about her.” Christina giggled. “I didn’t like the way she treated ‘the help,’ as she called anyone who did anything for her or the family, but I learned from the best when I need to pull out my entitled side. I should have Blake totally ignoring you before I leave. She’ll be too scared to browbeat you even a little.”

“Blake’s not that bad,” Mia said, then laughed. “Okay, at least she’s better than my last boss, who was actively trying to get me fired.”

Christina looked behind them. “I don’t know. I’ve met people like Blake before, and all they worry about is what they’re getting out of you. I’m not sure she’s on your side at all.”

Chapter 9

Mia found Christina sitting at the interview table in her office after the morning meeting. She was surfing the internet on her laptop.

Christina stood to get more coffee as Mia came inside. "You're not going to believe what I found. Come sit down."

Mia did what she was told, grinning at Christina's excitement about her sleuthing. "Can you bring over that pot? I need more coffee after that horrible meeting. My head is killing me. Blake is implementing more forms. A pre-evaluation of the event before it even begins. She's a horror."

"She finds comfort in numbers and forms." Christina filled her cup, then put the pot back. "Anyway, Suzanne Parker is a really common name, until you add in the Salem thing. Then the sightings fall into a straight line. Either this woman was three hundred and thirty-three years old, give or take, when she was murdered, or her family has a lineage tradition of naming the first-born daughters Suzanne Parker."

Christina showed Mia all the notations where a Suzanne Parker made the news. "And, most interesting, our current Suzanne Parker owns a plot of land here in Magic Springs."

"She has a house here?" Mia turned the laptop to see it.

"No, just an empty plot of land. She lives in a condo on Virginia Beach. I've seen the pictures from when it was on Zillow. You need to work for the National Office. Those people make bank. Of course, she bought it about ten years ago, so it's gone up in value, but she has a balcony and the building has a rooftop pool. I'm rethinking our move to Oregon." Christina handed her a folder. "I printed the stuff I knew was our Suzanne Parker. She reads a lot and posts reviews. She's not very nice in them, but sometimes she finds a book she kind of likes. If I read that many duds, according to her, I would give up reading."

"She lived on the beach, she reads, and her family owns property here in the area." Mia flipped through the pages. "You did a lot of work in an hour."

"You were gone for two. I was about ready to go find you when you walked in the door. Why did you say an hour?" Now Christina was studying her.

Mia waved away the question. "I guess I lost track of time because the meeting was so boring. I swear, at one point, I looked over and James had fallen asleep."

"Do you need to be here or is the event tonight dealt with?" Christina asked as she typed a message on her phone.

"Why, do you have a hot date?" Mia stood and sipped her coffee as she moved to her computer and started hitting keys. "This is good. Not like the crap Blake served at the meeting. How hard is it to make a good pot of coffee? I swear, we're in the hospitality field for a reason. According to everything I can see, my staff is ready for this event. I love them. Oh, and Matt sent us Suzanne's record from when she stayed in the hotel. It will show any room or dining charges, as well as who paid for the room, which appears to be the National Office, from their travel funds."

"Can you print that for me? Let's go check out this lot. Maybe you can sense something there." Christina stood and grabbed her coat.

Mia printed the invoice, then closed her computer. "Sounds good. I'm getting used to these low-key workdays."

After they left the Lodge, Christina drove them to a highway that headed out of town. Instead of going south toward civilization, this road headed west and, eventually, over Magic Mountain.

Mia rubbed her temple. "Man, this headache is not going away. Why is my necklace flashing? Tell me it hasn't been doing this for long. I never noticed. What good is it to have a protection spell if you can't see the warning light?"

Christina started to say something, but Mia's phone started chirping at her. She put it on speaker. "Sorry, this is Grans. She's probably found a potion and needs us to pick up something on our way home. Hi, Grans."

"Where have you been? I've been calling for over an hour since your necklace alarm went off. What is going on over there? Is Christina with you?" Grans barraged her with questions.

Mia held up the gently pulsing necklace, and it stopped beating. "It's been going off for an hour?"

"Blake had her in a meeting for two hours, but Mia thought it was an hour. The others in the meeting were asleep." Christina spoke toward Mia's phone. "I got her out of there when I saw the necklace blinking. She seems fine now."

"Well, Christina, you're not a doctor or a witch, so forgive me if 'seems fine' from you doesn't alleviate my concerns." Grans sighed so loudly, Mia heard it over the speaker. "Sorry. I don't mean to be short. Where are you now? Heading back to the academy, I hope?"

Mia locked eyes with Christina and responded. "No, we're going over to check out a plot of land that Suzanne Parker owned here in Magic Springs." With her head clearing from the fresh air and distance from Blake, she added, "Grans, is there any way Suzanne Parker was three hundred and thirty-three years old?"

"Of course. She works at the National Office. They don't like losing talent just because they grow old. They all use some sort of antiaging spell. I wish I could find that spell. I'd sell it to the makeup people and be rich. Or not."

"Or not?" Mia asked.

"Often pharmaceutical companies don't want the cure for something. It steals all their profits. They want to appear as though they're solving the issue without really fixing it. So they buy up these ideas and then stockpile the formula, keeping it from others, less unethical than they are. Humans are a weird lot. You're fine, so I'll get back to my work."

After putting her phone away, Mia turned to Christina. "You got me out of there on purpose?"

She nodded. "Your eyes didn't look right, and I sensed traces of magic on you. I don't want to tell you your business, but I think your boss is spelling you for some reason."

"You have got to be kidding me. Why do I keep thinking that Blake will react like a normal person?" Mia blew out a breath and then closed her eyes, focusing on her legs bouncing and her need to kill Blake. Okay, maybe not kill, but tie her up and make her understand she couldn't keep messing with her. Pushing her fantasies of torturing Blake aside, she opened her eyes and focused on Christina. "Sorry, she just makes me so angry."

"I'd be mad too if someone was messing with my head," Christina admitted.

"Well, I'm going to find out why, and if I don't like her answer, I'm going to let the coven know. They might not do anything about it, but in no world are you allowed to drug another witch." Mia peered at the address. "I think we're here, but that's not a vacant lot."

"They're paying taxes like it's bare land. I've driven down this road every day for almost a month but never saw this place." Christina pulled the SUV over on the road. "Do we want to knock on the door?"

"Why not? Work doesn't seem to be a safe haven, and we can't even go to dinner without having issues. My necklace is either calm or broken. Why not press our luck?" Mia laughed at the look Christina was giving her. "I'm kidding, a little. Let's just go knock on the door and see who lives there. With all the cars parked around the place, it looks like they're having some sort of party. We'll just crash."

"One, I'm not dressed for a party, and two, it's only eleven. Who has a party at eleven?" Christina turned off the engine and tucked her keys into her designer purse. "If your eyes go fuzzy again, I'm dragging you out of there. No discussion."

"I'm trusting you to do just that." Mia took a deep breath.

They walked up to the door and found it had been left open. Mia pushed the door farther open and stepped in. Chamber music filled the room, which buzzed with men and women in formal day attire. Suits, black dresses, and muted colors. She saw Finn checking the line of buffet trays set up on the side of the room. Christina recognized someone on the other side of the room, so she and Mia split up.

Finn was fiddling with a platter of food as Mia came close to the table. "The crab Rangoon is freshly made and we used Alaskan king crab for the filling." She looked up. "Oh, Mia, it's you. I didn't realize you were attached to this event. James got me a slot. You won't believe what these people pay."

"Let me guess; the event is for the Magic Springs Society for Magical Realism? Who's doing the catering? The Lodge?"

"No, James said it's a private company out of Sun Valley. All high-end products. The lady who hired me said they only do one or two events a year in Magic Springs, but she'd hire me full time if I wanted to travel around the Boise area." Finn's eyes widened. "Of course I said no. I'm happy at Mia's Morsels, but you know I need to fill in spots so I can get my own place."

"Relax, Finn, I'm not here to check up on you, and if you get a better offer, take it. Just make sure it fits into what you want to do." She glanced around the room and recognized a few of the coven members. Brandon Maxwell stood near the fireplace and watched her. He lifted his champagne glass in salute. Mia turned back to Finn. "What is this event? A meeting? Did they tell you?"

Finn pointed to the side of the room, where a picture of Suzanne Parker was propped on an easel. "It's a wake for that woman. It hasn't started yet. That photo gives me the creeps. It's like she's always watching you and you're failing miserably."

Mia knew that look. Suzanne Parker had used it on her from the moment she arrived at coven headquarters to the time Cleo came to end the testing—and probably check to see if Mia was still alive.

They were at Suzanne Parker's wake with the coven. Why would a local coven put on a wake for a National Office rep, unless Suzanne was a local member? Mia hadn't known that.

"Will everyone gather around?" Brandon called from his new standing spot near the picture.

Mia turned back to Finn. "Do me a favor and watch what goes on today. Come up to the apartment tonight and I'll cook. I need to know if anything weird goes on."

"I can do that, but I'm working the dinner service at the Lodge. How about breakfast tomorrow? I'm going into the Lodge around noon to help James with the prep for your event later that day." Finn rubbed her fingers together. "No fresh crab to shell for prep tomorrow, thank goodness."

"Don't tell Abigail I said this, but you work too hard." Mia took the plate Finn had made for her and walked over to stand by Christina. "Finn's here. This is a coven event."

"I found that out from Carolyn over to the left. She was in class with me. She said that Brandon never thought you'd come, so they hired an out-of-town caterer." She glanced around. "I think the level five thing is freaking people out."

"What, they think I'm going to blow up the building?" Mia smiled as someone came by to greet her. When they left, she turned to Christina. "Any idea who lives here?"

"Not a clue. Will you excuse me? I need to use the restroom." Christina walked to the back of the room, then pulled aside a woman who pointed her in the right way.

Instead of speculating about what her friend was up to, Mia focused on Brandon as he started talking.

"Suzanne Parker was a beloved elder in our coven. Her commitment to the coven and our way of life was strong. She moved back East to serve the National Office in the testing and verification of new witches everywhere. She mentored several witches during the time she taught at our old academy—many who have gone on to be leaders in our organization, including myself. I had the honor of taking potions from her all four years of academy. I was a mess in the class, but she never told me to give up. Instead, she gave me biographies of witches who took years to settle into their specialty. She was always telling me to focus on what I loved doing, not what someone else was doing better than me. Suzanne Parker, you will be missed." He held up his glass for a toast. Then the next speaker came up to the lectern and started talking. He too had been a former student, but his ramblings made Mia wonder if he'd ever given a speech before.

Christina came back around his fourth or fifth story that had nothing to do with Suzanne Parker or her life. "We need to leave. Finn should come too."

"I'm not sure she can; she's working." Mia took a look at Christina's face. "Oh. I think she looked sick. Let's get her out of here."

Finn didn't question the urgency. She went to the back, grabbed her keys, and told her boss she was throwing up and must have a stomach flu. The woman blanched, then shooed her away from the table.

As Finn and Christina got into the car, Finn looked back. "I hope they don't throw away all that food I made."

Mia climbed into the car after catching up with the group. "She won't. I told her you took a pregnancy test at home but left before it was done, and that I told you it was a test for the flu."

"She believed that?"

"I told her you were a little naïve." Mia shrugged as Christina laughed, and Finn groaned. "What? The next time you talk with her, just tell her you must have lost the baby early."

"I'm such an idiot, I can't keep a baby alive?" Finn got out her phone. "At least she knows I'm a good cook."

"A lot of people lose babies in the first trimester. That's why doctors say not to get too invested," Christina said.

"Oh, have you had that experience?" Finn asked, not looking up from her phone. "I just sent you a bunch of pictures I took of the house and the people who attended the wake. I have a cute one of you two as well."

"You're amazing." Mia grabbed her phone and opened the photo app. "Oh, Christina, why did we have to leave so soon?"

Christina shivered, digging through her purse as she drove. "I was looking for the main bathroom to find a medicine cabinet. Everyone keeps medicines near their bedrooms. Anyway, I found a bathroom that had another door. I looked in the cabinet and found these."

Mia caught the bottle of pills with Suzanne Parker's name on it. She didn't know the name of the medication. "This prescription was from last month. Did this woman stay here? Was the Magic Springs house a vacation home?"

"I don't know, but in the attached bedroom there were two beds. One seemed to be a hospital bed. A woman was hooked up to wires and stuff, including a breathing tube. She looked young." Christina paused as she stopped the car at a stop sign. "Mia, I swear the woman on the other bed was Suzanne Parker. She looked like the picture. What on earth is happening over there? Or did I just have a vision, like you did at the restaurant?"

"Those are both excellent questions." Mia texted Grans to see where she was. They needed a meeting of the society, and now. Some of the group needed to be caught up on the practices of the coven. "I don't know the answer. But maybe the society will."

Mia looked behind her and into Finn's eyes. One other member needed to be added to the group.

Thomas couldn't get away from the store until three, so Mia spent that time explaining to Abigail and Grans why they needed to drop Finn into the deep end of her witch education.

"She lives here. The ghosts have accepted her. And she knows we're not normal. She might as well know the whole thing." Mia stirred the batch of cookie dough she'd made to keep her mind off what could have been happening over at the house that shouldn't even be there. "Finn is either part of the group or we set her up in Twin Falls, where she'll be safe from all this. We can't just keep pretending that we're normal. She also needs to know the full truth about Dorian."

"You mean Damien," Grans corrected her. When Mia stared at her, she shrugged. "I think you're right. If Finn's going to be here, she needs all the information. If she chooses to leave, we'll wipe her memories and set her up in Twin. Damien will provide her with a war chest. He set aside money for years, and I mean years, for something like this."

"That's kind of you, or him, or you on his behalf." Mia laughed as she pulled out a cookie sheet. "Finn will be at the meeting tonight, then she can make up her mind. Unless you want to go chat with her now."

"I'll wait for the cookies to be done. I find disturbing news always goes down better when you have a little bit of sugar. Just like in *Mary Poppins*." Grans turned to Christina. "Now, before you reach for a second glass of wine, tell me everything you saw in that room."

Christina told Grans everything, just like she had to Mia.

After she finished, Grans took a breath. "Did you notice anything weird or off about the scene?"

"Besides the dead woman come back to life and the girl on the hospital bed?" Christina clarified as she took the last sip of her wine.

"Yes, dear, besides that. You said you recognized Suzanne Parker from the picture. What clothes was she wearing? A nightgown, a hospital gown?"

Christina blinked several times. "Huh."

"What's huh?" Mia put the tray of cookies into the oven and got out a second tray.

"In the picture, Suzanne Parker was in a classic Chanel suit. I know the suit. My mom bought one off the Paris runway that year and she still owns it. It's ivory, and I can't believe it still fits, but when she wants to look perfect, it's her go-to outfit. Suzanne Parker had on the same suit in the bed. Powder blue, but the same. She was wearing it as she lay in that bed. Mom wouldn't even sit down in her suit. She didn't want to wrinkle it. Now I don't think I was seeing some sort of body-swapping vision at all. The room was probably empty. I got sent a false vision, didn't I?"

"I believe you did. The coven doesn't have a body-swapping ritual, at least not one I'm aware of. Something triggered the glamour—maybe you sneaking off to find out who lived there. Or, more likely," Grans picked up the medicine bottle, "you removing this from the cabinet. Someone is going to great lengths to keep us from solving Suzanne's murder."

Chapter 10

Mia and Grans pulled Finn aside before their meeting. As they sat in the living room eating cookies, Mia watched Finn's face.

"Grans and I," Mia began, "well, we think we should talk about what it means to be a witch in Magic Springs. I want to make sure you know everything that's going on so you can make good choices. And maybe stay safe."

"You think it's dangerous here?" Finn let the cookie she was about to take a bite from drop back to the plate on the table.

"I don't know. But you need to know a few things." Grans started explaining the magic community to Finn, focusing on the people who were in their own magic society. When she told her that Dorian was a golem, she didn't bat an eye.

"He's a nice person, I know that." Finn shrugged as

she absorbed the information. "No matter what his history is. I guess the bigger issue is who I can trust, right?"

"That's exactly why we want you to know everything." Grans continued talking about the witches and ghosts around them and ended with Cerby and Tempest and their hellhound sides. "So if you have any doubts, we can get you a room in Twin Falls until this is all dealt with."

"I'm here and part of the group. Mia made me part of her circle. If there's trouble, I can help." Finn grabbed her cookie again. "It's like finding out I have superpowers. There's no way I'm walking away from that."

Mia felt better about their society as they met that night, mostly because she now knew they weren't hiding any *Rosemary's Baby* stuff from Finn. As she watched the group gather, she wondered how she'd ever thought that could be true.

Whoever had killed Suzanne Parker was blazing a trail with fire. They wanted Mia's group out of the picture. They weren't beyond trying to scare them away from the investigation with visions, which were getting worse by the day. Mia wasn't reacting like the killer wanted her to.

"What else do we need to talk about?" Thomas asked as they all gathered. Grans had told them about the discussion with Finn, and she'd been introduced to the group as a whole. Finn was one of them now.

Finn stood. "Hi. I'm Finn. I'm a witch. I don't know much about any of this, but I'm willing to learn and excited about helping in any way I can."

"You may regret saying that," Levi said as he playfully punched her in the arm. "Someone has to be the virgin sacrifice on Halloween."

"Levi Majors, what an awful thing to say to Finn." Abigail pointed at her youngest son. "Now tell her you were kidding. Finn's going to think we're awful people."

"I kid because I care." Levi grinned as he sat back.

"Don't worry about it, Abigail. I'll get him back when he's not expecting it." Finn tapped her finger on her chin. "What does Levi hate? Come see me with suggestions after the meeting."

Mia thought Finn was going to get along nicely with the group.

Thomas rubbed Abigail's shoulders. "Anything new on the murder? Did we come up with some suspects?"

"Did you hear anything at the shop?" Mia countered his question with a question.

"Not about the murder. Everyone's talking about Trent and his houseguests. I've been trying to explain that they are family friends and need a place to stay because the baby might have measles." He grinned. "Once you bring up a communicable disease, no one wants to gossip any more. At first, the rumors were about Trent having Sonja and Sarah living with him, and his new unconventional lifestyle, especially because Sarah is the police chief's wife. Now, everyone wants to know if the test results came back yet. I've been explaining that the CDC is running behind."

"What's crazy is that a measles outbreak might be true in today's reality. Trent is trending out there, or was, until you gave them all measles. Good work," Mia said as Thomas held up his hand for a high five.

Abigail pushed down her husband's arm. "On that subject, I haven't been able to find out who set up this whole at-home training schedule. I talked to Trent and he said that at first he was told that Cerby would have to do on-site training, even if it meant bringing his dragon. I don't think they thought that one through. Buddy would protect Cerby at all costs."

"So someone put the bug in Sonja's ear to do the home class, then Sarah came in and ruined her little romantic fantasy," Christina recapped.

"Nothing kills romance like a baby, a third wheel, and a couple of hellhounds," Levi added. He looked at Mia. "Not that Trent was looking for a side piece."

"Oh, don't let Sonja hear you call her that." Thomas shook his head. "I heard stories about her breakups. They're brutal, for the male, at least."

Abigail stood and wrote down something on the whiteboard. "Whoever set up the Trent distraction is still up for grabs. Innocent, poor planning, or intentional scheming? What else did we find out?"

"Christina found a property that has been in Suzanne Parker's name forever and indications that she's over three hundred years old," Mia said.

"Shut the front door, really?" Finn was sitting cross-legged on the couch, watching everything. "That woman in the picture? That was her house, right?"

Mia smiled but ignored the question. "Why did Suzanne Parker have a house in Magic Springs? Brandon revealed she was a local coven member in his eulogy. And that she'd taught here."

A book dropped from the ceiling and onto the coffee table. Finn jolted and moved her feet under her, staring at the table. Mia picked up the book. "Thank you, library. This looks like a yearbook. Who wants to bet that our favorite witch is in here?"

"I wonder if any of her friends are now in high places, like Brandon." Christina held out her hand for the book. "I speak high school. Let me see what I can find."

"You're scary sometimes." Levi pulled her and the yearbook back down on the couch they were sharing.

Finn sneaked another glance at Christina. Mia had noticed Finn doing that all evening. "Why do you keep looking at Christina like that?"

"I'm not looking at Christina. Well, I am, but it's not from a bad place. I promise," Finn stuttered, then stood, picking up the cookie platter. "Well, this is empty. I should fill it up." She hurried to the kitchen.

"What's with her?" Christina looked at Mia. "Doesn't she like me?"

"I think she likes you fine. She's probably just overwhelmed. Look, she'll be okay. Let me tell everyone about my day at work."

Mia explained about Blake's spell causing her to lose an hour and how Christina had noticed her necklace going off and had gently removed her from the Lodge.

"That's not done. We have a strict no-attack policy between witches. If someone found out, that witch would lose her powers, with no chance of parole." Levi stood and paced. "Someone's breaking all the laws around this death. It makes it hard to figure out who to trust."

"Which I think is the point," Mia pointed out. "The witch behind this is strong and getting stronger. We have to assume what we're seeing isn't real now when we go out into the world. Be careful out there. We don't know who the bad guys are."

After the meeting was over, Mia went and knocked on Finn's bedroom door. "Can we talk for a minute?"

The door opened and Finn waved her in. The room had a small sitting area with a table and a set of chairs. On the table was a pile of books and a can of soda.

"Sit down," Finn said. "Can I get you a soda? I've got a mini fridge over there in the corner."

Mia hadn't been in Finn's room since she'd told the girl she could move in. It looked like a college dorm room, but on the larger side. A rolltop desk was up against the wall. "Sure, a Coke if you have it, or root beer."

"I have Coke. I keep them for my migraine days. Caffeine and sugar work almost as well as the meds that are crazy expensive." Finn grabbed the soda, then sat down. "I guess you want to see how I'm handling the new world information you threw at me this afternoon."

Mia couldn't hold back her smile. "Basically."

"It was okay finding out I had some magical talent. Cool, even. But now, with all the stuff they're doing to you, I'm not sure I want it. It's like being in the mean girl's club at school. You see the new girls get hazed and wonder why didn't I, or when will they do that to me." Finn sipped her soda. "You guys—Abigail, you, even Christina—are normal. Well, she's not totally normal. She reminds me of the cheerleaders in high school. All upbeat, all happy, twenty-four seven, like a KHOP radio host. And now, well, she's going to have a lot on her plate."

"You should have met her at your age. She was all Goth. Black nail polish, the works. And those Doc Martens boots. Her mother hated it." Mia leaned back. "How do you know she has a lot on her plate? I suspect you're not talking about her wedding or the move."

"No, it's the babies. Can't you hear them chattering all the time? Sometimes they're worse than she is with the positivity. Every time I see her, I think of the happy baby yoga pose. The babies never stop giggling. It's weird I can hear them, right? I'm weird." She curled up in her chair.

"You're not weird, but this is a talent I haven't ever heard about. We should talk to Grans about it. You can't tell Christina yet. I don't think she knows she's pregnant."

Finn's eyes went wide. "How can she not know? She's a witch too, right?"

"We all have different abilities. Yours seem to be in the area of mind melding, to use a *Star Trek* word. Grans will know more." She sipped her Coke as she thought about what Finn had revealed. "So that's why you've been strange around Christina. Tell me what you think about the other stuff, 'the mean girls' club,' as you call it. Do you want to forget about this and just be human? I can fix that, but you'll have to leave Magic Springs."

"What about you guys?" Finn shook her head. "No.

This is the first time I've felt like I've had family in a long time. My mom tried, but she thought I was weird too. When I told her I could hear the baby she was carrying, well, that sealed the deal. What about this tester? That was her wake I was catering?"

"Yeah. I didn't know she was even from Magic Springs." Mia tapped her can thoughtfully. "I guess I need to find someone who knew her."

"You should ask the woman at Magic Brews. She knows everything. Once my magic was confirmed, she gave me a gift." Finn stood and walked over to the table. She picked up a dragon made of amethyst. "This. She said I might need it someday."

Mia hadn't talked to Marsha Fieldstone for a while. She seemed nice but very tied to the coven. "How did Marsha know about your magic? Did you tell her?"

"You're kidding, right? I don't need people thinking I'm crazier than they already do. No, one day, I was in there working on my recipe book, and she walked up with a box. The dragon was inside. She said it was lovely to meet a new witch, and if I ever needed help, I could call on her. She said she was on my side." Finn looked down. "Then she hugged me. I was shocked. She ran out of the dining area and back to the counter. I stayed away for a few weeks, but she chilled out after that."

"We need to have Grans check out the statue, and you should tell her about Marsha. I'll do some research on that too. Before we arrived at the wake, did you see anything?" Mia pushed away her questions about Marsha Fieldstone.

Finn shrugged. "I had some trouble keeping the sternos lit, but nothing weird about that. Some catering companies don't replace those containers often enough. Of course, people didn't start showing up until eleven. That guy Brandon who talked first came over and introduced himself. Said he was a friend of yours, and if I was considering joining the coven, he'd be glad to walk me through the process."

"He said we were friends, and he knew about your talents?" A pit formed in Mia's stomach. How had the coven found out about Finn? Did they know about Christina as well?

"I knew he was lying. One, he never comes over to the house, and two, he just had this liar, liar, look about him." Finn rolled her eyes.

Finn's description made her smile. "Good instincts. I haven't told anyone about your history, so I don't know how he found out you were training with Abigail, or how Marsha Fieldstone knew. I guess I need some coffee."

"Sounds like a good place to start gathering information. Coffee shops are the best place to find out about the community. Before I moved here, I'd stop at a shop for a few days to see if the town felt right." Finn looked up from rubbing the table with her jacket. "That was my magic talking to me, wasn't it?"

"You seem to have a strong intuition skill. Make sure you mention this to Abigail. Maybe there's some specific training around that. I only know kitchen witch stuff." Mia wondered how strong Finn really was with her magic.

"I don't think that's true." Finn turned around and found a worn paperback on her desk. "You should read this. The most important line in the whole book is 'Argue your limitations, and they're yours.'"

Mia looked at the copy of *Illusions* by Richard Bach. "Do you mind if I borrow it?"

Finn smiled. "I know where you live, so sure. Your library has been so generous with its books, I guess I can lend one of mine."

"You'll get it back, I promise." Mia stood. "I'm going to get that coffee now. I'd take you with me, but I want to talk about you, and it might be uncomfortable with you right there."

"Take Christina. You shouldn't be alone." Finn stood and followed her to the door. "Thanks for inviting me to your society. Things are starting to make sense."

"I'm afraid we might have put you in danger or on the wrong side of the battle, but you need to make your own decisions and alliances. I'm not even going to tell you to stay away from Marsha. I think you can figure out who is good and who's not." Mia held up the book. "Thank you for sharing this."

"Mia the good witch. It has a ring to it, right?" Finn giggled as Mia reacted. "You should see your face."

Christina was sitting in a booth at Magic Brews while Mia waited for Marsha to finish making the coffee. The dining room was empty. They had come at the exact right time to corner the coffee shop owner.

"Here you go." Marsha set a tray in front of Mia.

"Marsha, if you aren't busy, I was wondering if you could chat with us. I'd like to talk about Finn Shiley. She works for Mia's Morsels and now lives in the academy with us. She said the two of you talked?" Mia held her breath, half expecting Marsha to run out of the dining room to the back.

But the woman turned toward the large pot and filled a cup with black coffee. Then she put three cookies on a plate and gestured to the booth where Christina waited. "Let's get this over, then. I've been wondering when you would show up. I'm surprised it took Finn this long to tell you."

"Honestly, we've been limiting her witchy knowledge, so she probably thought you knowing and giving her the dragon was just cool. We sat her down today and filled her in on most things. Abigail's training her, and from now on, she'll be involved." Mia sat down and handed Christina her coffee. "So how did you know? Did the coven make an announcement?"

"An announcement? No. You must remember, I deal with the witch entrance log for Magic Springs. As soon as Finn arrived in town, I've been keeping an eye out for her. She obviously didn't know who or what she was for a few months. Now, I feel her power growing." Marsha took a cookie, then handed the plate to Mia. "I hope I didn't frighten her. I was just trying to be friendly."

"So, she showed up on the new entrance list. I suppose that's also how Brandon found out?" Mia took a cookie, then handed the other to Christina.

Marsha shook her head. "He already knew when he called me about two weeks ago and asked me when she arrived. The list isn't given to the coven. They have to work through me to get the specific information. That way, if a noncoven witch comes into town, then leaves without causing any trouble, the coven never knows they were here. It's a right-to-privacy issue, and it saves unattached witches from having to deal with coven admission coordinators in every town they visit. You've met Sabrina. You know they can be a little pushy."

Christina dusted the cookie crumbs from her hands. "When did the list show me?"

Marsha smiled softly. "I didn't realize you already knew your history, but the moment you showed up in town as a teenager. Wearing all that black. I was certain you'd realize your potential sooner rather than later. The funny thing is that no one in the coven has asked about you. Typically, if a witch stays longer than a year, the coven gets an alert, and they come to me for the specifics. Right now, it's like you're shielded. Mia, did you put that spell on her?"

Christina and Marsha turned to stare at Mia. She lifted up both hands in surrender. "It wasn't me, I swear. I wonder if it was Grans."

"Honestly, now that I'm up close with you," Marsha said, gazing at Christina, "the spell feels older. Like it was put on when you were a child. Speaking of children," Marsha started but saw Mia shaking her head, her eyes wide.

"Yes?" Christina asked.

"Oh, I was wondering how you liked the cookie. It doesn't have as much sugar as it normally has. I hope it's sweet enough." Marsha's words stumbled out.

Mia needed to talk to her friend soon to let her know she was expecting. Maybe all first-time moms were this clueless to what was going on inside their bodies, but Mia thought Christina would realize it sooner or later.

If someone like Marsha didn't blurt it out first.

Chapter 11

As they drove home, Mia kept thinking of ways to tell Christina. Mia was now certain of her friend's pregnancy because so many others had noticed it as well.

Christina pulled the car over into a slow-moving vehicle turn out and shut it off. "Okay, tell me what you don't want me to know. You keep watching me like I'm going to explode or something. Did someone predict my fortune and I'm going to die before my wedding? What? I need to know so I can deal with my future. Good or bad."

"It's good, but Christina, I could be wrong. It's just that other people are seeing it too, so I think you should know, so you can do something about it if you want." Mia took a breath. "You're pregnant. With twins."

"What are you talking about? I'm totally regular and I'm on the pill." She pulled out her calendar from her purse. "I track my cycles just in case and my last one was . . ." She flipped through the calendar app. "It looks like I didn't write it down. Probably all the excitement from the engagement and the move."

She fiddled with her calendar, then counted out the weeks aloud. "Eight weeks? How can I have missed it for eight weeks? Wait, why did you say twins?"

Mia didn't look up. "Finn can hear them arguing and laughing."

"That's why she's staring at me? She can hear the babies? But if they're that young, they don't have mouths or voices, or—crap, it's a witch thing, isn't it. The twins are probably witches too. Of course they are; their daddy is a witch, just as, apparently, I am. How is it that you knew, Finn knew, even the coffee lady knew, but I didn't? Marsha can't backtrack a line to save her life."

"I don't know why you didn't know, but now that you do, does it feel right? We're dealing in a time of false information, so maybe I'm wrong. Maybe everyone's wrong," Mia said, focusing on the hope she didn't feel for the idea.

Christina's hand dropped to her stomach. "I'm pregnant? With twins? I can't believe this is happening so soon. I mean, we've talked about a family. Levi wants a son to buy one of those little motorcycles. Just thinking about my baby on one of those makes me freak out. Wow. Pregnant. Me? I'm going to be a mom."

"I could be wrong," Mia repeated, but then she saw the glow on Christina's face.

"No, it's true. I can hear them now. Girls. Twin girls with an attitude. What are we going to do? I guess I'd better get a test and a doctor's appointment. And tell

Levi." She laughed. "I'm not sure he's ready to be a dad, but he'd better buck up. There's no way I'm going through this without him. I'd have to move back in with Mom and Dad and they would ruin the kids. Private schools, trips to Paris to shop, a housekeeper and cook? Maybe I'm not going to tell Levi."

Mia laughed. "You'd be back by the weekend. Your mom drives you crazy."

"Yeah, but these girls might send me to the loony bin sooner." She rubbed her stomach protectively. "I'm just kidding, girls."

"So you're okay with this entire thing? I feel like I keep asking people that question. 'Hey, your world just exploded, but are you okay? It's been a week.'"

Christina started the car and pulled into traffic. "Let's go back to the academy, with a quick stop at Majors Grocery for a test. Levi needs shampoo anyway. What did we learn from the coffee lady, besides the fact that she makes great cookies?"

Mia and Christina talked about the witch entrance announcement. Mia slapped herself on the forehead. "I forgot to ask her about when Suzanne Parker came to town. I wonder if she'd know about her living here and being part of this coven. I bet she does. Now I have to go back and ask more questions."

"You need a book. A notebook where you can write down this stuff," Christina offered an idea.

"I have one, but it means I have to look at it when I'm talking to people. I'll call Marsha tonight. I wonder if Grans started dinner yet. Does dinner happen if we're not there to remind people or actually cook ourselves?"

"Oh, I'm certain Abigail has dinner going. She's been pushing food on me all week." Christina sighed and hit the steering wheel with the heel of her hand. "My soon-to-be mother-in-law knows, doesn't she?"

"That I don't know, but if she's pushing food? Probably. Your mom would be taking food out of your hand, so you'd fit into a designer wedding dress," Mia pointed out.

"Twins. I'll be huge walking down the aisle if we wait. We need to move up this wedding, especially the one in Magic Springs. I don't want to look like a white whale in satin and lace."

When they got to the academy, Mia got out of the car and saw Buddy land in the tree.

"Do you think we had an escort?" Christina stood, watching the dragon.

"I don't think Buddy's going to be far from us until Trent gets released from almost solitary confinement." Mia walked over and rubbed Buddy's snout. "Make sure you check in on Trent and Cerby too. We're probably in for the night."

With those words, Buddy purred and rose back into the air. She disappeared seconds later, going into stealth mode.

"She listens to you." Christina joined Mia as they walked to the door. "I couldn't even get my dog to chase a ball when I was a kid. You have a dragon delivering messages and protection duties."

"I'm not sure it's my skills. I think Buddy is a lot smarter than we assume. I'm going to have to learn a lot more about dragons. I doubt there's a training camp for them nearby." Mia was met at the door by Muffy, who used the impromptu meeting to wander outside for a few minutes.

The academy smelled amazing, like Sunday dinner. Roasted chicken had to be in the oven, and it appeared that Abigail was cooking in the downstairs kitchen. Christina went looking for Levi for a little talk, and after Muffy came back in, Mia went to the kitchen with her on her heels.

"Welcome back. I thought I'd cook here so you didn't have to deal with the crowd when you returned. Finn left for work at the Lodge and Levi and his dad are out back, making plans to expand that garden of yours. Just don't let them know I told you. It's a surprise. Oh, and your grandmother and Damien are working on a potion in your lab." She looked up from the pie dough she was rolling out. "Where's Christina?"

"She went to find Levi. They need to talk." Mia went over to check the stove. Corn was in a pan, waiting to be cooked, and potatoes bubbled in another pan to make mashed potatoes. "Anything I can help with?"

"Get a bag of blueberry pie filling from the freezer, and check to see if we have vanilla ice cream while you're there. I thought I saw some, but now I'm questioning myself." She looked up after carefully setting the first shell in the pie pan. "Wait, Christina knows? Did she figure it out or did you tell her?"

"I told her. Marsha Fieldstone almost did earlier. I figured it would freak her out less hearing it from me. Besides, the twins are freaking out Finn. Now that Christina knows, maybe they'll quiet down."

"Maybe. Not all witch babies talk so early. Trent chatted the whole time I was carrying him. He wanted to know everything I was doing and seeing. He's always been my curious one. Levi's going to freak out a little. I can already see that."

"Babies. I knew they were coming, but it's a little sooner than I'd expected for those two." Mia came out of the walk-in freezer with the pie filling. "I put the vanilla ice cream on the shelf closest to the door."

"I love the idea of grandchildren, but this feels early to me as well." Abigail poured the fruit into the shell, then put the top shell on, cutting a leaf motif in the middle and sprinkling sugar on top. "Grab that bottle of chardonnay from the fridge and two glasses. We've got a little time before the pie and chicken are ready. Let's have a glass to celebrate the new arrivals. I always knew exactly when I conceived. My body told me the story. I even knew the day they would arrive, but Thomas never believed me."

As they sat at the little table in the kitchen, Mia poured wine and listened to Abigail's pregnancy stories. She wondered how many women had done this same thing. Sat in their kitchens, waiting for food they'd prepared for the family to be ready as they talked about babies and the magical process that brought them into the world.

"I thought Trent would be the first of my three to become a dad," Abigail said after a couple of sips. "He's levelheaded and ready for the challenge. Levi was always the baby. I just hope he's grown up enough for this."

"He has no choice. Christina won't let him slack off. The girl's a tyrant." Mia smiled as she thought of her friend as a mother. "As far as Trent is concerned, he's not even married."

"He might not be formally married to you, but you're as much a Majors as Christina is. The two of you just need to do the ceremony to finalize it." Abigail took another sip of wine. "But maybe right now is not the best time for more babies."

"Don't worry about it until we have something to worry about. All we can do right now is prepare as much as possible so we're ready. Getting Cerby and Tempest trained is the first step. I have a feeling that we're going to need Mark and Sarah in this fight. And Em will have babies to play with soon." Mia held up her glass. "To the future, whatever it might bring."

"You are definitely a kitchen witch. You have a positivity streak a mile long." Abigail smiled and clinked Mia's glass. "To our expanding family. May we welcome them with open hearts."

Mia wondered if Abigail was talking about someone besides the babies, but she let it go. The society was more than just a group of witches trying to survive in this world. They were a family.

The timer went off, and Abigail finished the last dregs in her glass. "Set the table out in the dining area and let's get this party started."

As they all gathered around the table, they made gratitude statements to the Goddess. It hadn't been Mia's family's tradition, but Abigail and Thomas did it every mealtime. Mia liked the ritual. It reminded her that no matter what was going on in her life, she had reasons to be thankful. They might be small in the scheme of things, but they were there. When it was Levi's turn, he looked at Christina first before speaking. When she reached for his hand, he started talking.

"I'm thankful for this woman who has chosen to bond with me and the new lives we're bringing into our world." Levi leaned over and kissed Christina.

"If you didn't get it from that convoluted announcement, let me be clearer. I'm thankful that Levi and I have been blessed with a pregnancy. Twins, I'm told." Christina grinned. "I get to tell my mother tonight over the phone. She can't kill me if she can't touch me."

No one at the table seemed to be surprised at the announcement, but everyone said the right things. As they transitioned into dinner, the group seemed just a little more upbeat than they had when the afternoon meeting had ended.

Saturday morning, Mia finished her reports, including the customer service surveys sent to the attendees of last night's catered event. Another one of Blake's new processes. She didn't mind evaluations, but the problem was that the complaints they received weren't about the food or the service, but about the topic of the event. Something she wasn't in charge of and couldn't fix for them. Mia had proposed that they only send evaluation forms to the people who had planned the event to survey how the night turned out in their eyes, but Blake didn't agree. At least Mia was learning what not to do without experimenting on her own catering company.

She needed to go into the office, but Christina was still in bed. Levi had left around midnight to return to the Adams's condo. If she waited a couple of hours, Mia and Christina could give Finn a ride to work as well. Everybody was a winner. Except Mia had done everything she could from the house.

She refilled her coffee and opened a new notebook to write down everything she knew about Suzanne Parker's death. Mia had some solid information and a lot of questions. She also made a list of interviews she wanted to do. Mark didn't mind her getting involved in a case if her involvement kept him from acknowledging the fact that witches lived in Magic Springs. Even though his wife and daughter fell into that genome, he thought if he didn't say it, it wasn't true. Of course the fact that the baby's new puppy was really a hellhound kind of ruined that mindset.

As she made a list of people to chat with, including Cleo from the testing facility and Marsha Fieldstone, she realized she hadn't looked at the report from Matt at the front desk. She opened her email and scanned the invoice.

Suzanne Parker had checked in Sunday night on the National Office's credit card. She ate in the dining room Sunday evening, Monday morning, noon, and dinner, and Tuesday breakfast and dinner. No lunch because she'd been busy tormenting Mia at the time. Cleo had probably provided her food, although Mia barely remembered eating that day.

From the charges, the meals appeared to be for one person. She wasn't buying anyone dinner on the bosses' dime. Suzanne Parker seemed to be a stickler for the details. No wonder Mia's quick ascension to level three, then level five, had upset her. It just wasn't done. She almost closed the file before she found the reservation notes. It showed Suzanne Parker's airline details for coming and going, with a note about needing a ride to the airport.

The dates were off. She checked in on Sunday, but her plane landed on Friday night. She should have checked out on Wednesday morning, but the shuttle charge wasn't till Thursday. And hadn't Mark said her rental car was in the parking lot for the cross-country trailhead?

Mia reached for her phone and called him on his cell.

"What's wrong? Is Sarah okay? Em?" He didn't give her a chance to even say hello.

"Good morning, Mark. Do you have a little time for a chat? I'll make you an omelet." Mia stared out the window, wondering if Buddy was out in the tree or still at Trent's.

"So they're fine?" He sighed. "Sorry, I'm a little jumpy without them here. Sure, I'll be right over with my files. Did you figure this out already?"

"No, but I have a question. Did you come by when I wasn't home and tell Grans I was a suspect?"

"No. Why would you be a suspect? Yes, you spent time with the victim, but from what I know of that whole testing thing, you were probably surrounded by your entire group Tuesday at midnight when the scores came out. You couldn't have been at the ski trail at the same time, right?"

"Exactly. Look, I'll fill you in on the fun we've been having here. I haven't gotten a lot of sleuthing done, but I've got some information on the victim that you probably don't have."

"All I know is that she worked for an educational organization and traveled all over, testing and certifying people, which we know isn't the whole truth. Let me grab my coat and I'll be over in a few minutes. Thanks, Mia."

After Mark hung up, Grans came into the room. She poured coffee, then sat down. No "good morning." Nothing.

"Are you okay?" Mia stared at her. She wasn't wearing the engagement ring that Robert had given her.

"No, I'm a complete idiot who likes making her life harder than it needs to be. How on earth did I allow Dorian to swoop in here again and fill my head with fairy tales? I have no future with the man. He just needs to go back to Boston and live his life. Not here, and not in your academy, where I have to run into him all the time." Grans sipped her coffee.

"What happened?"

Grans blinked and looked up at her. "What do you mean?"

"What happened? What did he do last night that has you this upset?" Mia was starting to worry about her grandmother's memory.

"Oh, dear, he's just being Dorian. You can change a man's name, but not his nature. I fell in love with him a few years ago for a good reason. Now, I just need to forget that reason and go on with my life. It won't be with Robert—I've burned that bridge—but I'm sure I'll find a perfectly acceptable substitute, if I can get Dorian to leave. He did what he planned. He stopped my wedding. He should feel good."

"I'm sure he didn't want to ruin your wedding, just because. Damien loves you. Tell me you don't have feelings for him and I'll tell him to leave. But I think you're in love with him as well." Mia moved the plate of muffins that Abigail had made yesterday closer to her grandmother's reach.

She took a muffin. Feeding Grans always meant just keeping her busy until she ate enough. She never even noticed food when she was in one of these moods.

"I packed all that up when we buried his first body." Grans broke open the muffin and put butter on it.

"Speaking of bodies, do you think there's any truth to what Christina saw at the house? Or was it just a way to scare people off?"

Her grandmother took a bite, then washed it down with coffee. "I've heard rumors about passing a soul from one body to another. But the body has to be someone willing, and nowadays people don't seem as receptive to having another soul in their bodies."

Mr. Darcy meowed from his place on the window seat.

"I think cats are less likely too, but Mr. Darcy doesn't blame Dorian. He knows it was an accident." Mia smiled at her cat. Now her grandmother had her asking where they got the young woman who was on the other table. Mia shifted in her seat. If Christina hadn't been imagining things, who was the girl in the bed? Or was this entire scene just playacting for Christina's benefit? Mia was beginning to think that the scene her friend had seen was just a re-creation of part of a movie. That neither Suzanne nor the girl were actually there.

Unless it was a past life transition. Was that how Suzanne had been able to live for three hundred years?

Chapter 12

Grans excused herself to go to the potions lab when Mark pulled up. Of course Damian had arrived at the same time and had walked in with Mark. As Mia and Mark went upstairs to her apartment, Mark rubbed his head. “That guy looks really familiar.”

“His brother lived here a few years ago, before he was killed,” Mia said, focusing on the stairs. She hated to lie to Mark, but he liked staying out of magical things. Damien was probably more magic than he could deal with at the moment, especially when Sarah and Em were at Trent’s, training their hellhound.

Humans could only stretch their belief system so far before they had to worry a little about brain damage, which was why Mia wondered how Finn was really doing with her life overhaul.

“That’s right. His brother was killed just before you moved here. You found his body at the food bank while you were trying to set it back up.” He looked less stressed because he had an answer. “Man, I’m not sure I could move to a town where my brother was killed.”

“Mark, you don’t have a brother,” Mia reminded him as she opened the door to her apartment.

“That’s right. I guess I’m safe, then.” Mark followed her into the kitchen. The table was clean, but Mia had the notebook and a file folder with a pen sitting by her coffee cup. “Can we set up here?”

“Works for me; that way I can talk and cook.” She held out a cup. “Coffee?”

“Please. I’m not sleeping well.” Mark didn’t elaborate, but Mia knew he missed his family.

“Just a few more weeks and we’ll all be back to normal here.” Mia poured his coffee as he sat down and pulled out the folder and a notebook.

Mark took a pen out of his breast pocket. “According to her travel records, she arrived Friday night and was to leave on Thursday, but that didn’t match the Lodge’s reservations.”

“Yeah, I saw that. Did you know Suzanne Parker owned a house here in town?” Mia glanced at the note and read off the address. “It’s lovely. They held her wake there on Friday.”

“ ‘They’ being your friends?” Mark wrote down the address.

Mia broke eggs into a bowl. “ ‘They’ being the magic coven that you know is here in town. Let’s not call them my friends because I haven’t found one person in the coven I like yet. Except for Marsha Fieldstone. She’s growing on me.”

“The woman from Magic Brews? She’s a witch? Huh.” Mark paused for a minute to take in the information. Then he continued with his report. "Ms. Parker rented a car at the airport in Boise, came up here, and was supposed to turn it in Tuesday night. Instead, she went to the trailhead, parked, and was found at six by the ski patrol making sure the trail was clear. She'd frozen overnight."

"How long does it take for someone to freeze to death?" Mia didn't know if she wanted to know the answer. She focused on putting together Mark's omelet while she waited.

"According to the coroner, when it's really cold, it can be minutes, but that's not what happened in this case. Someone doused her with water while she sat on the ground. I'm going to guess that she was sedated before the water was sprayed on her. He said she died around one on Wednesday morning." Mark sipped his coffee. "Right after your test results were posted. Do you think someone asked her to come and give you a lower score?"

"It doesn't work that way. Some sort of magical being does the scoring. All the tester can do is change up the questions, which Suzanne Parker did. The test felt a lot harder than the first one. I was worried that I wouldn't pass at all." Mia thought about that night. "She was here right after the results posted, mad as a wet hen."

"That's an unfortunate descriptor." Mark frowned.

Mia ignored him and continued. "She was here at midnight and Damien asked her to leave because she was threatening me."

"A lot of people must have seen her drive away. Remind me to look at your security footage before I leave. Anyway, if she was asked to lower your level, she failed." Mark scratched his neck. "Sarah has tried to explain what this means, you being a level five, but I don't quite get it. It's like you got a scholarship to study whatever you want, and they give you money."

"They say they give you money. I haven't seen any yet, although I haven't gotten into my online account yet to check. I've been busy." She put the omelet on a plate and added a square of hash brown casserole that she'd saved back from their breakfast. Then she put a big mound of fresh fruit on the plate. "Hold your fork over the plate; I'm going to snap a picture and send it to Sarah to prove you're eating."

"Proof of life is what they call it in my line of work." He laughed and followed her directions. "You're an amazing cook, Mia. Thank you. So that's all level five means? Why would someone want to stop you from reaching that level?"

"That is the big question, right? I need to bite the bullet and talk to Brandon again. I don't think he'll tell me the whole truth, but maybe I can get enough to show us what we're missing." Mia sat down and opened her notebook. "I found out a lot of the same things that you did, except I just learned that Suzanne had asked the Lodge for a driver the morning before she was set to leave, even though she wasn't still staying there. I bet Blake freaked on that one. She hates anyone using the Lodge's services if they aren't staying there that night. She says it messes up her bookkeeping."

"Interesting, but not at the level of I'll-kill-you interesting." Still, he wrote down something in his notebook. "It's been bugging me that you asked why I told people you were a suspect. I never did that."

"And yet several people, including Abigail and Grans, watched you come to the academy and do that exact thing."

Mark blinked first. "What the heck, Mia?"

"I know; it's very thought-provoking. But that incident is not the only time we've seen visions while awake. It's been happening more since this murder. I saw Sonja and Trent out to dinner in Twin Falls the other night." Mia watched as Mark frowned. Before he could say something, she continued. "I had Christina call Sarah, and she told me they were standing next to her, in Magic Springs. The spell caster didn't know Sarah was even staying at Trent's house, yet she or he knew that Sonja made me a little uncomfortable."

Mark considered what she'd told him. "They're making you see things?"

"Yeah, but let's make it clear, the spell caster doesn't have all the facts, so he or she is making mistakes. Like their impersonation of you. They know that you could make me a suspect, but they didn't know that we've been working together to solve these types of cases. Besides, you wouldn't announce your suspicions to my friends and family. You'd just come arrest me and play the strong, silent type."

"Not a lot of people know about our alliance," Mark admitted. "But you figured out that it wasn't me. So who was it?"

"It was the FedEx guy. I have no idea who's trying to fool us or why. But I know they're messing with me and my friends, and I'm going to stop them." Mia ate a muffin. "Oh, and I think my boss is spelling me."

"Way to bury the lede. Do you want me to do something about it? I could arrest her." Mark finished his breakfast and stood to rinse the plate and put it in the dishwasher.

"I'm not sure if she's using a potion or an actual drug, so not yet. I still want to find out why she's doing it. I didn't notice when it happened; Christina did," Mia admitted.

Just then Christina came out of her room all ready for work. She narrowed her eyes toward Mark as she got her coffee. "Good morning."

"How's my favorite Goth princess?" Mark leaned back in his chair.

"Pregnant." Christina sipped her coffee. "With twin girls."

Mia started laughing at Mark's face. "You look like you swallowed something big. Em should have some playmates soon."

Mark eyed Mia. "Are you pregnant too?"

"No. No way, no how. I'm good." Mia held up her hands like a barrier. "I wasn't going to say anything, but I guess Christina is letting the cat out of the bag."

"Congrats to you and Levi." Mark let out a breath. "Being a parent changes your world."

"I've had enough of change. I have no idea what to do, so who knows what will happen." Christina sat down and unwrapped a muffin.

Mark went on to tell Christina all his parenting war stories, including ones about the birthing process. Finally, when he left, Christina stared at Mia. "I can't do this."

"You can do this if you want. I'm not an angel, so I'm not trying to sway you one way or the other, but never say you can't do this. You're one of the strongest women I know. You made your own path even when dealing with your mother, and you've become an amazing young woman." Mia squeezed Christina's hands. "Ready to go to the Lodge and see what trouble we can find? I need to talk to Blake and find out what she's doing to me and why."

"And I need to get to work," Finn said, walking into the room. "Why were the police just here? I didn't come out because they freak me out."

"Mark's a friend. He came for breakfast. Now I have a list of people I need to talk to. Christina's driving, so let's go." Mia tucked her laptop and her notebook into her tote and threw Finn a bottle of water.

When they got to the Lodge, the great room was filled with check-ins for the hotel. A wedding was scheduled for Sunday, and Mia saw the mother of the bride standing by the counter.

Mia walked over and smiled at the woman. "The big day is almost here."

"I'm so glad to see you. I asked if we could meet, but they said I'd have to meet with the hotel director because you weren't here. I don't like that woman. She gives me the creeps. I just need a moment with you to ease my fears." Mrs. Edwards grabbed Mia's arm like she was afraid of falling.

"Let me get to my office and I'll come right back out for you. This is my friend and coworker, Christina Adams," Mia said. "Christina, will you keep Mrs. Edwards company while I find an empty meeting room?"

"I'd love to. Mrs. Edwards, your husband doesn't

work for Idaho Power, does he?" When the woman told her yes, Christina led her over to an empty couch. "I thought I recognized you. My father does legal work for the board."

Leave it to Christina to know everyone. Mia hurried to her office to drop off her tote bag and find a room. She booted up her computer just as Blake stepped inside.

"I'm glad you're finally here. I was wondering if you still worked here." Blake leaned against the door. "Your wedding people have arrived and the mother is freaking out."

"I just talked to Mrs. Edwards and we're going to go over the plans. I'm sure she'll relax in a few. I'm sending her and the groom's mother to the spa to relax and get to know each other better."

"Oh. That's a nice touch. I just wanted to make sure you were here." Blake started to leave.

"Blake? I know what happened at the staff meeting. Can you tell me why you spelled me and drugged the rest of your staff before I report you to the coven's ethics committee and put in my resignation?"

"I didn't drug the staff." Blake blinked, then sighed. "Please don't quit. I can't lose you. I'm sorry. I won't do it again, but I heard you had some issues with a succubus recently and I had to know if he was back. You know he freaks me out. I can't go through that again. I thought if I could find out what you knew, I'd feel safer."

"I don't know where you're hearing these rumors. I haven't had issues with a succubus, yours or any other one, recently. Someone is spelling visions for me. It's not you, is it?" Mia stared at her, trying to decide if she was being truthful.

"No. Even if I wanted to, I don't have that kind of juice. I'm sorry. I won't do it again." She turned again to leave the office.

"Blake, if you do anything like that again, I will report you. And quit." Mia met her boss's gaze. "I'm serious."

Blake held up her hand. "I hear you. I promise."

Mia scheduled the meeting in an empty room and called the kitchen to order coffee, juice, and pastries. "Put it on my marketing account with a note saying 'Edwards Wedding.'"

"Yes, ma'am." The person on the phone gave her a delivery time and then Mia headed out to gather her nervous mother of the bride to assure her that the wedding was going to be magical. The one thing about having weddings in Magic Springs, even for normal humans, was that the staff could pull off miracles in food and décor.

Christina was making Mrs. Edwards laugh as Mia returned to the lobby. Mia wondered if Christina had ever thought about opening her own event planning agency. She had the contacts in the area from her parents and she had the demeanor that put people at ease.

"We have a room. Christina, do you want to join us?" Mia offered because she knew her friend didn't have much to do except watch out for Mia this week.

"Sure, I'd love to. I've got to figure out what I want for my upcoming wedding too, and how to navigate my mother. I love her, but she wants a larger, more regal wedding than either I or my fiancé wants. It's a fine line, right, Belinda?" Christina had her arm linked with Mrs. Edwards's. She'd done it again. With Christina's help, this meeting might be more agreeable than Mia had expected.

Christina took the last croissant and followed Mia back into her office. "Don't look at me; I didn't have a big breakfast."

"I made you an omelet after I made Mark's." Mia held up her hands. "Your body, your rules. Thanks for the help with Mrs. Edwards. I thought she was going to demand changes, but all she wanted was some hand-holding."

"She just wants the day to be perfect for her little girl." Christina sighed. "I wish my mom had the same determination to make sure I was happy. Now she's pushing me to get my wedding dress so we can make sure that with the right support wear, no one knows. And she's moved up the wedding date. She's going to call me when she gets ahold of the event coordinator at St. Michael's Cathedral in Boise. She hopes they'll have a slot, but she's not optimistic. I didn't want to remind her that she was the one who pushed it out so far because of Dad's business meetings."

"As soon as you have a day for the wedding here, let me know and I'll put it on the Lodge's calendar. How's Levi doing with the whole baby thing?" Mia booted up her computer and started reading her emails. Most went into the trash.

"Surprisingly good. Somehow, I get the idea that he knew, or at least expected this. I thought he'd be all, 'I man, you woman.' But instead, he's talking about going back to school and getting a real degree so he can work in an office rather than as a first responder. I'm a little scared."

"Of Levi settling down? You should be. Although I think Abigail is more surprised than you are. She's always treated him like the baby and didn't give him a lot of responsibility until he had to take over the family magic line. Then she wanted him to act like a grown-up. I think he needed a reason to make those decisions."

"Like the babies." Christina closed her eyes.

"Yes and no. I think you are the reason. He loves you, and the babies are an added blessing." Mia focused on work as Christina took a book out of her tote and started reading. A knock on the door at noon made her look up.

"Lunch delivery," the girl said as she pushed in a cart with salads, sandwiches, a tureen of soup, and two entrées. "Where can I set this up?"

"We didn't order lunch." Mia stood and took the order sheet. It had come from Blake. Was the lunch her way of apologizing? Or was she just trying to look good to Christina? "I'd say the email from your company must have hit Blake's inbox."

"Whatever caused it, I'm starving." Christina cleared her book and papers off the small table. "You can set it here. Mia, do you have sparkling water in your fridge?"

As they settled and started eating, Christina paused between mouthfuls. "Did you and Blake talk yet? Because if not, maybe you should wait until after I stop being your bodyguard. James's food is amazing."

"We already talked. She's still freaked out about a succubus finding her. I've talked to her personal demon, and I don't think he's going to be bothering her anymore, but I guess even witches can have PTSD." Mia focused on her salad.

Christina didn't say anything for a few minutes. "She had a bad experience, huh?"

Mia didn't want to tell Blake's story because it wasn't hers to tell, but sometimes knowing that another person had their own battles helped people understand them. "Yes, she had it bad. It doesn't excuse all the stuff she's done, but it does help explain her behavior. I told her that she had one more chance and if I caught her messing with me again, I'd be gone. And I'd report her. Like Levi said, there's a rule against attacking other witches."

"I know I don't have a lot of knowledge about the coven system, but someone broke that rule both with your testing and with killing Suzanne Parker."

Chapter 13

With the rehearsal dinner menu in hand, Mia headed to the kitchen to see if Finn was ready to go home. She waved at her from the line.

"Sorry, I'm stealing your cook." James came up behind Mia and handed her a bag of cookies. "For your trouble and your friend. My staff says she's loving the food we've been delivering."

"Christina has always loved your food, James. But thank you for the cookies. Let Finn know if she doesn't have a ride home to call me and someone will come pick her up." She took the bag. "Her van is still being fixed. I think she's paying for a part and service after every paycheck."

"It's hard to be broke. Good thing she's young so working so many hours isn't wearing her down. Although as talented as she is, I don't think she'll ever want for a job. Has she considered culinary school?" James adjusted his watch as he glanced at the time.

"She's starting in the fall. She talked to Christina about the details, and if she stays with me at the academy, she should be able to afford it."

"I'm in a group of chefs that offers scholarships to promising students. I'll put her name in. Is she going to Twin Falls Tech?" James put a note on the planner he kept in the kitchen.

"I think that's the plan. You should tell her you're putting her up for the scholarship. It would mean a lot." Mia turned to leave, but James stopped her.

"I'm putting her in, which means she'll get one. Whether or not she gets another one is up to her. I'll drive her home after this shift. Thanks for the loaner." James watched the kitchen as he talked.

"You should be thanking Abigail, not me. I'm surprised Mia's Morsels didn't have an event today," Mia admitted.

"From what I hear, you're booked every other weekend this month." He shrugged when Mia turned to look at him. "I check on things. Especially things regarding one of my favorite substitutes."

"Well, you're more on top of the schedule than I am." Mia frowned as she said the words. She needed to know these things. Abigail may be Mia's Morsels's manager, but Mia was the owner.

"I'm just glad you're back to work. I guess you didn't have measles?" Now James was looking at her, and probably looking for spots.

Mia had forgotten their cover story. "Not according to the blood tests. I probably was allergic to some skin cream or something."

"As long as you're not looking for another job, I

don't care what your excuse for missing work is. I need you here." He sighed as one of his chefs tried to get his attention. "George needs me on the line. See how that all works? I'll be here tomorrow for the start of the reception dinner, then I'm going home to watch football."

"I never thought I'd hear you say that." Mia stopped in her tracks and turned to stare at James.

"What? My new beau is a fan." He waved her off. "Go have a life."

Christina spied the cookies as she met Mia in the hallway. "For me?"

"Sure." Mia handed over the bag. "Finn's still working, so James will bring her home. When do you think you'll go back to Portland?"

Christina stopped so suddenly, Mia thought something was wrong.

"What? Are you okay?" Mia scanned her friend from head to toe.

"I just realized that I don't want to be pregnant six hundred miles away from my friends. My mom, maybe. But you and Abigail? How on earth am I going to deal with everything?"

On the way home, they stopped at Magic Brews again. Marsha Fieldstone looked up as they walked in the door. "Second visit in as many days, what did I do now?"

"Maybe we just love your coffee. I want a large coffee to go. Christina?" Mia turned and let Christina order a large hot chocolate with whipped cream and two cookies. Mia didn't even look at her as she paid the bill. "I forgot to ask you about Suzanne Parker. When did she come into town, Monday?"

Marsha smiled as she made the drinks. "Now you're trying to trick me. Suzanne came in on Friday night. She often came in on weekends to spend time at her house. Of course she didn't socialize with the coven because she didn't want to seem partial, but she had friends who would visit. At least that was the rumor."

"Friends? Or friends with benefits?" Christina asked.

"Both. She had a very active social life for someone who lived in two different towns. I couldn't do it. Once I leave here, the only face I want to see is my cat's. I get too much peopling in the shop." Marsha wiped her hands on a towel.

"Was she friends with anyone we'd know?" Mia pushed as Marsha set down the coffee and hot chocolate by them and went to get the cookies.

"I'm not sure I know. Suzanne and Cleo were friends. Cleo doesn't have a lot of them; most people she's known have passed on. I think it would be hard to make connections, then watch those people age and die. Suzanne and Dorian dated for a while, but that had to be a century ago. I'm surprised your grandmother didn't mention that. Regarding her current lover, I heard rumors that she and Brandon were close. He can't trust most witches not to use his coven status for their own gain, but Suzanne was far beyond that. So he didn't have to worry why she was seeing him. Besides the sex. He's just average in that department. At least that's what I've been told."

The bell over the door rang and a bunch of tourists who looked like they just got off the ski runs entered the shop. "Come by anytime to chat," Marsha said as she turned her attention to the tourists.

As they left the building, Christina started giggling, and Mia joined in. "That was odd," Christina said.

"Odd is a polite description. So, what did we learn?" Mia settled into Christina's car and thanked the Goddess for the heated seats. "Suzanne Parker came to town a lot, and she might have been sleeping with Brandon. Is he the one who asked for my testing to be redone?"

"Maybe. I don't know. He's being weirder than usual. But then again, I don't know him very well." Christina pulled the car out on the street. "Home?"

"Yeah. Coven headquarters is closed until Monday, and I don't know how else to contact Cleo. There's something we don't know about Suzanne Parker, but I'm not sure it has anything to do with her death. On the other hand, if her murder didn't have to do with her past here, then we're back to my testing. I know I didn't kill her." Mia closed her eyes as Christina drove home.

"What does Mark say?"

"He thinks she was lured out to the cross-country trail, then drugged so she'd be stuck there. They covered her with water to make the hypothermia worse." Mia looked over at Christina, who looked horrified at the description. "Sorry, I shouldn't have been so blunt."

Christina swallowed hard before replying. "No, I asked. Does he have any suspects?"

As Christina pulled into the parking lot, Buddy landed on her favorite tree. "No, but I'm glad Trent is out of the picture this investigation. Now we just need to see why someone would try to frame me for the killing."

"Sure, easy peasy. Then we can figure out who killed JFK." Christina waved to Buddy and headed into the academy.

"When there is an obvious answer and a convoluted one, maybe the simple one is right," Mia muttered as she made her way into the house. "Night, Buddy."

That night, after dinner and when she was alone in the living room, Mia took out her Suzanne Parker notebook and added the few things that she'd learned. She sighed. It wasn't much. If Suzanne Parker had lived that many lives, maybe the library could access some sort of written record. Grans hadn't had time to get into the coven's archives yet, but if Brandon was involved in this, that information would probably be classified. She really needed to talk to Cleo.

The security alarm went off, and Mia didn't look at the monitor, assuming James was dropping off Finn. When the doorbell rang, Mia looked up, surprised. Cleo stood at the front door in a black cape and fedora.

Mia hurried downstairs with Mr. Darcy following close behind. She swung open the door. "Sorry, I thought you were Finn coming home."

"It's freezing out here. May I come inside?" Cleo didn't look like the snow had even touched her woolen cape, hat, or black boots.

"Of course, sorry. Would you like some tea? Or coffee?" Mia held open the door as the caretaker for the coven's headquarters came inside.

"I'd love some tea. May we take it in the library?"

"Upstairs? My library?" Mia was flummoxed.

Cleo looked amused. "Does the academy have a second library?"

"No, I mean, I keep some books in my apartment and in the potions lab, but no, there's only one library. I have to warn you, it's haunted and unpredictable." Mia followed Cleo, who was already on the stairs.

"Of course it is, dear. It's the academy's library. It's been haunted for years. Good thing you rescued the building from being torn down. Who knows what would have happened to the ghosts and all of the knowledge if the building was destroyed. I guess I would have had to move the books to headquarters, but that could be problematic when leadership changes policies." She paused on the second-floor landing. "The remodeling seems to be going well. Having Dorian's books here will be an asset to the building, and to your society. Knowledge is always power. You just need to make sure it stays readable."

It wasn't lost on Mia that Cleo had used Dorian's real name and not the cover name of Damien. When they reached the third floor, Mia opened her apartment door. "Do you want to come in while I make tea?"

"Just give me the library key. I'll wait in there. I'll do some looking around while I wait. It's been a while since I visited. Is Buttercup still there?"

Buttercup was a yellow cat who liked to sleep in the sunlight. She was also a ghost. Mia smiled as she gave Cleo the key. "Yes, she was there the last time I visited."

"Go make the tea and don't worry about me. I can entertain myself for a few minutes." Cleo took the key and headed toward the library.

Mia set the water on to boil, then got out a tray and her good tea service. She set sugar and cream in the matching bowls, along with cups, saucers, and spoons. Then she put her basket of tea on the tray and waited for the water to boil.

Gloria giggled at her sigh.

"I know a watched pot doesn't boil," Mia spoke the old adage, but just then, the whistle went off. Somehow, the water had boiled quickly. She looked at her kitchen witch. "Thank you. I hate to keep Cleo waiting."

She checked the tray after filling the tea kettle with hot water and added a couple of cloth napkins and the cookies that Christina hadn't devoured before heading to an early bedtime. It wasn't fancy, but tea was ready.

As she walked into the library, she saw the ghost of a young girl sitting at the table. Buttercup was lying on Cleo's lap as she read a book. The girl looked up and smiled before disappearing as Mia brought in the tea.

"Mrs. Julide would be horrified that we are having tea in the library. She was the librarian when I attended the academy so many years ago. I just think it's more civilized to have conversations like the one we'll be having with a nice spot of tea. Besides, the weather is horrible. I bet your dragon is loving the cooler weather."

"You know about Buddy? Of course you do." Mia took out an oolong packet and handed the basket to Cleo. "I forget that there are no secrets in Magic Springs."

Mia got the tea bag ready and then poured water in her cup and in Cleo's, as she'd chosen the same tea.

"That's where you're wrong. There are a lot of secrets in Magic Springs, just not that many that I don't know about. So, you're looking for information about Suzanne Parker? This book outlines all but her last life."

Mia took the book that Cleo handed to her. "That's helpful, but I'm really looking for information about this life." She didn't want to look stupid and ask the obvious question screaming in her head: How did Suzanne Parker have more than one life?

"A person's book isn't written until the life they're living ends. I thought you would have known that. How could we judge you at twenty when you were in a relationship with a mortal and working in what you thought was the apex in your career? Now, even without knowing the ins and outs of your magic level, you're so much more than you were then. If we'd written the book back then, it would be wrong. Just like if we wrote it today without taking in the woman you're going to become." Cleo sipped her tea. "Do you understand?"

What Mia understood was, she wasn't getting any closer to finding out who killed Suzanne Parker than she had been that morning. "Okay, the book isn't written yet. Can you tell me how you knew Suzanne?"

"I'll limit it to this life, but of course. We've been friends for ages. Literally. Before she took the job at the National Office, she threw the most wonderful parties. She was the local It girl in the sixties. Whatever Suzanne did, everyone wanted to follow. I never got into the miniskirts, though. My butt always felt a draft. But that's not what you want to hear. Her house had been in her possession since she bought it, and she kept it warded so the locals wouldn't realize she'd been living there for several generations. I always thought that was her mistake. She didn't change enough from one life to another. When the testing position opened, she moved to Boston. She majored in education through several degrees and thought our leveling process should have a more standardized testing." Cleo took a look at Mia, then sipped her tea again. "You surprised her."

"I never met her before the day of the test." Mia frowned, tapping her nails on the table. "I'm sure I hadn't."

"I don't believe you had, but a kitchen witch testing out as a level three? It's never been done since we started the testing process. Everyone was talking about you. Suzanne got it in her head that somehow, you cheated the test. When someone from the coven asked for a retest, she asked to be the second tester. I felt how hard the test was that Tuesday. No wonder you tested better. The test you got wasn't for a new witch, it was for an experienced one, so your intuition leveled up. You need to know that you're remarkable. I wouldn't be surprised if you didn't go up a level or two at your three-year testing."

"It's not what I want." Mia spoke frankly. "I just want to take on Grans's duties so she can retire and relax someday. I don't want to be part of leadership."

Cleo took a cookie and broke it in half, smelling it and then setting it down again. "I adore sweets, but this tea is going to keep me up for hours without even eating that cookie." She looked back at Mia, suddenly serious. "My mom always had a saying. 'You get what you get and you don't throw a fit.' Sorry, Mia, but this is your destiny. Why do you think you have an elder as a familiar? She's less a familiar and more of a counselor. You are Goddess chosen. Something we all dream of but never dare to hope for."

Mia sipped her tea, deep in thought. She'd had a feeling that Gloria was more than a familiar for a while now. She was part of Mia's circle of trust. Her own personal coven of spell casters. But she couldn't even imagine her future as what Cleo called "Goddess chosen." She'd have to believe that she was more than just Mia.

"Honestly, I don't know what to do with what you just told me, so can we go back to talking about Suzanne Parker?" When Cleo smiled in agreement, Mia went back to the story. "She left Magic Springs for Boston but kept her house here for weekend trips now and then."

"She's been home a lot more this year. When I asked her about it, she said something was brewing. A change. She didn't know when or how, but she needed to know that she was on the side of good. The side the Goddess would bless. The problem was, she didn't know which side that would be. You were flying under her radar until the test. I don't think she had a clue how powerful you were, or that your academy society was going to be the side the Goddess blessed."

"How do you know we are blessed? How do you know we are on the right side in a fight I can't even see coming?" Mia knew they'd fallen away from the subject of Suzanne Parker again, but she needed to know what Cleo thought.

"You wouldn't have two hellhounds and a dragon for protection if you weren't. The Goddess gives you what you need to survive and thrive. Have you asked her your questions?"

Mia fidgeted. It was one thing to believe in a Goddess that was somewhere out there, taking care of the world. It was far different thinking that the deity was using Mia and her friends as chess pieces, or that she'd speak directly to Mia.

"I haven't. But I will."

Cleo stood. "I need to be back home before the clock strikes midnight. Just call me Cinderella."

Mia glanced at her watch. The time was later than she thought. "Can I come on Monday if I have more questions?"

"Make it Tuesday. You're going to be busy Monday."

Mia followed Cleo to the front door, then watched as she climbed into a Grand Wagoneer that had been running. She had a driver, something that Mia hadn't noticed before. After Cleo left, Mia noticed that Buddy was awake and watching.

The Goddess had sent her two hellhounds and a dragon. And two new witches that would be joining the clan next year. This society was feeling more like a family, and Mia was feeling more out of control.

When she closed the door, she heard Gloria's laughter.

Chapter 14

Mia felt like a truck had run over her the next morning when she finally pulled herself out of bed. She couldn't sleep, so she had opened the book on Suzanne Parker and read late into the night, or early into the morning.

"Mia? Are you okay?" Christina knocked on her bedroom door, then opened it. "Wow, you look bad. Did you need to go in for the Edwards's wedding?"

"Thank you for the pep talk. Give me thirty minutes to shower and change and inhale a cup of coffee, then we can head into the Lodge. I should be there for the ceremony and the beginning of the dinner. Mrs. Edwards can be a little much." Mia eyed the coffee cup in Christina's hands. "Is that for me? Or did you lace it with sugar and cream already?"

"Black like your heart," Christina teased. "What were you doing last night? I got up around three and your light was still on."

Mia took the coffee. After a couple of hot sips, she opened her eyes and pointed to the book. "I was finding out about our victim, Suzanne Parker. She was a child when her mother was hanged in Salem. Then she lived as a servant. If anyone deserved a life do-over, it was that child. I got through all but her life before this one. She was kind of a badass."

"Do you know why she was killed?" Christina picked up the book, then dropped it quickly. "The book feels wrong."

"Really?" Mia set down her coffee and picked up the book again. Nothing. She looked at Christina. "Is Abigail here? Tell her what just happened."

"I'm not picking up that book again." Christina backed out of the room.

"Drama queen. Just ask her. She can come in here and get it if she needs to." Mia picked up her coffee again. "I'm heading to the shower."

When she got out and dressed, she noticed the book wasn't in her room anymore. In the kitchen, Grans and Abigail were huddled over the table. Christina was in the living room. "What's going on?"

"Cleo gave you this?" Grans looked up and stared at Mia. "Let me see your hands and arms."

She held them out. "Nothing. I didn't react. I couldn't sleep, so I read for hours last night, probably too long to be productive at work this morning. Hopefully, the wedding will go off without a hitch, because I don't think I can solve a problem to save my life right now."

"The book probably drained you a little. Christina felt it more because of her current state. Her body is trying to keep three people alive, not just her." Grans met Abigail's gaze. "Cleo must have thought that the book's power had died with its subject, but I think there's some still in there. One of the ways Suzanne Parker kept coming back was that she'd use the book to drain energy from the people it came in contact with. Life energy. Just a little from everyone. In a school full of rambunctious kids, the book would probably fill up fast, keeping Suzanne alive. It's an amazing spell."

"When you're not the one being drained!" Christina called from the other room.

Mia rolled her eyes and Grans laughed. "She's not wrong. I think we should return this to the library and get it away from you. Your face is a little pale."

"I didn't finish reading about her last life," Mia said as she refilled her coffee cup, "but I didn't find anything that explains why she was killed. No revenge plot building. Is the book true?"

"It's a historic rendering, yes. Maybe you can read the rest tonight or Monday, when you're a little stronger. I think the book's power is slowly waning anyway." Abigail picked up the book and carried it out to the apartment door. Grabbing the key to the library, she called out, "I'll be right back."

"I'm not going to be the one to tell Thomas that his wife was sucked dry by a dead woman's book." Christina picked up her plate and headed to the kitchen. "Let me know when you're ready to go."

Mia's phone buzzed. Mark.

Do you know if this was a magic killing or not? Can't believe that's my question.

Mia smiled as she texted back.

From what I can tell, I don't think so. I need to expand my investigation today. Any tox results back yet?

It's the weekend, so no.

Heading to work, then I'll pull out my notes. I'll let you know if I find anything.

Weird thing is, the mayor's not sticking his nose in this murder. Does that mean that it's not magical?

Don't know. But it's interesting, I agree. Chat later.

Mia set down her phone near the food that Grans had set in front of her. She was starving. Probably due to the book draining her life force. She looked up and saw her grandmother watching her. "Have you figured out anything on who would want to kill Suzanne Parker? On the coven side?"

"She was powerful. The coven originally thought the attack came from us, but since your level went up, I'm sure that ended that discussion. We didn't have a reason to kill her unless she nullified your testing. She was the one who tested you and the result was higher, so, well, there goes that logic."

Grans sat down across from Mia. "I do think you need a stronger protection spell. I don't like the fact that Blake was able to put you under a spell for over an hour. She could have planted anything in your head."

"She said she was sorry and she wouldn't do it again." Mia flinched as the words came out of her mouth. The words didn't sound like something she'd say. "Can you tell if she did anything to my head?"

"What do you think I am? An emotional X-ray machine?" Grans shook her head. "Dorian, I mean, Damien has a potion that might clear any unwanted programming. He's been working on it in the potions lab. We'll see if that works."

"Cleo knows about Dorian and Cerby and Buddy, and she has to know about Sarah and Em because she said two hellhounds." Mia looked down at Muffy. "Unless you're one in disguise."

Muffy barked, then Mr. Darcy yawned, and they both went back to sleep.

Grans rubbed his belly. "I think that's unlikely. Cleo knows a lot. She also holds a lot of secrets. I don't worry about what she knows, I worry more about what she tells us. What else did she say that has you on edge?"

Because Christina was in her bedroom talking to Levi, and Abigail hadn't come back from the library yet, Mia quickly told her grandmother about Cleo's assumption that Mia was Goddess chosen. "It's not a label I want."

"I think Cleo's right on this subject. You get what you get." Grans looked at the kitchen witch doll hanging in the kitchen. "We need more direction from Gloria if this is true. I'll find the right spell and we'll see if we can have a conversation with our elder with more than just the giggling."

Abigail came back into the apartment. "The library sent me back with a book. Dream walking? Is this for one of you?"

Mia stood and took her plate to the sink. "I guess I have more reading tonight. I've got to get to the Lodge before Mrs. Edwards's head starts spinning around like a top."

"It's good practice for Christina's wedding." Grans grinned as Abigail refilled her coffee. "Her mother is going to be a nightmare. Thank the Goddess that you got out of Isaac's clutches before we had to deal with her."

At the Lodge, things were going better than she expected. Mia checked in with the not-horribly-anxious mother, made sure the deliveries of wine and food were ready for the dressing party, and walked through the chapel, where the ceremony was to be held. Jeani, the decorator for the Lodge, had done an amazing job. Everything that Mrs. Edwards had listed off had been done. The chapel had looked lovely yesterday, but today, the room almost glowed. With those tasks checked off her list, Mia went to the reception ballroom and made sure things were set up there too.

Blake came up to her. "Everything looks good."

"I think our clients are going to be very happy." Mia looked up from her clipboard. "I realized today that you could have done a little meddling in my head while you were in there looking for your answers. I don't know what your game is, but I'm reconsidering letting bygones be bygones."

"I didn't add anything to your head." Blake's anger flared just a little and her face reddened. "But I did find something you should know about. Someone has been feeding you fake memories. Not a lot, so I was confused at first when I found them. Your grandmother should be able to clear them quickly. It's weird; they're like little patches covering up holes in your memories. Like they took something out and put these in."

Mia thought about the vision she'd seen at the restaurant. What if something else had happened? "Blake, could this have happened during my testing?"

"No. The National Office wouldn't allow . . ." Blake stopped and tapped a finger on her lips, a sign she was thinking. "I don't think Parker could have done it during the test, but you got breaks, like lunch. What did you have for lunch that day?"

Mia shook her head. "I don't remember, but it was something Abigail sent over."

Blake studied her, then took her wrist, holding it between two fingers. "Don't tell anyone I said this, but yeah, I think it might have happened during your testing."

After Mia made sure everything was fine with the wedding, she headed back to her office. She had questions, and she didn't know if she could trust Blake to tell her the truth. She needed to go home and talk to Grans and Abigail.

Christina was reading when Mia went into her office. She set down the book. "Now what?"

"I didn't say anything." Mia crossed the room and grabbed a soda from her fridge. She needed the sugar or she was going to faint. Right here. Splat.

"You didn't have to. You look worse than you did after that book got hold of you. Don't tell me that Blake attacked you again. I'm going to go kick her butt three ways to Sunday." Christina stood, putting her bookmark between pages to save her place.

"Sit down. She didn't attack me. We talked, and she told me something she didn't say before. I have holes in my memories, and someone planted new, fake ones. She thinks it happened during my testing."

"I didn't think that was possible." Christina sat down but didn't open her book.

"Let me finish up this email and we can get out of here. Then we'll talk to Grans and Abigail. There has to be a test somewhere that checks for something like that, and maybe something that can fix it." Mia shook her head. Maybe this was why she hadn't been feeling well since the testing, and why she couldn't see clearly enough to help Mark solve his case.

What did the flight attendants always say? Put on your own mask before helping others. Mia needed to get her mask on quickly.

At home, Mia hung out in the living room downstairs while Christina gathered the group. Whatever was going on, it was getting worse. Even the protective wards on the academy weren't making her feel right. She felt like she hadn't eaten in days and, worse, like her head was going to explode. She grabbed a bottle of Tylenol out of her bag and went to the bar area near the wall to get a glass of water. She had the pills in hand when she heard footsteps.

"Don't take that. If your memories have been tampered with, we need to see what's going on." Damien hurried over and took the pills out of her hand. "I should have seen the signs, but I was too focused on my need to get your grandmother to take me back."

Mia set down the water and leaned over the bar counter. She was going to be sick. She closed her eyes and whispered, "I don't feel well."

When she woke, she was in her bed and in her favorite Snoopy pjs. Trent sat on the bed next to her, Cerby by his side. "What are you doing here?" Mia asked.

"Checking on you. Buddy said something was going on, but she couldn't reach you or anyone inside the academy to find out what." He looked worried. "What happened?"

"According to Blake, someone messed with my memories. Wait, you can't be here. Don't you have to stay at the house?"

"What Sonja doesn't know won't hurt me. Sarah and Em are keeping her busy right now, and technically I'm not here. We're still at home. I'm dream walking, which Sonja still considers against the rules but whatever."

"This is in my head? Can you see the missing areas like Blake did?" Mia should have read the book the library had given her, but she'd been busy.

"I'm not in your head, no. This is a dream world. You and I are somewhere else. Oh, and Cerby. He didn't want to miss seeing you. Buddy's perched outside your real window, watching you to make sure no one hurts you while we're here." Trent smiled as Mia glanced at the window and saw the dragon watching her. "A part of her is here too. I don't know how animals do it, because Cerby's watching my bedroom door and he's here. It's weird."

"Everything is weird lately." She reached out and stroked the little dog and felt his tongue on her hand. "Am I okay?"

"That you're going to have to ask your grandmother. Damien did some sort of reverse spell and has been dosing you with a potion for the last few hours. Levi reached out to me as soon as he saw you. You had a lot of people worried."

"Not my choice. When did this happen? Blake said she thought it was during my testing, but I'm not believing most of what comes out of her mouth. I thought I was protected if I stayed home." Mia felt the connection wavering between them.

"We think it happened before we knew you were being retested. You need to look at who you met with that day and see who had access to you." Trent shimmered. "I think you're waking up. I love you and we're watching out for you."

Cerby barked his goodbye, and Mia heard Buddy chuff as well.

She opened her eyes. She was in her bedroom and in her Snoopy pjs. That much had been spot on.

Buddy's face filled her bedroom window. She smiled and held up her hand. "I'm okay, girl. You just make sure you're not seen."

The response sounded like laughter. Apparently, Mia's concern over Buddy was hilarious to the dragon.

A knock sounded on the door, and Grans stepped inside Mia's room. "Gloria said you were awake. How are you doing?"

"I feel like a train hit me. What did you guys do?"

She tried to sit up, but the nausea made her lie back down.

"Dorian said several pieces were missing. He tried reaccessing them and got a few, but your memories of the testing and the Monday before are mangled. This potion should help you get past the effects of the spell." She held out a small cup of what smelled like strawberry jam. "Drink this. You should be back on your feet later tonight."

"Did Suzanne Parker do this to me?" Mia asked the one question that kept circling.

Grans sighed. "Maybe. It's totally against coven code, but she was the only one who knew you were going to be retested. I still can't see why someone would kill her for that. Again, unless it was one of us."

"That doesn't make sense at all. If someone killed her to protect me, why didn't they tell me about the memories? Blake only mentioned them because I threatened her." Mia drank the potion and immediately felt the world shifting a little.

"Maybe Blake did this." Grans stroked her hair as Mr. Darcy jumped up on the bed and cuddled. "Can you trust her, really?"

"I don't know. But if Blake did this, how did she find out I was being retested? She's not part of coven leadership. She doesn't trust them." Mia felt herself sinking into the pillow.

"I'm calling Cleo. We need to find out who knew about your retesting. Once we have that list, we should be able to narrow it down," Grans said as Mia drifted off to sleep.

In her dream, Buddy's chuffing became words, or she spoke the language of dragons. "Be careful who you trust, Mia. They want you weak. The Goddess can only send protectors to you. She can't protect you herself."

Chapter 15

The kitchen was filled with people and noise when Mia got up from her potion-infused nap. She realized it was dinnertime and Abigail had made lasagna, garlic bread, salad, and what looked like a cake. Her stomach grumbled as she found a chair. A plate was set in front of her and the talking stopped as she picked up a fork.

"What? Did you think you'd get rid of me that easily?" Mia said.

Levi laughed as Abigail shushed him. "Dear, you were in bad shape. Thank goodness for Damien and your grandmother. They make quite a healing team."

Mia looked around and realized neither one of them was at the table. "Where are they?"

"Your grandmother's resting and Damien is downstairs, unpacking the books that came this afternoon. His kind doesn't need to eat much to keep going." Abigail glanced around the table. "On the other hand, I cook when I'm worried, so we already have a soup chilling in the fridge for tomorrow's lunch and several dozen cookies in your cookie bin."

"The cookies are amazing," Christina said, looking up from her lasagna. "I forgot to tell you that."

The volume of cookies Christina was devouring was going to catch up with her, but Mia wasn't going to be the one to tell her friend. Let the doctor do his job. Mia smiled and took another bite of dinner. Her phone buzzed. Trent had texted a message.

Glad to know that you're awake. Eat dinner. You need the fuel.

She replied quickly.

You're not the boss of me.

His **lol** made her smile and she put the phone away. Her kitchen witch doll was swinging on the rope that held it on the baker's rack. Gloria was happy too.

"What's been going on today?" Mia asked. "Besides what happened to me. I want to eat before I start asking questions."

"That works, because your grandmother said we need to wait for Cleo to arrive before we talk about your missing memories. She's doing some research at headquarters and should be here around eight," Abigail filled her in.

Thomas glanced at his watch. "I'm heading back to the shop. Trent put in an order, and I'm going to fill it tonight and then head over to see my son. I'm worried what being locked up in that house with all those women might do to him. I can catch him up on the excitement here."

Mia smiled at the mention of Trent, but she didn't

say anything. Levi, on the other hand, met her gaze and smiled back. He knew that Trent had already visited her via the dream walking.

After dinner, while Christina and Levi cleaned up, Mia went downstairs with the dream walking book and started reading. She still needed to finish reading Suzanne Parker's book, but with everything that had happened today, she thought putting it off until tomorrow might be prudent. As she read, Damien came downstairs to grab a bottle of water.

"You look better than the last time I saw you." He sat down in one of the wing chairs, leaning forward, watching her.

"I hear I owe you my thanks for fixing me." She set down the book.

He picked it up and smiled. "I have a better book. Newer, at least. I'll bring it up to your apartment as soon as I unpack it. And, unfortunately, I didn't get you fixed. I restored most of the memories, but only time will tell on the others. Tell me about your boss, Blake Sandburg. What do you know about her?"

"You can't think Blake did this." Mia leaned back in her chair, thinking about the last week and her interactions with her. "I mean, she's all about her, but she's not dangerous."

The look Damien gave her told her he wasn't convinced, so she went through everything she knew about Blake: her coven in New England and her attack by the succubus when she was in high school. "She reacts to life like she has PTSD from the event. I've met the guy who attacked her and, yes, it was horrible at the time, but I think he's changed."

"Succubi may grow old and slow down, but they never change. They crave sex, adoration, attention. It's not something you just get over with them." Damien looked thoughtful. "I have another book on the succubus. I'll find it too. You need to know the monsters in the world sooner rather than later, I'm afraid."

"That's what I keep hearing. Blake also told me more about Suzanne Parker. You knew her in another life?"

He shook his head. "I've only had one life. Suzanne Parker manipulated it so she had several. She liked her twenties a lot. She'd start over at twenty when *she* decided that she was old. I don't mind looking older, so I just aged very slowly. I think this new body is going to be the same."

"Okay, nice to know, but tell me what you knew about her in this last life. Who was she close to here in Magic Springs? Loves, enemies, children?"

"From what I know, she didn't have children. I think that would have been too painful for her because she would have lost them. As for loves, she kept most of her affairs light. No attachments. She had a few friends: Cleo, Sabrina, I'm not sure who else." He frowned. "What are you looking for?"

"A reason for someone to want to kill her. She was left in the cold with a bucket of water poured over her to make sure she didn't survive. Water kills witches, right?"

He shook his head. "Water doesn't melt witches, not like in the *Oz* books. Suzanne's death might have been an accident."

"Maybe, if not for the water. Someone lured her out

there, drugged her to keep her outside, and then poured water on her. That's premeditated." Mia paused for a minute. "Was she dating Brandon? He seemed very comfortable in her house."

Damien laughed and shook his head. "Sorry, you're going to have to ask someone else about the social lives of Magic Springs. I've been away, and I never really fell into that crowd anyway."

The rest of the group soon arrived, and Levi watched for Cleo. When the clock struck eight, a knock sounded.

"Now that's a little creepy," Mia said as she watched Cleo enter. The woman was always dressed immaculately and today, she had on what Mia assumed was a fake fur coat that swept down to the top of her boots. Witches didn't wear the skin of animals unless it was absolutely necessary. Cleo handed it to Levi, who put it on the coatrack. Muffy came up and sniffed it, then went back to lie by Grans.

When Cleo got closer, Mia stood. "Thank you for coming tonight."

"Let's get down to it, then. I can't believe I didn't notice this before, but we have been busy around here, right?" Cleo lifted her hands and placed them on both sides of Mia's head. As she did, Mia felt woozy. Memories ran through her head like a slideshow: her buying the academy, her first catering event, finding Dorian's body, laughing with Trent, it was all there and all mixed together. The vision of Trent with Sonja at the restaurant came into focus.

Cleo said, "Ah, here's one."

The vision faded away and the process started again. Over and over, Cleo extracted the false memories. Mia couldn't tell if the memories that she put back were in the right place or not, but as Cleo replaced one for another, she heard a pop in her head.

Of all the things she'd done and seen since becoming a kitchen witch, this was the weirdest.

"I should have mentioned that you should try not to think while we're doing this. Just relax, Mia. The weirdness will be over soon. I think there's just one last memory." As Cleo said that, a memory of eating lunch with Suzanne Parker and Cleo on testing day materialized at the front of Mia's mind. Cleo brought in soup and a sandwich for Suzanne and the lunch that Abigail had packed for Mia, and then stayed and sipped coffee as they ate. Suzanne and Cleo talked about old times, and Cleo told Mia about how they both wanted to get involved in training young witches. Then Suzanne's phone rang, and she turned bright red.

"I need to take this."

As Mia felt Cleo's fingers leave her skin, she looked up at the witch in front of her. "That memory is new."

"It shouldn't be, but I think they blocked it. Whoever called Suzanne Parker that day when we were having lunch is probably involved in her death. And in building your false memories." Cleo stepped back and stumbled a little.

Levi took her arm and led her to a chair. "Can I get you something? Tea? Water?"

"A cup of tea on a cold night would be lovely." She patted Levi's arm. "You're going to be such a good dad."

Levi blushed as he followed Christina into the kitchen to make up a tea service.

Abigail took Mia by the arm and sat her back down as well. "Any idea who did this and when?"

Cleo closed her eyes as she sorted through what she'd found. "I can give you some impressions. I believe it's a male. Suzanne wouldn't have blushed so hard if the phone call was just business. And it had to have happened after Mia's testing but before the coven reassigned the protection spell, which was Friday night."

"What? I thought it would go on as soon as the testing results were announced." Abigail met Grans's gaze. "She was unprotected for three days after testing?"

"Her original test was to be on Friday, if you remember. Suzanne changed the testing but didn't update the protection spell implementation time. It wasn't part of her process. The coven should have updated that as soon as the new testing was announced." Cleo smiled as Christina brought out the tea. "I'll look into why that didn't happen as soon as I get back to headquarters."

Mia's first thought was that Cleo spent a lot of time at coven headquarters. Her second thought was that she should have been thinking of all the people she'd talked to while she was unprotected. "Abigail, do we know when Cerby's house training was set up?"

"I talked to Trent. He got the call the weekend before your test." Abigail frowned as she thought about the timing. "He said he mentioned it to Sarah, and she called the training office to get Tempest in the session with Cerby. She didn't realize they'd be locked up for six weeks. At least Tempest didn't have to go to the camp. Em's very attached to her puppy."

Mia wanted to listen more but found herself drifting off, and when she awoke, she was upstairs in her bed with Mr. Darcy curled next to her. She smiled as she rubbed his head. “Some level five witch I’m turning out to be. I can’t even stay up past nine.”

He reached out a paw and rubbed her hand. He knew she’d been through a tough event, and she was being hard on herself. The images he sent her made her smile. Her cat thought she was a warrior.

“I’m not sure that’s true, but I like the way you think.” She glanced at her watch. It was just after three. “Let’s sleep in tomorrow and make a huge breakfast.”

He curled closer, but it took Mia a few minutes to fall asleep. She hoped she was over the worst of the reactions from her memory wipe.

When she got up the next morning, she hadn’t kept her promise to sleep in. Instead, she was up at six, waiting for the rest of the crew to come to the kitchen. After she put a batch of muffins in the oven, she sat down with her coffee, her Suzanne Parker notebook, and her newly restored memories and made a time line from the weekend before the test to today.

When Damien had started remodeling, a lot of people were in and out of the academy. She needed to find out more about his contractor, Nathan Boyle. It would probably be an exercise in ruling someone out, but that had to be done in order to find a suspect you couldn’t find an alibi for.

She decided to start there and opened her laptop to see what she could find on Nathan. His website looked normal, but it had one clue. He had a local Magic Springs discount code. Did that mean he was part of the coven? Or just a local?

Mia had just started to look at his Facebook posts when Christina came in.

She held up her hand. "I know, I know, I need to limit my caffeine, but on Sundays I'm doing a mocha first thing, then I'll switch to fruit tea or water."

"Your body, your decisions." Mia stood. "Do you want me to make some fresh hot cocoa to mix with the coffee?"

"Add a dollop of whipped cream and you have a deal." She sat down and looked at Mia's laptop. "Why are you looking at Nathan Boyle?"

"He's one of the people who were in the academy last week."

Christina shrugged. "Yes, I saw him here. I talked to him several times. He's a friend of the family. Or his dad is. He works with my dad, so I met him years ago at some event. Mom tried to fix us up, but we were always just in the friend zone. He was dating some girl from Magic Springs, and that's why he started his business here. Then they broke up and he stayed for the mountain life. He loves to hunt and fish."

"Is he human?" Mia stirred the hot cocoa mix into the milk. She was going to have a mocha too.

"That would be an odd question from anyone else but you, but yes, as far as I know, he's human and comes from a well-off family from Boise. He got his degree in business management, but building has always been his love. When he was in college, he refurbished a little house up in the north end. He took it down to the studs and rebuilt everything. It's amazing. I wonder if he sold that or is just renting it."

"Looking for a Boise house?" Mia asked as she mixed up two mochas and finished them off with whipped cream.

"No, but I think we're going to look for a Magic Springs house. Maybe Nathan can help us remodel it before the babies come." Christina smiled as she took the cup. "I called and talked to my boss in Portland last night and told her about the babies, and that I didn't want to move now. She's okay with me working from here with a little bit of traveling. Not horrible, but when a new hotel opens, she wants me there for a couple of nights to make sure my plans are implemented."

"You're staying in Magic Springs?" Mia set down her cup and hugged her friend. "I'm so happy I could cry."

"Well, we have support here. If we moved, we'd have to find babysitters who we could trust, a house, and all the stuff. So you're stuck with me. Now I just have to break the news to Mom that I'm not moving back home." Christina sipped her mocha. "She's going to stop taking my calls. First, it was the engagement, then the babies, now the nonmove. Change is not in Mom's wheelhouse. She likes steady, dependable, boring—like Isaac is, now that he's not with you."

"I never saw him that way, but he would have hated all this. Trent takes everything in stride. Can you imagine Isaac's face if I told him his dog had conjured a dragon for a pet?" Mia laughed as she shut down the laptop. She could do more sleuthing on Suzanne Parker later. After a chat with her friend and breakfast.

When everyone had scattered for the day, Mia decided to head to the Lodge to see how the wedding party was doing. The bride and groom would already be on their way to the airport and their Hawaiian honeymoon. Mr. and Mrs. Edwards were staying one more night to decompress before returning to Boise and their lives. Mia knew that empty-nest feeling well after Christina moved out to start her Portland life with Levi. Now, they were back in town, if not in the academy.

She knocked on Christina's door. "Do you want to run with me to the Lodge? I want to check in with the happy parents from yesterday's wedding."

"I'm here to be your wing man, so the answer's yes. Is Finn working at the Lodge today? Does she need a ride in?" Christina set down the book and pushed herself up from the bed.

"We can check when we get downstairs." Mia headed to her bedroom. "Let me change into jeans and a nice shirt. I can't wear yoga pants to represent the Lodge."

"You could, but I think you want your job for a while longer," Christina teased as she grabbed her purse and got out her keys.

As they went downstairs, Finn was already ready for her walk into town. They'd caught her just in time. "Want a lift?" Mia asked. "I need to check on some things from yesterday."

"That would be awesome. Christina's car is the bomb. Even when my van is running, it's not even half as dope as hers."

"Don't expect cooking to get you a car like that. Christina's family spoils her," Mia said as she looked at her little compact sitting in the back of the parking lot.

It had chains on the tires so that she could get to work when Christina wasn't chaperoning. It was a just-enough car. One that got her where she needed to be. Not a car to enjoy being in.

Finn shrugged. "It's nice to be able to afford things like that, but I love cooking. If I had wanted money, I would have gone into something like finance or web design. I want to mix flavors and come up with something amazing. Things aren't as important as experiences."

"Spoken like a true believer. Let's go get this party started." Mia hugged Finn, and they made their way into town. Sunday felt like a new beginning.

Chapter 16

As soon as they arrived at the Lodge, Finn excused herself from the others and headed to the kitchen. Sunday brunch was starting soon and she needed to be on the line, cooking. Mia glanced around at the people enjoying coffee and pastries in the great room. Mrs. Edwards was sitting by the fireplace, and she waved Mia over.

"I was hoping to see you before I left. The wedding was just what Alicia wanted. So pretty, and yet we felt like we were at home, only with a larger dining room for the reception. Thank you so much." Mrs. Edwards stood and pulled Mia into a hug.

"I'm so glad you were pleased. We work hard to make your special occasions exactly how you envision them." Mia let out an internal sigh of relief. With all that had been going on, the Edwards's wedding hadn't been top on her priority list, at least not in her head, which was one of the reasons she dropped in yesterday and today. She had built a solid plan for the event, and even without her steering the boat, her staff was able to implement all the moving parts without incident. She was proud of that. "Well, I just wanted to check in and make sure you two were okay."

"I'm going skiing as soon as we get some food." Mr. Edwards stood and wrapped his arm around his wife. "This one's going back to that spa of yours with a novel. We all decompress differently, right?"

Mia thought Mrs. Edwards had the right idea, but she let it go. "Make sure you tell them to charge the buffet to your room. I have a credit there for you. I wanted to buy your first empty-nest breakfast."

As they walked away, Christina looked back at the happy couple. "I wish my parents would be like that after I get married. Instead, Dad will go back to work the next day like it never happened and Mom will get involved in the next charity event. They won't take a minute to breathe or to reevaluate their lives together."

"Some people are more relaxed than others." Mia didn't want to say that she thought Christina's dad was work-obsessed and her mom hid her unhappiness by always being busy. Christina already knew her parents' faults. "All you can do is choose who you're going to be as a couple."

"What's next?" Christina brushed a tear away from her cheek as they walked through the employee hallway.

"I left my planner here yesterday and want to make sure I'm ready for Monday's meeting." Mia paused at the door to her office. It was open. "Didn't I lock this?"

Christina frowned at the door. "You did. I waited for you while you found your keys at the bottom of your tote. Should we call security?"

"I don't hear anyone in there." Mia pushed the door open.

The office was a disaster. Paper was everywhere. On the floor, on the table, on her desk. She walked over and saw that her desk was open and the drawers had been emptied out onto the floor. Had someone been looking for something? Or just playing around? Her planner sat closed in the middle of her desk.

"I think you should call security now," Mia said.

By the time they were back home, Mia still didn't know why anyone would have destroyed her office. Her planner was in her tote bag, and it didn't appear to have been touched, but every file in her desk had been opened and the pages scattered around. After security had taken pictures and told Mia they'd search the tapes for anyone who shouldn't be there, they'd told her she could put her office back in order. Christina had convinced her to ask housekeeping to send someone to gather all the papers and set them on her table. She was taking Mia home.

As they came into the academy, Mia rubbed her face. "One more mystery that doesn't make any sense. Why not?"

"The security guys will find out who did this," Christina said.

Mia realized Christina had said the same words to her several times. Mia was scaring her friend. "I'm sorry, I'm repeating myself, aren't I?"

The relief on Christina's face was noticeable. "Just a little. I was starting to worry that you were in shock. Do you want a drink? Tequila? Beer? Wine? You should take a drink to calm your nerves. I'd join you, but . . ."

She left the reason unsaid.

"No, I'm going upstairs, taking a long bath, reading something fictional that isn't attached to my coven training, and then getting on my jammies. I'm ordering pizza, so let everyone know if they don't want that for dinner, they're on their own." Mia started up the stairs, her legs feeling like hundred-pound weights.

"Levi and I are going to Abigail's and Thomas's house tonight. She wants to talk baby stuff, like what happens if both twins have power. I think we already know they will from their chattering." Christina sighed. "They aren't even here and there's nothing I wouldn't do for them."

"I'll check with Grans, then. She's picky about what kind of pizza to order." Mia shrugged. "Finn said she's going out with friends and will be home late. Everyone's deserting me tonight."

"We're not deserting you." Christina focused on her as they reached the second-floor landing. "We can change our dinner plans. I haven't had pizza in forever. Abigail will understand."

"Don't be silly. There's no reason to change your plans because I'm feeling blue. I'll be fine, and even if Grans and Damien have plans, you know I'm never really alone here." Mia not only felt blue, she was also still tired from yesterday's work with Cleo. She'd probably eat, then go curl up in bed and read until sleep took over. Which might be minutes.

"That should be more comforting than it is." Christina hugged her as they finished climbing to the third floor. "But I'll take you at your word. I hate that Trent's confined to his house during all this. I feel like we're missing a part of our core group."

"Once Cerby and Tempest are trained, we'll all be safer. It needed to be done." Mia rubbed her face. "I just hope Buddy doesn't have to go to a training. That could get messy."

Christina giggled. "I never thought I'd be chatting with you about the correct training methodologies for hellhounds and dragons."

"Oh, I'm sure that's not the craziest thing we'll ever talk about. Christina, I wanted to tell you how much your friendship has meant to me over the years. When Isaac and I broke up, you could have just picked sides." Mia opened the door and found Muffy and Mr. Darcy sleeping in the living room.

"I definitely picked a side. I chose you. My brother barely talked to me anyway. You were the one who made me feel seen." Christina's hand dropped to the gentle curve of her belly. She'd been doing that a lot lately, unconsciously. "You're the closest thing I have to a real sister."

"You two are getting mushy. Did something happen at the Lodge? Or are Christina's hormones kicking in?" Grans came out of the bedroom in a blue shimmering cocktail dress. "Stop looking at me that way, it's not a date. We're heading over to the Sun Valley Country Club for dinner. Dorian has a membership."

"Damien?" Mia reminded her.

Grans rolled her eyes. "I'm not sure why we're putting up the false identity. Obviously, the coven knows he's back."

"Because some of the humans, like Mark, saw Dorian Alexander be buried." Mia settled on the couch between the dog and the cat and grabbed a remote. "We live in a small town, but not that small."

"I'm trying to remember, and when I don't, I just look old and forgetful. A stereotype that helps keep his secret." Grans rubbed Muffy's head. "I've already fed both of these rug rats, so don't let them con you into a second dinner. Muffy just went outside, but he'll probably have to go again in about an hour or two. Maybe when your pizza comes."

Mia didn't even want to ask how Grans knew. "Sounds like a plan. Be careful while you're out."

"We don't have the bull's-eye on our backs like you do." Grans paused a minute, thinking about her words. "I wonder why that is. Abigail is certain that whoever is behind this is trying to isolate you. Maybe we should just stay home."

"As long as I stay on the property, I should be fine. I'll put a lead on Muffy before I let him out so he can't be tempted to wander." Mia saw the concern growing on her grandmother's face. "And I'll text you every time I open the door."

"And when you're back in the apartment?"

Mia rolled her eyes. "I promise. Go have fun. I'll be fine here."

She didn't add "alone" because, as she'd told Christina, she wasn't alone. She had Mr. Darcy, who had a connection with Damien. She had the academy ghosts, who could tell anyone anything. And she had a new *Project Runway* season that she hadn't even watched the first episode of yet. Add in a supreme with extra veggies and a beer out of the fridge and she'd be just fine for the two or three hours she'd be alone in the academy.

When neither Grans nor Christina moved, she picked up the remote. "I promise, I won't take off for any reason. Even with Cleo's intervention last night, I still feel like the world around me is staged. I know what I see might not be reality. I'll call someone first before jumping into deep waters." She held up her hand in a Girl Scout symbol. "So help me Goddess."

"You're not funny. But I think you are clear enough to not fall for a vision. At least I hope so." Grans called out to the kitchen. "Gloria? If something goes down, will you reach out to me?"

An old James Taylor song wafted through the room: "You've Got a Friend."

"I'll take that as a yes. Be careful and I'll see you no later than nine." Grans kissed Mia on the cheek, rubbing off the lipstick as she stood up. "And you, Christina. Go change into something pretty. Levi's almost here."

Mia smiled as she curled up on the couch. She had people who worried about her and people she worried about. She had family. No matter if they were blood-related or not, they were united. She watched the security monitor as Levi's Jeep came into the parking lot and Damien's car left. Then Christina blew through the living room in a maxi dress and boots and rushed out the door.

Mia paused the show, then got up to get a soda and threw the dead bolt on the apartment door. Stupid, she knew, but it made her feel better. No one would get in the front door without a key, and she wasn't going to open the door for anyone.

She resumed the episode and got busy trying to figure out who was her favorite in the new cast of designers. So many were cast as the love-to-hate reality stars this season. Nailing down a favorite to go all the way was going to be hard.

She ordered pizza and breadsticks after the first episode was over. When she saw the pizza delivery guy pull into the parking lot on the security monitor, she also saw Mark Baldwin's truck pull in afterward. She picked up her phone as she went out of the apartment and called Sarah.

"Do me a favor, call Mark and ask him where he is right now?" Mia asked as soon as Sarah answered the call. "Wait, ask Trent to call him."

To her credit, Sarah didn't even ask why. Mia waited to open the door until Sarah returned to the phone. "Mark says he parked in front of your school. Is there a problem?"

"No, just tell him to say, 'Tempest is a hellhound' when he reaches the front door." Mia snapped on

Muffy's lead before she opened the door and gathered the pizza. She set it on the foyer table and waited for Mark to come up to the door. He nodded to the pizza delivery kid, who gave him room on the sidewalk.

When Mark got to the door, he looked back to see if the kid was in his car, then dropped his voice. "Tempest is a hellhound. What is this all about?"

Mia called Muffy in and he greeted Mark as well. She shut the door, then tapped a finger on the top of the pizza box. "Want some dinner?"

"Sure." Mark followed her into the living room.

She set down the pizza on a table and grabbed paper plates and napkins from the bar. "I have cola or lemon lime down here. Or root beer."

"Root beer, please." As he sat down and took off his jacket, he laid it on the couch. "Are you going to tell me why I had to have a password from my wife to talk to you?"

"I told you I was having some visions and unsure what was real." Mia set two cans on the table and opened one to take a drink. "I'm alone, so I didn't want to be surprised if you turned out to be someone else."

"I didn't think this place was ever empty. You collect strays like you run a dog pound." He opened the pizza box and took a deep sniff. "This smells amazing. I don't know why I didn't think to order pizza one night while Sarah's been gone."

"She probably has a compelling spell on the house to try to get you to eat healthy." Mia took a slice, watching Mark's reaction. Maybe she shouldn't have told him that.

Instead of getting upset, he shrugged and grabbed a slice. "I wouldn't put it past her. Anyway, I thought you dealt with the visions."

"I think I have, but a girl can't be too careful. Why are you here, besides the fact that it's dinnertime and you thought you'd get invited to eat?" The pizza was just hot enough and had a thick crust, which made it taste so much better than if it had a crunchy, thin crust.

"One, yes, I thought dinner might be around this time. And two, I wanted to update you on what I found out about Suzanne Parker. She did own a house in town. Funny, the county records show it as vacant land. She has a will, but her attorney is out of town until late next week. So is her boss, who sent her here from Boston on assignment. Only he can tell me what her assignment was or who she was meeting. Being human, I can play dumb well. After talking to his assistant, I got a call from the large attorney firm, which told me not to contact their clients directly but filter all questions through them. So, I sent them a full page of them. No response yet, but the boss is on vacation, according to the lawyer. Who was this woman besides your tester? Is that job enough to get this kind of celebrity cover-up? I haven't seen this kind of back peddling since we had that murder of a low-level actress in Sun Valley."

"She was a powerful witch, I know that much. She lived a long time here in Magic Springs, and she loved being part of a new witch's education. Except for mine, I guess. She was upset that I'd tested so high on my first test and thought I pulled one over on the first examination guide. He was lovely, by the way. Then someone asked for a retest. Parker came and gave it. Then I tested higher. I don't know why that or her death happened, but I believe someone wants me to step away from my magic."

They ate in silence for a few minutes, then Mark set down his pizza. "You think this is about the magic? You usually can tell me if my victim was killed by magic or not. This seems like a bad rewrite of *The Wizard of Oz*."

"I don't know. I don't know if it's because of this guy or girl messing with my memories," Mia circled around her head with an outstretched finger, "or because of my level from the test. Or maybe it had nothing to do with Suzanne Parker's professional life and she was just here when the killing happened. She'd lived here for many years, so I'm sure she must have made some friends and enemies. I just can't find either."

"That's not normal." He finished the pizza on his plate, then went back for another slice. "I know Magic Springs isn't normal, but we have a pace to life here. This seems like it's coming from somewhere else. The whole murder was set up to highlight that she was a witch, if you didn't know anything about witches."

"Could it be about the property? Christina said it's on a road on the way to her parents' condo. I assume that's all high-end property from the way the house looked at her wake." Mia picked the loose toppings off the box. She wasn't hungry, but it tasted so good.

Mark brightened as he finished his slice. "This is why I love talking to you about these cases. You hit on a possible normal motive. I've heard rumors that a developer wants to buy up two million-dollar lots, combine them, and then build even bigger, ten million-dollar houses. I wonder where Adam Boyle was on Tuesday night."

"He's the developer?" Mia asked for a bit of clarification because she was lost in Mark's line of thinking. "Wait, is he related to Nathan Boyle?"

"Nathan is his son. Adam mostly works in Boise, or he used to before he started sniffing around Magic Springs."

Chapter 17

Monday morning, as Mia waited for Christina, she signed on to her work email and went through the last week and the upcoming one. The wedding had been perfect, according to all the evaluations from the family. Mia loved making someone's special day just a little less stressful. As she went through her calendar, matching up emails and meetings, she realized for a holiday month, this week was fairly light. Thanksgiving was a big buffet day for the Lodge, but without the snow that the weatherman had predicted, the ski slope wasn't being booked as quickly. And people who had booked were backing out and going somewhere the snow gods had blessed.

Mia figured they'd have another storm or two soon, but she didn't think it was going to fix Blake's November numbers. With the weather warming up again—a fake fall, Grans liked to call it—the cross-country trails would turn from snow-packed to mud. If Mia's test had been scheduled one week later, Suzanne Parker might still be alive. Of course the method of murder wasn't the motivation behind the deed, so she might still be dead, but by other means.

Had the murder been planned out? Or spontaneous? Anyone who lived here knew that snow didn't always stay on the ground. Idaho was famous for its late fall summer days, when the sun would melt the snow and tan the few skiers who didn't mind going downhill in slushy conditions.

Mia pulled out her Suzanne Parker notebook and wrote down what she'd been thinking about: *Weather reports, not a local?* She wondered if she could talk to the testing department at the National Office and see when this retest was planned. Was it spontaneous too?

As she put down her pen and went back to making sure her planner matched her work calendar, she noticed a meeting invite from Blake. Hesitant to accept, she opened the invite to see what the topic was and if anyone else was invited. Of course other people in the meeting hadn't stopped Blake from scheduling them to sleep while she played with Mia's mind.

The meeting was just for two, but the description made her stop. "Meeting with Carl Hagen from National Testing Office re: Suzanne Parker. Mia and a guest." And it was set to be in Mia's office. Who had called Blake to set up the meeting?

She wished for a meeting and now here it was? This was getting weird.

Her phone rang. The caller ID indicated the call originated from coven headquarters. "Hello?"

"Gloria said you needed a meeting with Carl, so I set one up for tomorrow. Does that answer the why?" Cleo asked.

Mia knew Cleo from her voice, not that she introduced herself. Grans did the same thing, jumping right into a conversation as soon as someone picked up the phone. Mia looked up at the doll, who was swinging on her broom. "I didn't realize she was listening to me."

"My dear, Gloria's always there. She's trying to help you settle into your new role, but I admit, if you're not used to the connection, it can be disturbing. I'll talk to her about slowing down a little. Why are you interested in the testing schedule?" Cleo shuffled some papers on the other side. "Never mind, it's all about justice with you humans. I forgot. Look, I've got the memos for the last month from the coven to headquarters. The answer on who asked for the retest should be in there. I'd assist, but I'm only allowed to provide materials, not interpret them, so I wouldn't be much help. I'll send the package over to your house later this afternoon."

After Mia hung up with Cleo, Christina came into the room. "Abigail said she's going to be a little late this morning. I've already texted Finn, so I think we can go. Let me fill my coffee and get a muffin for the road."

"Sure, I'm just finishing up my schedule. Does Mia's Morsels have any catering events this week? That you know of?" Mia glanced at the kitchen calendar, but besides the deliveries, nothing was scheduled for the entire month. If that was true, Mia would be working at the Lodge a lot longer than she'd expected.

This should be their busy season. Why weren't their weekends full? Hadn't James told her that her catering business was busy doing events so he'd miss Finn?

Christina opened her phone calendar app. "Yep. They have a small gathering on Friday night, a holiday dinner for the local charity group on Saturday, and the Magic Springs Quilt Club luncheon on Saturday. Didn't Abigail send you these to your calendar?"

"What calendar?" Mia turned the page on her planner to show the month view. Nothing was listed besides Thanksgiving at Abigail's.

"Not your paper one, the online calendar she set up this fall." Christina leaned over Mia's laptop and opened a new tab. Then she keyed in the Mia's Morsels website, went to Staff Only, and opened the calendar app there.

Abigail had the events blocked out, as well as cooking and delivery days. As Mia watched, several invites from Abigail popped up to see if Mia was available to work an event.

"This is amazing. We're booked through the first two weeks of January." Mia sifted through the catering events, adding them to her monthly planner.

"You don't need to duplicate it all, just add your stuff to this one. It will only show you your events, not everyone's." Christina keyed in Mia's work schedule and put it on Repeat for Monday through Friday. "You can connect this one to your work calendar too. No need to check your planner, it will all be here."

"I like my paper planner. It helps me decide when I'm too busy and when I have time for fun," Mia objected. Even adding the events to her planner was making her nervous. What if she double-booked herself and didn't realize it? No, she was definitely keeping the paper version of her life. "Let me just add these events and answer Abigail's invites. I know I can help Friday night and Sunday for lunch, but Saturday might be an issue."

"I told her you'd say that, so she's already hired a few servers. She'll probably need some prep help in the kitchen Thursday and Friday if you have time." As she'd talked, Christina had gathered her stuff and now had her keys in her hand. "Ready to go to work?"

Mia finished adding the last December event to her planner. "I'm ready when you are. I think we can make it a half day at the Lodge today and probably tomorrow, so we can help with the cooking then. I was starting to get worried."

Gloria giggled as Mia tucked everything into her tote. Grans wasn't up yet, so she left her a note. Muffy had already been fed and taken out.

As they went out the apartment door, the elevator doors opened and Grans stepped out, her purse by her side. "Oh, I thought you'd be at work by now."

"Just heading there." Mia stopped in front of her. "I thought you were still sleeping. Where did you go this morning?"

"None of your business." Grans brushed by her. "Has Muffy been fed?"

"I left you a note, but yes. Fed and out already." Mia paused and watched her walk to the apartment. She wanted to ask if she'd come home last night, but she'd already been told it was none of her business, so she let it go.

At least until after she and Christina got into the car and headed out of the parking lot. "Did we just see my grandmother do the walk of shame?" Mia let out a breath.

"I wasn't going to mention it, but I think so." Christina started to giggle. "I guess her date last night went well."

"She'd probably say they were working on some spell or potion at her house." Mia leaned back in her seat after turning on the heater. "Grans says you don't have a spell perfect until you've done it at least eight times. I'll stay in my bubble and think they were working on potions."

"Okay, live in your G-rated fairy-tale world. I like my romance steamy." Christina went on to talk about her latest favorite author find.

Mia tuned out the chatter and thought about Suzanne Parker and potions. Maybe she wasn't drugged but put under a potion spell. Was there one that would make you more pliable to suggestions? And what about the water? In order for her to have that much water on her, the killer would have had to bring a bucket or more to pour over her. How did they get that on the trailhead? The cross-country ski trail was an old logging road, so they might have brought a vehicle. Did the police find tracks?

She pulled out her phone and texted Mark her questions. Something about this whole thing didn't add up. It was looking more and more like magic had been a part of Suzanne Parker's death. Mia wasn't liking that theory at all. She might just be a kitchen witch, but in her opinion, magic should be used only with good intentions.

Maybe she was too much of a Pollyanna for this life.

When Mark didn't answer right away, she put the phone away.

"I know you didn't just order the book I've been talking about since we left the house. Were you listening at all?" Christina asked as she parked the Land Rover at the Lodge. As they got out, she looked up at the sun shining in the clear blue sky. "I'm glad I didn't move my clothes to Portland. I would be without a jacket for today and would have had to wear my puffer or gone without. You know it's going to be cold when we drive home."

"The weather has been strange," Mia agreed. She'd ignored the question about the book because Christina was right, she hadn't been listening at all. The guy at the front desk waved her over. "Ms. Malone, you have a visitor waiting to talk to you."

Mia glanced over to where the man pointed, and Brandon Maxwell sat on a couch, looking at his phone. As she walked over, he stood, smiling.

"Brandon, how can I help you today?" Mia asked. "Do you need to plan an event?"

"Not unless you're agreeing to join the coven. Then we'll throw a huge bash, but we probably should wait until the solstice or at least a full moon. so more power will be available for us. Miss Adams, how are you feeling?" Brandon turned his cat-that-ate-the-canary smile on Christina.

"Fine, thanks. Mia, I'm going to grab some breakfast. I'll meet you in your office," Christina added as she narrowed her eyes at Brandon. "Unless you need me to stay."

"I'll be fine." Mia sat on the couch across from where Brandon had been sitting. "I'm sure we can deal with this out here, in the open."

Brandon blinked, realizing that he wasn't in charge of the meeting, and sat back down. "I'll be quick and you're perfectly safe with me. I can't believe you would even think otherwise."

"Brandon, a woman is dead and we don't know why. I've heard that maybe she and you were an item, so forgive me if I don't think meeting you in a private, secluded spot is a great idea. Speaking of that, I wanted to ask you who assigns hellhound training slots. Is it you?"

The change of subject surprised him, forcing him, as Mia had hoped, to give a true answer before he could think about it. "No. I don't deal with the animals. Familiar issues are handled by Aaron Harding, but hellhound training runs through Marsha Fieldstone. She's amazing at keeping the scheduling and records, and since she had an incident with one many years ago, she has a vested interest in making sure the animals pass their certification. I thought you knew that because she was part of Cerby's original discovery."

"Marsha schedules the training too?" Now Mia was confused. If her theory was right, the hellhound training was specifically scheduled to keep Trent out of Mia's life for six weeks.

"For the last twenty years. Although Cerby and Tempest are the first hellhounds we've had arrive in

Magic Springs for more than ten years. Because the McManns' training program is in our area of concern, the coven uses Marsha to coordinate with the other covens who send animals to be trained. We like to have a heads up on hellhounds coming into the area. Just in case they get loose. Why are you concerned about the training? Isn't it going well?" Brandon asked. It was obvious that he hadn't expected to be chatting about hellhound training.

"It's fine. I was just wondering who coordinated all that. Do you handle the witch testing? Or is that someone else, like Sabrina?" Mia continued to pepper him with questions, hoping she'd continue to get honest answers.

"Sabrina does the recruitment, but someone else schedules tests. Sabrina isn't keen on completing tasks or following through unless it's to go out to eat or coordinate a party. No, the scheduler is someone on her staff. It used to be a woman, but she was promoted to National. All our strong witches are, which is why I believe you'll be leaving the coven for a better position as soon as you decide to join."

"If I decide to join. Is Cleo the test scheduler?" Mia tried to steer him away from talking about her possible commitment.

"No, Cleo's too busy for that. Let's see. When Karen left, who took her spot? Oh, Jullian Barnes. I'm not sure you've met. He doesn't much care for the parties or meetings. He mostly just works. He's a favorite of the old guard, though. Between you and me, I think he has a benefactor in the coven."

"A benefactor?" Mia leaned forward. "Who?"

"Now, listen to me spilling all the coven secrets to an outsider. Of course if you joined, I wouldn't have to worry about what I said." He met my gaze. "Would I? I'm just here checking in to see if I can answer any more questions about joining. Your first level five payment should be in your account by now. Have you looked?"

"No, I've been a little busy." Mia thought Brandon had led her down the primrose path, but she was too smart to fall for his trickery. If she joined the coven, it would be because she thought it was best for her, not because Brandon wouldn't tell her something. She could find out what she needed without him. She had in the past. "If that's all, I'd better get to work. I have a staff meeting coming up."

"Of course. Thank you for taking time to talk to me. It was most . . . illuminating." Brandon bowed slightly and then headed to the door.

Mia watched him leave. Whatever he'd come for, it wasn't just to ask her if she'd received the money from Nationals. He'd been looking for something, and her questions had distracted him. Something that he hadn't had to deal with for a long time. As he was coven leader, people usually deferred to him and answered his questions directly. Mia probably just frustrated him. She headed to her office.

A piece of paper was taped on the door, and she ripped it off as she unlocked the door and went inside. She set the note on her desk as she took out her planner and put away her tote. She hung her jacket on the coatrack, then opened the note. She read it aloud. "'What have you done? Come to my office as soon as you arrive.' "

Blake had scheduled the meeting with the National Office tomorrow. Mia wondered if Blake thought Mia had turned her in for what she'd done. Or she might have seen Brandon sitting in the lobby, waiting for Mia. Whatever it was, Blake was freaking out. The handwriting was even a little shaky.

Mia booted up her computer and answered some emails. She wanted Christina in her office before she went to see Blake to verify the time Mia spent with her boss. She didn't trust Blake not to put her under a spell again, which, as she thought about it, was not a very good sign for their professional relationship. She knew why Blake didn't trust easily, but that didn't excuse what she'd done to Mia.

As the saying went, Fool me once, shame on you. Fool me twice? Shame on me. She wasn't going to be the girl who was too stupid to live, like some of the characters in Christina's books.

"I brought you coffee and an apple turnover. I bought two, but I already ate mine," Christina said as she came into the office. She set down the bag and coffee carrier and hung up her coat, setting up her temporary workstation as she talked. "James is so cute. He really knows his stuff in the kitchen. He just hired a new pastry chef. Maybe I should have gone into that instead of event planning. I love a good cookie."

"Sorry to break into your dessert dreaming, but I need to go to Blake's office. Can you time me?" Mia held up her watch. "If I'm gone more than ten minutes, go to the kitchen and get James to come with you to get me. Tell him my grandmother called and she's sick or something. Just get me out of that office."

"You don't think she's going to try to read you again, do you?" Christina checked her watch and wrote down the time. "I'll set an alarm too."

"I don't know what she's planning. I just don't trust her. I'm probably overreacting, but . . ."

"Fool me once," Christina said, mimicking Mia's earlier thought.

Mia met her gaze. "Exactly."

Chapter 18

Blake Sandburg totally remodeled her office when she came on board last year. The wood paneling and heavy dark furniture that was Frank's version of a 1920s gentleman's den was lightened with a coat of peach paint, and the furniture was a white reproduction of the French baroque period. She had installed a wall of bookcases on one side of the room and put a floral love seat there with a small coffee table in front, for a coffee or tea service.

Mia noticed that not only was the coffee service fresh and hot but Blake had also ordered scones from the kitchen for their meeting.

Usually, Blake only got out the good presentations for customers who were planning large events at the Lodge. Mia's typical meeting was five minutes at the desk with a pile of papers shoved at her at the end. Today, the room smelled of Christmas trees and peppermint cocoa.

Now she was concerned. Maybe Blake had another meeting right after theirs.

Focused on her computer, Blake hadn't seen Mia arrive, so she knocked on the open door. "Blake? You wanted to see me?"

"Oh, Mia. I'm so glad you could squeeze me in today," Blake said as she got up and moved to the couch. She waved her over.

Mia wasn't sure if the opening had been sarcastic or not, but she decided to assume it wasn't. No use starting a fight when her boss seemed to be offering an olive branch. This version of Blake had not been what Mia was expecting from the note. "I got your message. It seemed urgent."

"No more than any of the other messages I've sent you. Of course we are all swamped with holiday events and parties, but you know that. You've been managing your job duties well, especially considering what you're going through in your personal life. How's Trent doing with his familiar's training? He's lucky the coven made a special dispensation for Cerby to be trained at home. Well, with the dragon and Sarah's new hellhound. It's quite a team you're building. Almost like you're preparing for something big."

Mia didn't know who had told her about the in-home hellhound training or about Buddy, but she didn't like her boss knowing this much about her personal life. The announcement of her new level had been broadcast all over the witching world, so there was nothing she could do about that. The National Office loved presenting new witches and their skill level to the entire group of covens. Mia thought it felt invasive, especially when she didn't know how to use this new power or what it meant for her.

"I'm just a kitchen witch," Mia said, ignoring the question and statement about her team. One of Grans's tricks to surviving the testing was to answer the question you want to be asked, not the question they ask you. Maybe her trick had worked too well.

"Of course you are." Blake smiled as she patted the couch. "Coffee? Or a scone?"

Mia walked over as Blake poured coffee into two of the fine china cups. Mia perched on the edge of the love seat. She had ten minutes before Christina would come looking for her. She planned on being out of this Martha Stewart–designed office way before that. "Sure. What can I do for you, Blake? As you said, we're all really busy with upcoming events."

"I know we've gotten off on a bad note. I was too worried about keeping my identity here secret and I didn't want you to look at me differently. I thought maybe we could spend some time getting to know each other better." Blake picked up her coffee and sipped it. "What are your plans now that you've tested higher? You realize there are only three or four witches in the state at your level or above."

"I didn't know that." Mia needed to talk to Abigail and Grans again. They should have told her this, not her boss. "I'd love to sit and chat, but my day is really packed. We have events all week."

"You're right. But you made time for Brandon Maxwell this morning. What did he want?" Blake's eyes went dark, and Mia could feel the power behind the question. "And why are you meeting with the National Testing coordinator tomorrow?"

"You didn't just try to compel me to answer those questions, did you?" Mia stood and took a step away. "I'm sure you didn't, because that would force me to report you to the coven, and we both know you don't want to deal with that headache." Mia paused again. "Brandon was making sure I knew that opportunities would be coming my way if I joined the coven, which I haven't, yet."

"Mia, I didn't mean to push. I got carried away." Blake stood. "Please don't take offense."

"I'll take your word for it." Mia walked to the door. "Now, unless you have some work issue to talk about, I need to get back to my office. So much to do. Thanks for the coffee, though."

Blake just waved as she left. Thank the Goddess Mia hadn't drunk any of the coffee. It probably didn't have a potion in it, but with the compel spell she felt coming from Blake, she was glad she didn't take the chance. Her boss was testing her, and Mia didn't like it.

The bad part was that right now, she needed the money.

Unless the allowance for level five was more than she expected. But if she counted on that money, she'd still be under someone else's thumb.

Mia went back to her office. Christina looked up from the book she'd been reading. "You feel like you're going to set something on fire. I take it the meeting didn't go well."

"She tried to compel me to answer a question." Mia sat behind her desk and checked her calendar. "Look, I'm upset, so let's just go back to the house. Nothing pressing is on my plate right now, which is weird, but I'm not looking this gift horse in the mouth. Maybe I won't feel like blowing up Blake tomorrow morning."

"We could do a yoga practice," Christina said as she gathered her things. "Yoga always calms me down. Especially after I chat with my mom for a few minutes."

"Sure, let's do some yoga." Mia set her email to Out of Office with a note to text her cell in an emergency, then she shut down her computer. She would try again tomorrow. Besides, she would soon have a pile of copies of memos to go through from Cleo.

As they walked out of the Lodge, a light snow was falling around them. On impulse, Mia turned to Christina. "Hey, do you want to go to coven headquarters with me? Two people going through those memos should be faster, and that way no one can filter our findings. I don't think Cleo has sent them to the house yet."

"Can I go?" Christina leaned her head up and let the snowflakes hit her face. "I love Magic Springs, even in winter."

"I think the name explains it all." Mia thought about Christina's question as she walked over to her friend's Land Rover. "I guess we'll see if your magical heritage is enough to get you a day pass. Otherwise, you can drop me off and then come back when I call you."

"Sounds groovy either way. I'm curious to see what headquarters look like. It's not every day you find a place where magic is regulated." Christina turned on the SUV, then pushed buttons. "Heated seats, heated steering wheel. We might need a place where we can sit and go through what we find, if anything. If I can't get in, I'll wait for you in the car. I've got some work and a book."

When they arrived at coven headquarters, Cleo was standing outside and waved them both inside. "If it isn't our latest level five. I don't think we've had a kitchen witch test out so fast for centuries. Gloria might have been our last one. She was a level seven the last time they tested her. She might be higher now. Christina Adams, welcome. Are you here to do some genealogy?"

"Actually, if you haven't copied those memos, we'd love to look at them here. At least until the roads get bad." Mia held out her hand for a snowflake to land.

"Oh, this is just a gift from the Goddess. The roads will be fine tonight." Cleo held the door open for them. "I haven't bundled the memos yet. I've been distracted with this gift."

Mia headed inside and heard Christina's audible gasp. "It's beautiful, right? Cleo decorated it," Mia said. The room looked like it had been lifted from a high-end hotel lobby in Greece, not from any current building. She half expected centurions and satyrs to walk through the room as they talked, if not bunnies or deer.

"I swear I was in this building a few years ago and it looked like the DMV. Of course that was what I was looking for. A woman sent me two buildings down." Christina spun around, taking in all the angles. "This is breathtaking."

"I'm glad you like it. When humans enter, they have a different experience than anyone with witch heritage. You must be special to be able to see this now, before your first test. How long have you known about your history?" Cleo headed over to the counter and grabbed a set of keys. "Follow me, I'll get you set up in a request room. Christina, please let Mia lead you here. Making the right request makes all the difference."

"I'm learning that there are a lot of things I need to understand." Christina smiled at Cleo. "I've known about my family history for a while, but I never realized that I could have any talent. My mother—my adopted mother, I should say—thought magic wasn't real. She thought it was a fun party trick, but not something serious to study, like art or music."

Mia laughed. "I don't think Roxanne thought my gift was fun or a party trick at all. She would have died of embarrassment if any of her friends had found out her son had married someone who 'believed' themselves to be a witch. Off to the mental hospital for that daughter-in-law."

"Witches have been persecuted for their beliefs for years. Only in recent history could someone call themselves Wiccan without being seen as crazy or worse, a devil worshipper. Our Goddess is definitely not evil." Cleo shook her head. "I'm wasting your time. You have other tasks ahead of you today. Come, let me get you settled."

After Cleo had left them in a request room, Christina sat at the table. Like the last time Mia came for information, the room was empty except for the table and, now, two chairs along with two pens and notebooks. "I don't understand. Does someone else come and get your request?"

Mia smiled and shook her head. "Keep your hands inside the car, kids. The ride is about to begin."

Christina watched as Mia picked up a pen and, after a minute, wrote down these words: *All correspondence between anyone in the Magic Springs coven and the National Office regarding Mia Malone and her testing, including complaints about her level.*

She showed the paper to Christina, then pushed it toward the front of the table. It disappeared, and almost immediately paper started floating down to the table. Christina caught one that hit her on the head.

"So, you tell it what you want and the information appears?" Christina glanced at the memo. "Someone doesn't like you much."

Mia scanned a few more memos. "I think a lot of people didn't like my testing. Weird. I would have been happy for someone who tested higher, but these people seem to think in a scarcity mode. If I test higher, they think they don't get what they want, but nothing could be further from the truth. A rising tide raises all boats, not just mine." Mia started stacking the negative emails. There were a lot of complaints, including one that surprised her. Thomas Majors had sent a memo complaining that Mia's level made it harder for people who were raised in the magic community. "Seriously? I wonder if Abigail knows about this."

"If she doesn't, she needs to. Thomas can have his own opinion, but he needs to be honest to your face if he feels like you're taking jobs away from his son." Christina bit her lip. "Except Levi isn't looking for a job with the Magic Springs coven. When this was written, we were in Portland and he was looking for a job with a fire station. Mia, I'm not sure this is real."

Chapter 19

Mia took a picture of the memo with her phone. "One way to find out."

She looked at the pile of complaints and found another one she wondered about. It was from Sabrina, the woman who had just been over to the academy to congratulate Mia. She snapped a picture of that one too. Finally she found one from the National Office to Brandon explaining that because so many complaints were filed, they were sending a new tester rather than Hugh Charlton, the man who was in charge of Magic Springs's testing for years. Suzanne Parker would redo the test. The memo also said that Brandon could stop the testing if he thought this was a nonissue.

"Huh." Mia sat back in her chair. "Why didn't Brandon just stop the second test? And even if he didn't agree with the first test level, why the dog and pony show when I got my second set of test scores? This doesn't make any sense." Brandon knew Mia didn't want to join the coven. Why would he keep asking if he didn't think she deserved the levels she was testing at?

"Ready to go ask some people what they really think?" Christina asked, skimming through the memos.

"Almost. I need to know who requested the house training for Cerby and Tempest." She handed Christina a new stack of papers that had just drifted down from the first question. "You go through these. I need to ask a second question."

As Mia formulated the next question, she tried to narrow it down as much as possible without limiting the answer. She had a feeling she might know where the house training request came from, but she would rather know all her enemies than think some of them were friends.

She wrote down the question, then pushed the paper forward to the edge of the table, where it appeared to fall off. Mia knew she wouldn't see a paper on the floor if she looked down. Her question had disappeared into a metaphysical slot. Mia couldn't see where it started or where it went.

A new paper floated down to the table. Mia waited for others to drop to pick it up, but only the one page dropped. She picked it up and read the memo aloud. "'Per your coven president's appeal to the National Office's department of hellhounds and other magical creatures, due to the special circumstances, the office has approved a home study course for both hellhounds.'

"Brandon authorized the at-home training program for Cerby. And Tempest. He knows about Sarah and her powers, and maybe Em." Mia tried to think. What special circumstances could he have found out about? Buddy? Why had he requested this? She turned to Christina. "Anything else we should know? Is the governor or president against us as well?"

"One more. Blake sent in a complaint too. For someone who's trying to hide from the coven, she's sure busy getting into your business."

"Let's get out of here and get some visits done. We'll leave talking to Blake about the letter for tomorrow. Right now, I like knowing I'm employed. After we talk, I might have to actually join the coven for the monthly payments, because if this is true, I can't work with her." Mia took a picture of the survey. She couldn't believe all Blake wanted was to stay out of the limelight. The complaint not only outed her as a witch but put her in Magic Springs. Two things she said she didn't want the coven to know. What a liar.

"Where are we headed first? To find Brandon or to talk to Thomas?" Christina stood as she straightened the papers on the table.

"Let's go to the store. If they falsified Thomas's complaint, maybe some of the others were false as well." Mia followed Christina out to the lobby. Cleo was nowhere to be seen. Mia shrugged, and they left coven headquarters. "Something feels off about this. Would Thomas submit a complaint without telling Abigail? If he'd told her, she'd be in the third bedroom in the apartment."

"You're right about that." Christina grinned as she unlocked the doors to the Land Rover. "Mama don't take kindly to people attacking her family."

Mia smiled as Christina started the car. As they pulled

out of the parking spot, she saw Cleo standing in the window, watching them leave. What had Cleo wanted them to find? Were Mia's questions on point enough for the magic answer room to give her the answer she needed? Sometimes in Magic Springs, Mia thought she might do just as well with one of those Magic 8 Balls. *Your answer is inconclusive. Try again later*.

As Christina drove the short distance to Majors Grocery store, she was quiet as well. She parked the car in the lot and then turned to Mia. "You really don't think Thomas sent that complaint, do you?"

"Honestly I don't know. Levi said something earlier about his dad. Maybe we should listen to the people who know him rather than relying on what we think we know." Mia had a few mottos to live by, and one was when someone shows you who they are, believe them. Was Thomas showing his true feelings? She stared at the big windows in the store. He'd taken over the management of the store grudgingly for Trent when Sonja put him on house arrest for Cerby's training. Levi said he was old-fashioned. Maybe he didn't believe a kitchen witch could obtain a level three without cheating.

She turned to Christina. "You don't have to come in. If he did do this, maybe you don't need to know."

"Mia, you're my best friend and basically my sister. What you know, I need to know. You can't protect me forever." She squeezed Mia's hand. "Whatever this crazy life brings, I hope we're always together to fight the battle for the right side."

Mia squeezed back. "Let's just hope the Goddess tells us the right side before we start the fight."

"The fact that you're even questioning which side is right tells me you'll make the correct decision. People who don't, well, they're usually wrong." Christina turned off the car. "Let's go talk to the man who might be our future father-in-law, whether he likes it or not."

Thomas Majors was standing by the customer service counter, talking to a clerk. When he saw them arrive, he checked his watch and frowned, but then finished his conversation and walked over to them. "Are you here to shop? You could have called in the order and I would have brought it when I came back from work."

"No, we're here to talk to you. Can we use Trent's office?" Mia pointed toward the back of the store. She'd been to his office several times and knew where it was located.

"Of course." He held up his hand and got the head clerk's attention. "Farrah? I'll be in the back for a bit. Can you handle the front?"

The woman rolled her eyes. "Yes. I've done it before."

Thomas chuckled as they walked to the back. "Farrah's a little put out that I'm here. She thinks that Trent should have put her in charge while he was training Cerby, but the door does say Majors Grocery. She'll get over it. Come on in. I just made a fresh pot of coffee. Don't tell Abigail; she thinks I cut myself off after the cup at home."

"No coffee for me, thanks." Mia sat down as Christina waved away the coffee as well.

Thomas looked confused but sat at the desk, watching them. "Okay, so not a supply run and not a social call. Why are you two here?"

"Christina, show him the memo, please." Mia watched as Christina handed over her phone.

He took the phone and read the memo. Shaking his head, he read it again. He handed back the phone to Christina. "I didn't write or send that memo."

"You weren't upset that Levi wasn't being put into coven management?" Mia asked, watching Thomas's face.

This time he laughed before he answered the question. "Levi? My ski instructor-EMT driver Levi? That boy likes change way too much. He lives on the chaos. He would die in a desk role."

Christina met Mia's gaze. "That's true. Levi has never expressed a desire to be part of management. In fact, he said he was happy that Trent took on running the grocery store. He would have hated it."

"If I wasn't looking for a place for my son in coven management, why would I worry about a kitchen witch taking a spot? Besides, I know you don't want to join the coven, even if they offered you Maxwell's job. You like cooking and feeding people. That's your gift. Not managing a group of people who don't want to be managed and attending the parties that the coven holds." Thomas pointed at Christina's phone. "Whoever did that made it seem like I didn't approve of you and Trent's relationship, which isn't true at all. Trent loves you. Any fool can see that."

Blushing, Mia pushed the statement away. "We're not here to talk about my relationship with your son."

"Are you sure? Because that memo could have caused a fight. A fight someone wanted to happen. Maybe between you and Trent. Maybe between me and Abigail. Someone is playing us. And the National Office. Did you find more of these complaints?" Thomas leaned back in his chair, his fingers steepled to his lips.

"A lot. Some I questioned, like yours and Blake's, my boss. She swears she's trying to keep off the coven's radar, so why would she file a formal complaint and out herself over my rating?" Mia said.

"Anyone else stand out?"

Mia answered. "Brandon Maxwell. He's been welcoming and pushing me to join because of my rating. Why would he complain? Doesn't it make Magic Springs special to have higher-rated witches as part of the coven? I asked him if he knew who had complained, and he made it seem like he never knew about the complaints. The research room showed us a whole pile."

"Maybe he was hiding his complaint in plain sight. If enough were submitted, Nationals would be forced to send a new tester." Thomas tapped his fingers against his lips.

"There's one more thing. I asked Brandon point-blank if he knew who had requested a house training for Cerby. He said he had no clue, yet he was the one who sent the formal request. Was he lying, or was he unaware the request went out under his signature?"

"This all seems so random, but I'm sure there is some type of pattern here." He leaned forward and glanced at his watch. "I've got some work to do before I go home. Do me a favor and tell the others about this.

I think keeping everyone in the loop is smart right now. Lack of information tends to lead to mistakes, and then bad decisions happen. We need open communication between us. I think it's the only way we're going to keep us all safe. You should talk Trent into relocating into the academy for a while. Until we find the person behind all of this."

"It's going to put back Cerby and Tempest's training. We can get through this. They only have three weeks plus a little more."

"Mia, a lot can happen in a short amount of time. I want Cerby trained as much as you do, but we have to protect one another. We can't protect Trent or Sarah or the baby when they're so far away." Thomas met her gaze, and she broke the connection first.

"Fine, but I'm telling him it was your idea. What he does with that is up to him and Sarah." Mia felt like she was losing the game.

Thomas stood and swept his arm to the doorway. "Ladies first. And Mia, this isn't a game. Not by a long shot. No matter what's going on, I'm going to be on your side, as will the rest of the Majors family. We take care of our own."

When Christina and Mia got back in the car, Christina fiddled with the heater controls, delaying their departure. "Do you think he was being honest?"

Mia thought about the question, staring into the windows of Majors Grocery. Thomas was talking to the woman at the counter again. "If he was a stranger, I'd say he was lying through his teeth, but I think this is just Thomas. He tells you what he believes, without any filtering. He doesn't say much, but his values and beliefs always stand behind his decisions. I need to talk to Trent."

"Are you calling him or do you want me to drive you to his house?" Christina still hadn't moved the car. She stared at Mia.

"Let's go to the house. If Sonja throws a fit, we'll know where we stand." Mia shrugged. "Then it will be up to Trent and Sarah to make the decision. Besides, I haven't seen Cerby in two weeks. I'm missing some puppy hugs."

Christina put the car in motion and they started toward the outskirts of town, where Trent had a ranch house on several acres that butted up against National Forest land. If you were going to have a dragon, his house would be perfect. Mia wondered if Suzanne Parker had time between the threat and her death to notify Nationals about Buddy. No matter what, she wasn't going to go to a zoo. She and Cerby were bonded. Not to mention she treated Trent and Mia as part of her pack as well.

"What are you thinking about?" Christina asked as they turned onto the road that would take them to Trent's.

"Buddy. How long did it take for me to fall in love with that little dragon? Minutes? Days? I have to accept that my life here will never be normal. I'm drinking the Kool-Aid, so to speak." Mia turned to Christina. "Maybe you should rethink your decision to stay. You'll be in the Abby Normal world too. Just like in *Young Frankenstein.*"

Christina chuckled. "I'm already there. It's going to

be my world, because we've decided to start looking at houses at the first of the year."

"Are you serious? What about Portland?" Mia knew they were thinking about staying for the babies, but buying a house here sounded longer.

Christina shrugged. "It's all on hold until I make a final decision. My boss was pretty sure she could make a case for me working remote due to the circumstances. Mom's furious. She wanted me out of here and into a larger city where she and Dad could visit."

"And Levi?" Mia asked.

"He was following me. He said he can be happy anywhere as long as I'm there. Isn't he the best?" Christina wiped a tear from her eye. "Man, are there wildfires somewhere? The smoke is bad here."

"It's not wildfire season." Mia frowned and looked around. "But something's burning." They pulled into the lane that led to Trent's and saw the fire.

Trent's house was burning. Or at least the left wing of it. Buddy, Cerby, and Tempest were crowded around a baby car seat. Sonja had a water hose, and Trent and Sarah were using magic to douse the flames and rebuild the house.

Mia jumped out of the car. She called to Christina as she ran. "Get Em in the car, just in case. Then back down the hill. Take the dogs too. Buddy? You need to follow them and protect Christina and Em."

Buddy took off and hovered over Christina's car. The dogs followed Christina as she grabbed Em's car seat handle and took off.

Sarah looked back, and relief filled her face. When

Mia joined the group fighting the fire, she said, "Thanks, Mia. I've been distracted between the fire and Em. Knowing she's out of the danger is helpful."

Trent looked down at her. "Cerby and Tempest got a little carried away today with their training. Now, I can't get the fire to stay out."

"It's not my fault," Sonja yelled over the noise of the water as it hit the fire. "We do this training at the camp all the time."

Trent rolled his eyes. "Any suggestions here would be amazing, Level Five."

"Shut up." Mia smiled at him and then focused on the building. "You're fighting the fire. You should be joining it."

She walked toward the part of the house that was in flames and started talking to it. "Fire, fire, burning bright. Warm our toes, cook our food, keep us safe, and stay contained. The house is your home as well. Take good care of it and us." She raised her hands, trying to enclose all the fire together. "We support one another. We are one. We support each other. We are one."

Slowly the fire went out. Mia waved her hand at the water hose, and the water stopped flowing.

"Hey, we need to get all the embers." Sonja waved the limp water hose at her. "Turn it back on."

"We don't need it, and having the water running tells the fire to keep burning. To keep fighting. We are one. We support one another. We take care of all of us." Mia took a breath, and she could hear the pop as the house went back to normal. Prefire. She didn't know what it looked like inside, but Trent could fix whatever was wrong with magic.

With the house safe and the fire cut off, Mia texted Christina to come back. Then she turned to Trent. "What on earth happened?"

Sonja threw down the hose and stomped over to where the others stood. "The hellhounds are out of control, that's what happened. I should never have agreed to this unconventional training method." She shook a finger at Mia. "I thought I made it clear that no one was supposed to bother us here. You need to leave, now!"

Chapter 20

"You are the one who needs to leave," Trent said to Sonja. "You've been trying to pit the hellhounds against each other since you got here. We aren't teaching them to be mean; we're trying to get them to control their other side. You caused this, and you should be thankful that Mia was here to fix the fire. The entire forest might have gone up."

"I told you when I came that outsiders were not allowed during the training process. It was bad enough that you brought the second hellhound here, but then Sarah and the baby? We were at summer camp, not hellhound school." Sonja glared at him. "I don't know what I ever saw in you."

"That's good, because there was no way you were going to get me to leave Mia and even have a short relationship with you. We are not compatible. At all. If this was your plan, you were way off base. Now go get your things. I want you out of here before I get back." Trent turned his back on Sonja and went to join Mia in Christina's car.

Sarah packed Em and Tempest into her car and followed Trent and the rest back to the academy. Now, they were all sitting around the front room, waiting for Mark to get out of a meeting and come to the academy to talk about the hellhounds and their training.

"If you hadn't come, I might not have a house." Trent put his arm around Mia. "And the forest might have burned down. The drought has kept everything powder-keg dry out here this winter. Cerby and Tempest weren't out of control, Sonja was. I don't think it helped that I kept Cerby in my room at night. He barked several times in the middle of the night, and I suspect Sonja was trying to get inside. She has a thing for me."

"Really." Mia rolled her eyes.

"Yeah, one of those sad, unrequited-love types of things." Trent held up his hands. "I was good, just ask Sarah."

"Your man was a perfect gentleman to all the women in the house, which made Sonja even madder. He put Em to bed every night, then he'd go to his room with Cerby without coming back down to the living room. Sonja freaked out the first time. She kept asking what was taking so long. When I got your text that you were safely tucked in, I headed upstairs myself. I bet she sat there for another hour, waiting for you to come down." Sarah sipped her water. "We worked well together, I think."

"Brandon Maxwell sent the letter asking for the

house training," Mia added to the discussion. "Then he lied to me and told me he didn't."

"Why would he want Cerby trained at home?" Trent asked, but then he looked around the room and realization hit him. "So Sarah and I would be taken out of play. Two less people to worry about. Whoever this is was trying to isolate you."

"I bet he didn't count on me coming back," Damien said as he stood and refilled his glass from a crystal decanter of what Mia assumed was whiskey from the smell.

He, Thomas, and Grans were all sipping the liquor. Trent and Levi had beers. Christina was drinking sparkling water. Sarah was on soda and Mia had just switched to a wine cooler. No one was driving tonight. Mark would pick up his family, but not until they talked about the murder. First, they needed to get Trent and Sarah caught up with what had happened since they'd been quarantined.

"You're lucky you still have a house. That's why hellhounds are trained far away from structures in the woods or the desert." Thomas leaned back on the couch with Abigail by his side. "If you remember, I wasn't a fan of this plan."

"But it kept Cerby home. I think he's done. Having Tempest there accelerated the training process. Sonja kept denying it, but even she could see they learned quicker together. Now, without someone egging them on to fight, they should be fine."

"She was using a cattle prod," Sarah said. "I was planning on pulling Tempest tomorrow once I saw that.

Sonja denied using it, but I saw it in her bag. She tortured them to get them to fight. It's not right."

"And it's against training protocol," Thomas said. "If you don't mind telling your story again, I'd like to report this to the National Office. If she's doing it, maybe the rest of the McManns are too." He stared at his drink. "No animal should have to deal with mean trainers."

"Nor should humans," Grans added. "Even though Suzanne Parker's dead, I filed a complaint against her testing methods. I don't know if anyone else in the department uses the methods she used on Mia, but leadership needed to know." Grans absently leaned into Damien's side and closed her eyes.

He met Mia's gaze and smiled. His plan was going well, it appeared.

"Okay, so we know that Brandon set the house training program in motion, and we know he was at least one of many who complained about my level from the first test." Mia was trying to think this through, but she was tired and hungry.

"I think he hid his complaint with all those other fake complaints," Christina added. The doorbell rang and she stood to answer it. "That's either Mark or pizza. No offense, Sarah, but I'm hoping for the pizza."

Both had arrived. As the Baldwin family got reacquainted, Mia and Christina retrieved plates and napkins from the kitchen. The group paused the discussion and took a few minutes to eat.

Mark broke the silence. "Suzanne Parker's death has been ruled an accident. The mayor came by with the report, and the recommendation that I close the case. I believe he tried to mind wipe me as well. I didn't know he was part of your social circle, Mia."

"Not my circle," Mia reminded him again as she took another piece of Hawaiian pizza. "If he did push the magic button, we know the killing has a magical component—not just in the method but also in the motivation. Huh. This is the first time I haven't been able to tell you that a murder isn't related to magic. I'm not happy. I like it when 'my' people are good and kind and don't kill others. How do we punish someone in the magical courts? Does the coven have a Mark I can take this to?"

"The Mark in the coven already knows about the human ruling. Now, that person is working on making sure the killer is found and punished," Thomas explained. "Mia, I'm surprised the office holder hasn't reached out to you before. I guess they assume if you cleared it from being magic-related, they had no reason to tell you."

"You're saying 'office holder.' Does that mean you don't know who it is? As a full member of the coven, you don't know?" Mia's head was hurting. The food hadn't helped like she'd hoped.

"Mia," Abigail started gently, but then sighed as Thomas met her gaze. "We have a sheriff, I guess you'd call it. Someone who handles rule breakers. We have prisons and trials, just like humans. But the person who brings a rule breaker to trial is kept secret. That way, if you're interviewed, you won't know who to lie to and who to tell the truth to. It's complicated, but it works for us."

"So all we can do is wait for the office holder to make a decision and put the killer up for trial? How do we give them what we know?" Mia curled up her legs under her. She hadn't gone this far to find Suzanne Parker's killer to stop now and trust that someone else would do the job.

Mark was pacing with Em in his arms. He'd missed his little girl. "Believe me, I feel the same way. It's like working hard to get an A, but then not being told your score—just that you passed and not to worry about it."

"So that's it? We're done?" Mia couldn't believe this was happening.

"Think of it this way," Abigail said. "If Brandon, or maybe even Sabrina, killed Suzanne Parker and you gave him the evidence you've collected, he could get rid of it. It's better for everyone to stay out of this now."

"It's not right, and I hate it, but from what you're telling me there's nothing I can do." Mia pushed away her unfinished pizza. "Sorry, Trent, but if it's okay with you, I need to get some sleep. Are you going back to the house?"

"If you don't mind, I'd rather stay here for a few days. Even though we fixed the damage, the smoke smell takes a bit longer to get out." Trent looked at Cerby, and the hellhound covered his head with his hands. Tempest inched closer to Sarah. The dogs were sorry.

Mia laughed at the dogs' reactions. They knew they were in trouble. "I'd love to have you stay. I've missed all of you. But for now, I'm beat."

"You're still recovering from the test," Grans said as Mia stood to go upstairs. "Don't worry, I'll keep this group from throwing a kegger while you sleep."

Mia laughed. "That was one worry I never had. Thanks. Now I'll be listening for blaring hard rock."

Sarah stood and gathered up the baby's car seat. "We're heading home too. If I'm right, I'm sure the house is a disaster. Mark and I have some work to do before we head to bed."

"To my defense, I thought I had a couple of weeks before I needed to start cleaning." Mark took the car seat and handed Sarah the baby. "Come on, Tempest. Let's go home. And no fire games. I don't have top-of-the-line, premium home insurance."

Tempest barked in response, then turned and barked at Cerby. The two had become fast friends.

Mia was on the second floor when she realized Damien was following her with Mr. Darcy. She turned in the foyer and shook her head. "I'm fine. Tired but fine. You don't need to follow me."

"I'm not. The library asked me to come up and get the academy's original blueprints. There's something we need to know before the remodeling is finished." He put his hand on her back as they started up the last flight. "As tired as you feel, I'm surprised you didn't take the elevator."

"It's funny that the library helps by giving us books with information, but they don't just flat out tell us what's going on. It would be a lot easier if they manifested as a sweet old lady librarian who told us what we needed to know and then gave us cookies and reading recommendations." Now Mia knew she was tired. She was manifesting more creatures to live in her home. "Maybe she could . . ."

Mia never knew what she was going to suggest because she slumped over onto Damien's side and he swept her into his arms. She felt herself being carried into her apartment, then nothing.

When she woke up, the morning sunlight made her blink. She sat up in the bed and saw that Trent had slept on the love seat in her room. His legs stuck out and angled toward the floor, and Cerby lay next to him. Mia looked out the window and saw Buddy perched on her roof. The dragon waved a wing and cooed through the glass. Mr. Darcy opened one eye from his place on the end of the bed, stretched, and then curled up again. Apparently, it was too early to get up.

Mia threw off the covers and went into the bathroom to get ready for the day. She wasn't sure she'd go to the Lodge. Did her sudden tiredness come from her meeting with Blake? Or had her body just given out after all the stress and torture she'd gone through in the last month? What she needed was a massage, and maybe a trip to an island somewhere with rum drinks and sea and sand.

That would be nice. But first, coffee. She groaned as she realized the testing guy from Nationals was going to be at the Lodge to meet with her. She had to go in.

Grans sat at the table with Cleo, talking quietly over coffee. Both looked up as Mia walked into the kitchen. She poured herself a coffee, added a few teaspoons of sugar, then sat down.

"Why did I fall flat on my face last night?" she asked.

"I believe it was the stress from the testing and everything else that has happened since," Grans said, looking to Cleo for confirmation.

"Somehow, Suzanne Parker had the codes to lower headquarters' sensitivity to danger to the testing witch. I'm not sure she could have killed you, but she came close. Each time, you bounced back. I didn't notice until I went back and viewed the tape of her testing. She had disabled the alarms as well. I had a bad feeling all day, but I thought it was from the retesting itself, not the way she handled it. I knew Suzanne. She was solid. Fair. Someone got it into her head that you cheated. Someone she trusted." Cleo put her hand on Mia's. "I'm sorry I didn't step in. If the system hadn't been tampered with, you would have been pulled in the first hour."

"Well, I guess it's a good thing I'm strong, then," Mia said, then she shook her head. "I'm not mad. I just want to find out who forced a second testing because I think that might show us the killer."

"You can't continue to investigate this," Grans warned. "It's dangerous."

"I can't not. Someone put me in danger, then killed the woman they sent after me. It's all tied together. Now that Mark's been sidelined, I'm all there is." Mia sipped her coffee. It was warm and comforting and—her eyes popped open. "You spelled the coffee?"

"I put an energy potion in, dear. It's not a spell. You need to be more precise in your language." Grans filled Mia's cup and then dumped the pot. "The rest of your group doesn't need this. They'll be bouncing off the walls for days. You, on the other hand, need that to get through your day."

"You're a remarkable woman, Mia," Cleo said. "I knew that the first time you came to visit your grandmother and she brought you to the coven library. You were so curious. You're going to make an excellent addition to the historical rolls of the kitchen witch." Cleo stood and put on her coat. "Thanks for the coffee this morning, Mary Alice. I needed a pick-me-up."

"You gave me Gloria." Mia didn't know how she knew, but she knew. Gloria's next song choice proved her right. Helen Reddy's "I Am Woman" filled the kitchen.

"Gloria gave you Gloria." Cleo smiled. "All I did was deliver the doll. We've been watching you for a long time. We knew the Goddess was sending us a warrior. I'm glad it's you."

Mia watched as Cleo headed out of the apartment and to the first floor. "She's pretty amazing."

"You should have seen her in her prime." Grans smiled. "She was magnificent, and the strongest witch I have ever met. She had to give up a lot of power to become the library keeper, but she says it was worth it. Spells and potions are her life. And now, she has a bit of a seer in her. It's a good thing she likes you. A lot." Grans pushed Mia's coffee closer to her. "Go ahead, accept her gift."

"Cleo brought the energy booster?"

"Why are you surprised? She's the closest thing we have to a doctor in our world. She called me last night when you went upstairs. She said to let you sleep and she'd be over in the morning to fix this." Grans pressed her lips together. "Funny, that was after Dorian followed you upstairs. If he hadn't been there, you would have fallen."

"Maybe Dorian has a bit of seer in him as well. Or the library felt what was happening." Mia sipped her coffee. Now that she knew a potion was mixed in, she could taste the ingredients. She started listing them off in her head, but she couldn't name the last one. As she tried to isolate it, Trent walked into the kitchen and sat down after he saw the coffee was still brewing.

"Magic Man" from Heart played in the kitchen.

He smiled at the kitchen witch doll. "Nice choice, Gloria."

"Don't encourage her. She's been into the older rock all week." Mia kissed him on the cheek. "How did you sleep? And why didn't you just sleep on the bed? You looked uncomfortable on that love seat."

"I was fine. I didn't want to wake you. By the time I came upstairs to go to bed, you finally had some color in your cheeks." He rubbed his finger on the side of her head. "I should ask you how you're doing. You scared us last night."

"Sorry. Maybe quelling the fire drained too much of my energy." She turned to her grandmother. "I didn't cast a spell or make a potion, but I harnessed the fire and water with my hands and my mind. I helped Trent rebuild the house while trying to convince the fire to go out. Sonja waving around that hose wasn't helping."

"The McManns never understand anything but brute force." Grans stood to refill her cup and get Trent some coffee. "Sonja was pushing for another outcome. I hear she's been banned from participating in hellhound training for an infinite time period. Thomas works fast."

"She's going to blame me for that, and for getting you out of the house, but really, the fire's to blame. I was just there to help put things back together." Mia leaned her head on Trent's shoulder. "Like every good kitchen witch should."

Chapter 21

Carl Hagen from the National Office showed up at the house an hour before his appointment at the Lodge. He was a short, pudgy man with a few hairs on his head and a smile that warmed Mia from the inside out. They met in the living room after Christina had provided coffee and treats for the visitor.

"Cleo called to let me know you'd be here. I heard you had quite a day yesterday, and I thought it might be easier to meet you at your home. The academy seems very happy under your stewardship. I didn't attend here. I'm from Central California. We had our own boarding school on the beach. It was the best six years of my life." He sipped his coffee, looking around the great room. "I feel so many happy memories here. Are you with ghosts?"

Mia frowned a bit at the wording. "Yes, the academy is haunted. They mostly hang out in the library."

"Probably trying to finish their to-be-read pile." He smiled at her. "I know mine is larger than several lifetimes."

Mia couldn't help but laugh. Carl Hagen had a way of making people comfortable. It was probably his gift, like Christina's.

"Mine is getting that way too," Mia said. "I'm just a few chapters away from finishing a book and things keep getting in the way. Thank you for coming. I have a few questions about my testing."

"I want to apologize on behalf of the entire board. If we'd known this was some kind of vendetta, we never would have sent Suzanne. Hugh is furious about the method of testing she used. He sends his regards. He said you were lovely, and you are." Carl smiled. His eyes kept returning to a corner of the room with nothing in it, at least not anything Mia could see.

"He was amazing as well. He made the test so easy. Please send him my best wishes." Mia set down her coffee cup. "I've done some research and found that retesting is rarely done."

"You're right about that. The issue was the amount of complaints we received and, of course, the push from local leadership."

Mia thought about his response and then continued. "One question before I go into the leadership issue. Did you verify that any of the complaints were valid? Did you talk to anyone who sent in a complaint? Directly, I mean."

Carl turned away from his fascination with the corner. "No. It's not in our process to verify that the signer actually sent the complaint. We assume that the local leadership has a finger on the pulse of their coven, so when Brandon and Sabrina sent in their own complaints, we assumed the rest were valid too. Now that I'm saying it aloud, I realize our mistake. The complaints were fake."

"At least a few. I haven't verified all of them, but one was from Thomas Majors, who told me he didn't write or send the complaint that had his name on it. I was planning on asking the others, but I've been under the weather." Mia watched him for a reaction.

He rubbed his face. "I'm truly sorry. You shouldn't have been put through another testing yet. Although with your increase in level, I'm thinking your third jump will also be large and happen soon. We'll make sure Hugh does all of your tests from now on."

Mia didn't want to test again, but like she'd told Christina, maybe she should keep a door open. You never knew what you might want in the future.

Carl stood, breaking her thought process. "I promised Cleo I wouldn't stay long and wear you out. I also need to chat with the office holder before I leave. Apparently the local coven here is having some issues. I'm sorry you got caught up in our politics."

"Thank you for coming to me. I know you have processes for finding out who killed Suzanne Parker, but I still have a lot of questions. I feel like I was in the middle of the whole thing." Mia stood and followed him out. "I need to get control of whatever virus I have, because I'm missing way too much work."

"I'm sure it's just the stress." He reached out his

hand, and as they shook, his eyes widened. "Well, isn't that special. Take care, Mia Malone. I'm sure we'll be hearing good things from you, sooner rather than later."

As he walked out, Trent came out of the kitchen, where he'd been listening. "He was a man of few words."

"Yes, but I think we found the hole in the process. Maybe I can save someone else the embarrassment." She went over to the elevator. "I'm still not up to this. I'm heading upstairs. Want to watch a movie with me?"

"Desperately." He put his arm around her and they stepped into the elevator car. "You feel worn to the bone. Are you sure you can stay awake?"

"If I can't, I'll just rewind when I wake up." Her watch buzzed with a notice that someone was at the door. "We need to go back down. Someone's at the door."

"I can go." He held the door open when they reached the third floor. "Go in and get the movie set up. No chick flicks. Okay, maybe a rom-com, but it better be funny."

"I'll ride down with you. I haven't seen you in weeks." She brushed his arm away from the door, then pushed the button for the first floor.

"You're stubborn." He pulled her into a hug. "I'm so glad you're okay."

"I've got a few steps before I'd say 'okay.' Standing and not crying is more my mood today." She kept her head on his chest and listened to his beating heart as they made their way down.

A flower delivery was at the door. A beautiful blue-and-silver bouquet with a note. *Happy birthday, Finn.*

Mia frowned and looked at the flowers. "I wonder why Abigail didn't tell us Finn's birthday is today."

"Maybe she has a surprise party planned for later. Is Finn even here?" Trent checked his watch.

"I don't know. She's probably at the Lodge. James has been giving her tons of hours." Mia paused by the corner Carl had been watching and closed her eyes. Could she feel anything?

"Are you okay?" Trent's hand was on her arm.

She didn't look at him as she answered. "Fine, but Carl Hagen couldn't stop staring at this corner. Why?"

"Could be many reasons. He was attracted to the power? He had a lazy eye? Maybe he just thought he saw something."

Mia thought about Trent's explanations. "Damien was getting records, no, blueprints of the academy from the library last night when I fell. Did he get them?"

"I don't know, but we can check. What are you doing with the flowers?"

"I'll put them in her room, then talk to her as soon as she's home from work." Mia looked up at the stairs. "Want to make a stop before we watch the movie?"

"Sure." He waited for her to drop off the flowers, then they took the elevator to the second floor.

The workmen weren't there today. Damien must have asked them to stay away to give Mia some peace and quiet. She and Trent walked down to the new suite Damien had carved out for himself. The door to what appeared to be a library or office was open, and Damien was there, going through boxes. This room was complete, with wall-to-ceiling walnut bookcases, wood floors, a large desk, two large wing chairs on an Oriental rug, and spotlights over the chairs to add reading light. It was a perfect room for someone in love with books.

Damien looked up as they came to the door. "Welcome. This room is almost done. I had them start here so I could get my books out of storage, especially because I'm sleeping over at your grandmother's house. I swear, Mary Alice thinks we live in Victorian England."

"Too much information." Mia held her hands over her ears, then let them down. "Did you get the blueprints from the library?"

"This morning. Last night was a little hectic, with you swooning into my arms. Purely platonic, of course, but I'm glad I was there." He stood from the chair where he'd been unpacking a box of books. "I have the prints over here on the table. Nathan is supposed to come over this afternoon to take a look. I'm not sure what the library wanted me to see, but I thought he might see it through his construction lens better than I could."

Damien unrolled the many-paged blueprint. "This is the outside front view of the plans. Each floor should have its own sheet."

"Can we see the first floor?" Mia glanced at Trent, who was staring at the pages. "Is something wrong?"

He shook his head. "No, but something's off. These are different from the original prints."

Damien looked at him. "Good eye. There's a second wing that doesn't show on the prints. The gym and main kitchen were added a few years later."

Trent let the answer settle. "That must be it. Where's the first floor?"

"Here it is." Damien smoothed out the prints. He pointed to the left side. "This ends right where the living room ends now. Mia's office is back here. The kitchen and gym addition is shaped like an L."

Mia pointed to a spot on the page. A drawing. If she was right, it was where Carl had been staring. "What's that?"

Damien squinted at the symbol, then at the legend on the side. "Weird. That's where the original dumbwaiter was located. It went from the basement to the top floor and ran through what is now your potions lab. It was probably closed off and boarded up so the kids wouldn't mess with it when the building was changed into the academy."

"Wait? It wasn't always a school?" Mia looked up at Damien.

He shook his head. "The building was supposed to be coven headquarters. It was changed to a school when new leadership was voted into office a few years after the building was finished. That was when Suzanne Parker was leading the coven. She was voted out and a whole new board came in. She never forgave the people who turned on her."

"That wasn't in her life book." Mia glanced at Trent. "Damien? Were you two an item then?"

"Was she wearing my class ring?" He chuckled. "Kind of. We saw each other, but I know she was also seeing other people. She hated the thought of becoming attached. Of trusting someone. I wonder what changed her mind later. She seemed to trust someone a lot."

"Carl said the building was filled with happy memories." Mia didn't know what he could sense when he was here.

"Carl Hagen? From Nationals? He was here?" Damien turned to stare at her. "When?"

"Just a few minutes ago. He came to talk to me about Suzanne Parker and my retesting. He said she went rogue. Why?"

Damien turned back to the blueprints. "Just a name from the past. Carl was one of the guys Suzanne was dating back then. He offered her the testing job after she was removed from coven leadership. That's why she moved to Boston and when we broke up."

When Finn came home, Mia was downstairs reading. Well, that's what she told herself. Really, she was waiting to talk to Finn. Trent had left after lunch to check on his house and give Buddy some flying time in the forest. She figured he'd stop by the store and chat with his father as well. She expected him back for dinner.

Finn saw Mia and walked over. "Hey, I thought you'd be working at the Lodge today. Everything okay? James asked if you were all right."

"Nothing a couple of days of rest won't fix." Mia closed the book. She'd finished a few minutes ago and had been thinking about the ending ever since. She put the book on the table. "Hey, come sit down for a minute. I have a question."

"If it's about your offer to let me live here while I go to school, I say yes. James told me I have a scholarship to pay the tuition, and if I can stay here and pay you rent, I'll be able to save most of my paychecks so when I get a job, I'll have money to get set up." Finn flopped into the chair next to Mia. Her hair was bright pink and braided today. She wore a Hello Kitty shirt and jeans.

"I'm glad you've decided to stay, but that's not the question." Mia leaned forward. "Finn, is today your birthday?"

Finn frowned, then looked at her phone. "November 16. It is my birthday. I've been so busy with work, I didn't even know what day it was. Not that I've been a big one to celebrate anyway. My mom always forgot too. I guess it's easier to forget because she didn't actually give birth to me."

Mia hated that Finn's eyes went sad at the mention of her adopted mother. "Well, happy birthday. We'll have a special dinner for you tomorrow. Sorry, we would have surprised you if we had more notice. If you want to invite anyone, let me know. Otherwise, I'll just invite the society."

Finn stood and stretched. "That would be fine. Like I said, it's not a big deal."

"Oh, someone sent you flowers. They were in a vase, so I put them in your room." Mia stood and put the book on the shelf. Tomorrow, she'd start reading a new book. Something fun.

"Someone sent me flowers? For my birthday?" Finn shook her head. "No one who knows my birthday knows I live here."

"Hmmm. Let's go look at the card. Maybe you put the address on your job application? Maybe it's from Abigail?" Mia had a bad feeling in her stomach.

"I gave her a fake date. It was just habit. I didn't mean to lie," Finn explained as she walked to her room with Mia by her side.

"Fix it now." Mia smiled. "First, let's see if the card's signed and we'll go from there."

They walked into Finn's room and Finn headed straight to the flowers. "The card isn't signed, but the florist is next door to the coffee shop. Do you mind driving me over so I can see who sent them?"

"Not a problem." Mia needed another cup of coffee anyway. The potion from Cleo this morning was wearing off and she wanted to go back to sleep, but she didn't want to sleep her life away either. "Let me grab my keys from the apartment and we can go."

When they arrived at the florist, the woman who had taken the order was gone to lunch. Mia looked at the clock. "It's almost time for her to be back. Just come over to the coffee shop and I'll buy you a coffee while we wait."

Marsha Fieldstone's face burst with joy as they walked inside Magic Brews. Mia waved. She'd been so excited to get any information, she hadn't looked at who was supplying it. The coffee shop was empty, so after they ordered the coffee, Mia took a chance and asked Marsha about the flowers. "Does the list of new witches also give you details like their date of birth? How did you know when to send Finn flowers?"

Marsha jerked at the question and spilled coffee on her hand. She grabbed a towel to sop it up. "No, the entrance/exit report just says that. Who's in and who's out. How did you know about the flowers?"

Mia smiled as she walked through her guess. "You gave Finn a dragon statue. You talk about her like she's amazing. And you almost glowed when we walked in here today. On her birthday. You don't have much of a poker face."

"As a level five, your intuition is on high alert all the time. You'll find this happening more and more now." Marsha turned to face Finn and took a deep breath. "I've always known Finn's birthday because I'm the woman who gave her up for adoption. Finn, I'm your biological mom. I know you don't have any responsibility to talk to me, but I just wanted to tell you how proud I am of you and the woman you've become."

Finn stared at her. "You're my mom?"

Marsha shook her head as she answered. "I know your adoptive mom gets that title. I'm just hoping we can develop some kind of friendship. I never wanted to give you up, but things were complicated."

Mia and Marsha were floored when Finn went over and hugged Marsha. "Thanks for telling me. Now, my witch talent makes more sense. Thank you for the flowers."

"You're welcome. It was the least I could do. Does this mean you might want to continue talking?" Marsha looked at Finn with hope pouring out of her.

Finn looked up at her with wet eyes. "As long as you're fine with it. I know having me show up after all these years is probably a shock."

"More for you than me." Marsha hugged her again, then stepped back behind the counter. "We all need coffee."

Chapter 22

After the coffee was made, Marsha went over to the door, locked it, and turned the sign to close the shop. When she sat down at a table with Finn and Mia, she took a sip of coffee. "Do you have any questions for me? I'm not going to push to be part of your life; I just want you to know I'm here."

Finn focused on her drink, but then looked into Marsha's eyes. "Who's my dad? Why did you give me up?"

Marsha sighed. "I got pregnant in high school. Ken Forney. He was a beautiful boy. We were just kids, experimenting with emotions we should have locked up for years. It was summer at the lake and things went too far. By the time I knew about you, he was off to college and I was a pregnant high school junior. It was a hard year, but I knew I wanted to have you and give you the best shot at a great life that I could. So I gave you up for adoption. Ken signed the papers when he came home for spring break, and that was the last time I saw him. He was killed in a motorcycle accident on his way home from college the next year."

"I'm sorry for your loss," Mia said, trying to keep the conversation going.

Marsha shrugged. "We were too young to fall in love and know what it meant. You look like him, Finn. Dark hair, dark eyes. He was a beautiful boy."

Finn didn't say anything.

Mia looked over at Marsha. "Not to change the subject, but you told me that Brandon already knew about Finn coming to town. How did he find that out?"

Marsha leaned back, tapping her finger on the table. "I've been thinking a lot about that since you brought it up. I don't know. He shouldn't have known unless he looked at the in-and-out book. I'm supposed to be the only one who has access, but maybe that's not true. Maybe the leadership has at least one access spot. That's all I can think of. Nationals is very clear on why this assignment needs to be a nonleadership position, but I don't think they check."

"Brandon has been breaking the rules quite a bit lately." Mia texted the information to Abigail. "One more question: Did you file a complaint about my original level three ranking?"

"No. Why would I? I'm a level three, and I chose to stay there, officially. I'm sure if I retested, I'd be ranked higher, but who wants the headache of being a higher level? A lot of people just stay with their original level so they don't have to deal with the bureaucracy of coven life." Marsha smiled at Finn. "Any time you want to talk or just hang out, let me know. I know you've had a lot thrown at you this year."

"Let's see, I'm a witch, I've signed up for culinary school, my van died, Mia invited me into her circle, and I found out I'm an excellent chef. Oh, and the library is haunted, but it likes me." Finn shrugged. "You being my bio-mom sounds about par for the course. I need some time to think about what we are to each other, but I'll start by coming in for coffee once a week or so. We can chat then."

"Sounds like a plan." Marsha glanced at her watch. "Classes are just getting out. I need to reopen so I don't miss the after-school munchy and coffee crowd."

Mia stood. "Thanks for talking with us. About everything."

Trent texted as soon as they left the coffee shop.

Where are you? Is Finn with you?

Mia decided to call instead of texting. When he answered, she jumped right in. "Finn and I went for coffee. I'll explain later, but yes, today is her birthday. I told her we'd do a family dinner tomorrow night, so let everyone know, especially Abigail. Finn needs a cake."

"I do not need a cake, or a dinner." Finn spoke loudly, so Trent could hear her too.

"Okay, so she doesn't need it, but we need to do it. It will be nice to have a celebration dinner. With the babies coming, an upcoming wedding, and Finn's birthday, we have three reasons." Mia smiled as Finn shook her head.

"Sabrina's here. She needs to talk to you. If you're

done party planning, can you come back to the academy?" Trent asked.

Mia didn't mention that his question dripped with sarcasm, but she'd tell him later. "Sure. We're on the way. We should be there in five."

After she hung up, she groaned. "Hopefully Sabrina's not there to try to strong-arm me into joining the coven. We could let your heritage slip and she could start bugging *you* about it."

Finn's eyes widened as she shook her head. "No way. I'm not sure what's going on in my life. Sabrina can be a bit pushy. I've watched James have to deal with her while event planning. The woman wants what she wants, and it doesn't matter if it's possible or not."

"I think you should relax and decide after you get your career in place. If you test out and become a coven member, you might live in a different area. No need to jump now." Mia pulled into the parking lot and saw Buddy sleeping in a tree. "I'm just happy for you. I don't know how you feel about Marsha, but at least you know where you came from."

"I was a mistake made by two high school kids," Finn stated.

"I don't think that at all. Marsha may not have been ready to raise a child, but if you weren't conceived that night, your bio dad would have died with no kids. And, as Marsha said, he was a beautiful boy."

Finn laughed. "That is true. I need some time. Like Marsha said, a lot has happened this year. I need to settle in and see where I want to go, and who I want to be."

"I understand more than you know." Mia turned off the car and stepped out into the day, which was warmer than usual. "Let's go see what Sabrina wants."

"I'm going straight to my room, then I'm taking books back up to the library. Do you think it will have more for me?" Finn shut the car door and followed Mia inside.

"I'm sure it will, especially now that you warned it you were coming." Mia took off her coat and saw Sabrina sitting in the living room. All of the academy society was sitting in chairs around Sabrina and watching the new arrivals. "Well, I feel like I'm late for the meeting," Mia said.

Sabrina spoke first. "Sorry about barging in unannounced, but I needed to talk to you. And your friends."

"I'll see you later, Finn," Mia said, dismissing the girl. Hopefully Sabrina still thought Finn was just working for Mia's Morsels and didn't know about her heritage.

Finn took the hint, disappearing down the hall and into her room.

Mia heard the door close as she sat down on the couch next to Trent. He kissed her hair and then asked, "Do you want coffee?"

"That would be nice." She let him stand and get her a cup. Then, with the coffee in hand, she focused on Sabrina. "What's going on?"

"Brandon is crazy. He's colored over the lines before, but now it's getting bad. I just found out that he forged a letter from me to Nationals about you, complaining about your level. I'm not sure what you've heard, but I was ecstatic with your level jump this time.

As well as your original test results," Sabrina added quickly. "I also found some emails between him and Suzanne Parker. I think they were involved. I hate saying this because it makes me look like a complete idiot because I thought we were getting married. The power couple, you know. But he was sleeping with Suzanne and she's old. A lot older than she looks. Why would he do that to me?"

Christina pushed a box of tissues closer and Sabrina pulled out several to wipe the tears she hadn't noticed before off her cheeks. Along with a lot of her makeup.

"That part is not your problem. I'm just an idiot." Sabrina tried to compose herself and let out a long breath. "I've reported his duplicity to the National Office. I'm sure that's going to get him kicked off the leadership board, if not a harsher punishment. Which means Nathan Boyle will be stepping up as leader. I hate that fact, but he's next in line. With Brandon out, Nathan is next in seniority."

"Nathan Boyle, the contractor?" Mia met Damien's eyes and he shrugged. Apparently this was news to him as well.

"I'd call him a developer, but yeah. He's put in a bid for Suzanne's house to redevelop the area. I hope he gets that approved before they ask him to step in for Brandon." Sabrina's phone buzzed. "That's Brandon now. I'd rather not have him know I'm here, talking to you all. He's very sensitive when it comes to you, Mia."

After Sabrina left, Finn popped out of her room and headed upstairs with a pile of books for the library. Mia and the group were still in the living room.

"Do you think Brandon is the killer?" Trent asked after Abigail had brought in more cookies. She shook her head at him. "I know, we're supposed to stand down and let the office holder deal with this, but I'm thinking it's Brandon who killed Suzanne Parker."

"Why? If Sabrina is right, he was sleeping with her. Why kill her?" Mia shook her head. "What led Sabrina to even look for this evidence? The fact that she found out that he wrote the complaint about my testing?"

"It fits," Abigail said. "But we're supposed to stay out of it now. The office holder—"

"Doesn't know what we know." Mia shook her head. "I can't just stop and hope for the best. I have two more people I want to talk to. After that, I'll let it go."

Abigail started to speak, but Mia held up her hand.

"Two more people, then I'll give it up. Suzanne Parker almost killed me during my testing, and if Blake or Brandon started that chain of events, I have to know. One, so I can quit my job and come back to run Mia's Morsels. And two, it would make my decision about joining the coven an easy no. Sabrina won't give up, even if Brandon is replaced by Nathan."

"I didn't know Nathan was even a member." Damien shook his head. "I'll go with you to talk to those two."

Trent stood and reached for Mia's hand. "No, you stay here and help get dinner ready. Mia and I will go. If something happens, you and Dad can come for us. We'll keep you apprised of where we are at all times. The Lodge first?"

"Might as well. Then I'll know if I'm still employed and if I can go back to work tomorrow." Mia stood and looked around at the group. "From what I've heard and learned these last few weeks, we're on the side of the Goddess. This might not be our last fight, but we need to know who is on our side and who's not. It's time to go on the offense and unmask some of the players."

"Good analogy," Levi said. "It's kind of a mixed metaphor, but good all the same." Levi hugged his brother as Christina hugged Mia.

"I should go with you," Christina said.

Mia shook her head as she touched Christina's belly. "Not now that we know what's happening. I don't need three people to watch over. You stay here and help Abigail with the cake. I know I told Finn the dinner would be tomorrow, but let's do it tonight. I'll use that as an excuse to go to the Lodge and invite James."

"I'm almost offended by your statement, but also, I understand your feelings. I don't want to put the girls in unnecessary danger. If you think you'll be okay."

Trent kissed Christina on the cheek. "We'll have a dragon nearby. What could go wrong?"

In turn, Christina was polite enough not to mention Trent's house fire. Mia grabbed a coat from the closet and slipped the small spray bottle she'd gotten from Grans in her pocket.

At the Lodge, Mia and Trent stopped to invite James and a few other staff who could get away for dinner. One was a boy who had a twinkle in his eye whenever Finn's name was mentioned. As they walked out of the kitchen, they ran into Blake.

"Oh, I thought you were home," Blake said, looking nervously from Mia to Trent. "And I thought you were involved in hellhound training."

"It's completed. The advantage of having two go through it together rather than isolated in their cages is that they train faster. I'm going to write a letter suggesting the process for future training." Trent leaned against a table in the hallway.

"Oh, well, Sonja is a good trainer." Blake looked at her watch. "I have dinner plans so . . ."

"Sorry, that's not what we came to talk about." Mia pulled out her phone and showed Blake the letter of complaint sent to the coven with her signature. "Did you send this?"

Blake sat down and took the phone, reading the letter carefully. She handed the phone back to Mia. "I didn't send that. You know that I don't interact with the coven any more than I have to. That's the reason I was upset you were talking to Brandon. He'd called to set up a meeting that morning, then he talked to you before coming to my office. I don't want to be involved in coven politics, and that's what I told him that morning."

"Brandon set up a meeting? What did he ask you about? Me?" Mia knew standing over her boss looked intimidating, but she just couldn't sit and act like the conversation was casual.

"You, a little. He wondered how you were doing with your level five label. Were you freaking out? Or handling it? I told him I wasn't the best judge of how you were doing, and that I'd made mistakes in dealing with you. He said he understood and he'd underestimated you as well." She leaned back into the chair, resting her head against the wall. "This town was supposed to be easy. A small lodge to run where I could hide. You all make it hard to stay invisible."

"You didn't write a complaint about my testing level?" Mia asked, simplifying the question.

"No, I didn't. And I wouldn't." Blake looked into Mia's eyes. "I'm being truthful here."

Mia studied her. The body language and the message from her eyes and words all said "trust me." She looked over at Trent to see if he saw anything different. He shook his head.

"I think she's being truthful," Trent said as he broke eye contact.

"I am. I promise. And I wasn't lying the other day. I need you here at the Lodge. Please stay. I'll put your name in for a raise tomorrow morning," Blake assured her, even though it wasn't a normal raise period.

Mia thought the woman was being honest. "That's what I needed to know. Thanks for being truthful with me."

Blake blew out a breath. "It's hard for me to let anyone in. I'm sorry I kept breaking your trust."

After Blake left to go to dinner, Mia and Trent stayed in the deserted hallway for a few more minutes.

Mia broke the silence. "One down, one to go."

"We could stop here. You have a job. You know she didn't go to the coven. No one would have been able to lie after you put that truth potion on them. I didn't see you touch her, though. How did you do it?"

"I put it on the phone." Mia took out a bottle and sprayed the phone again. "Let's go find Brandon."

They didn't have to go far. Brandon was in the lobby of the Lodge, sitting on a couch with a drink in his hand. When they approached, he waved over a waiter. "Please bring my guests a drink too."

Mia and Trent ordered, then sat down. "You've been expecting us?"

"I figured I might as well come to you so you didn't have to drive to my house." He looked toward the windows. "I hear a storm's coming. I have a room here. I've got to talk to a few more people tonight."

"Like Nathan Boyle?" Mia guessed.

Brandon smiled and nodded. "Like Nathan Boyle. I'm afraid your renovations aren't going to be completed as quickly as he promised because he's going to jail after our conversation."

Mia blinked several times, processing what he hadn't said. "You're the office holder."

Brandon waited for their drinks to be delivered. A glass of wine for Mia, a beer for Trent. He told the waiter to put it on his bill and the guy left. "I am tonight. Now that my cover is blown—thanks, Mia—I'm going to have to pass the office to someone else, which will be a relief. I'm pretty sure Sabrina's ready to break up with me. And I already bought her the ring."

Mia didn't want to get involved in his relationships. "I wouldn't tell anyone, well, outside the academy society. You didn't kill Suzanne Parker, did you?"

He shook his head. "But all signs pointed to me. I was supposed to be the fall guy. When I realized that, I knew it wasn't you or any of your 'society.' You didn't even know about the office holder until Thomas and

Abigail let it slip. I told you that there were some coven secrets I couldn't tell you."

"Someone was framing you for her murder. Leaking the affair. Tying you to the mess that forced the retesting. Even getting Sonja to do a training at Trent's house, keeping him away from me. They couldn't blame me because I had too many people watching me, so you were the next patsy."

Brandon leaned back in his chair to explain. "They didn't expect you to see through the visions they were sending. You didn't react the way you were supposed to react, and you had a solid alibi all along. I was the next logical choice, and the frame would have worked, except for one, maybe two main hiccups. I'm the office holder. Magically, I'm bound to not do anything illegal or immoral during my term of office. I physically can't. The magic of the oath I took stops me. It's a good way to keep the foxes out of the chicken house."

"What was the other hiccup?" Trent asked as he sipped his beer.

"Suzanne Parker wasn't my lover. She was my mother. After all those years, she slipped and had a baby with Carl Hagen. He didn't know about the baby, but he remembered the love he'd felt for Suzanne all those years ago. That's why he was so willing to come and talk to you about your test. In the hundreds of years he has been in that position, I don't think he's ever talked to a test taker. Ever. Until you."

"The person who sent me the visions didn't know about the relationships I had with people. That's why I kept thinking it had to be someone outside of Magic

Springs. Someone who didn't know how close I was to Mark Baldwin or Sarah. Or that I trusted my friends. Or that you had a mother." Mia reached over and squeezed Brandon's hand. "I'm sorry for your loss."

"Thank you." He glanced at his watch. "So, to pull it together, because I know you'll be chatting with your magical society later tonight, Nathan wanted me out of leadership. He first went for you, because your level was too high for a kitchen witch. He thought you were aiming for a spot on the coven board."

"He was wrong there," Trent snorted.

Brandon agreed and added, "When someone wants power, they don't understand someone who, like Mia, doesn't want to wield it. After he met you and realized you didn't even want to be part of the coven, he changed his plans and focused on me. If he was in coven leadership, he'd be able to control the land deals in the area and make some money. A lot of money. Starting with Suzanne's house. He found it on the tax rolls and thought it was an empty lot."

"Hold on a second; did he plant the false memories in my head? He wanted me to leave Magic Springs." Mia thought about all the work she'd done to the academy since she'd moved to the area. "He was in the school when I was 'hiding.' He probably caught me before and after the testing."

"I think so. The academy is prime redevelopment land. I believe Nathan and his father tried to buy it before you won the contract. With you and Suzanne gone, he would have been able to start his Magic Springs development plan. That was probably more Adam than Nathan. The guy loves controlling real estate development. He's the one who started building high-end houses in Eagle years ago." Brandon looked at Trent and Mia, noticing their confusion. "Sorry, I get in the weeds when I get excited. Basically Nathan and his dad wanted to control Magic Springs."

"Nathan seemed so nice." Mia squeezed Trent's hand. "And yet all he wanted was for me to walk away from you and Magic Springs so he could take over the coven. I guess this level five comes with a bit of fear factor for other witches. I mean, they fear me."

"Between you and Mark Baldwin, you've become a strong investigative team," Brandon acknowledged. "You made my life as the office holder easy."

"You're welcome. But I like working with my catering business and the Lodge more than making myself a target for crazy killers." Mia took in a deep breath. It was over. Cleo's words echoed in her head. *You get what you get and you don't throw a fit.*

"We've got a few minutes before I need to leave to collect some people, but I wanted to say one more thing. I believe Nathan was part of a collective of witches who were trying to bring down the coven. I talked to Carl before he left, and several people have been removed from office lately for wanting to start enforcing the magic-to-one-child rule. I think by figuring this out, we've stopped an upcoming fight for power."

Mia took a long breath. If Brandon was right, there would be no war. At least not today. The Goddess had intervened, and they were all safe. "Thank you for telling us that. I'm sorry you're going to have to vacate your office holder position."

"Don't be. I'm sure someone will step up, someone younger and more willing to hide part of his life from everyone he knows and loves. I'm not that man anymore. Or I won't be, once I propose to Sabrina. Maybe we'll even have kids. My mom said I was the best thing she'd ever done. That's hard to live up to." He stared at the door. "My security force is telling me that Nathan is in the parking lot, valeting his car. Poser. I have work to do."

Mia and Trent thanked him for his time and stood to leave. Nathan walked in just as they were walking out, and Mia felt the man's eyes on her. The mystery was over and a killer was on his way to being caught.

"Let's go have dinner. I want cake." Mia leaned over and kissed Trent. "It's time to celebrate life, not just solve murders."

"Who are you and where is Mia Malone?" Trent joked as they walked to his truck.

Chapter 23

The gym at the academy had been transformed into a magical woodland scene. Even though it was still cold and snowy outside, the area where the wedding guests sat appeared to be a sunny meadow on a perfect early summer day. White chairs with sprays of flowers were lined up on a patch of grass so green it looked fake but felt real, if a guest were to reach down to touch it. Jeani had gone all out on the decorations. The budget had been blown, but no one minded. It was a special day.

Mia was getting her hair done while the others in the room helped Christina into her dress. Her mother and Jessica had declined to attend this wedding, claiming that the Boise one would be their chance to celebrate with the bride. That wedding would be held tomorrow, delaying the happy couple's departure to Hawaii for the honeymoon by a day. Mia didn't think Christina minded. The girl loved all the ceremony around the wedding.

The bridal showers, the bachelorette party, the teas with all the parents and grandparents. Christina shone in the spotlight, and the babies were doing their best to make sure she didn't look five months pregnant until after the wedding. Having two ceremonies just made the event more magical. And she bought two dresses.

The hairdresser laid the wreath of baby's breath on top of Mia's head and started to pin it in so it wouldn't fall. She turned to her grandmother, sitting next to her in the other chair. "Are you sure it's not too much?"

"You look beautiful and special." Grans reached over and squeezed her hand. "I can't believe we are doing this."

"It makes sense. Christina has to get two of these done before she starts showing." Mia reached down to touch her own belly. "And with ours following along soon after, we need to get hitched before the secret comes out."

A few weeks after Nathan Boyle was arrested for killing Suzanne Parker, Mia had finally taken a test when she kept falling asleep during the day. She was pregnant. Not quite as far along as Christina, but close. The second test hadn't taken it out of her; the baby growing inside was draining her life force.

The baby let out a laugh. He or she wasn't letting Mia know their sex, but the bug did talk to her a lot. Like Gloria, they liked to talk in giggles.

Gloria had recently moved from songs to actual conversations, particularly when Mia was in the potions room practicing. She had created eight elixirs that Grans had approved for her to write down in her grimoire. One was a protection spell and the other the truth potion she'd used on Blake. She continued to use it off and on with her boss, just in case.

Fool me once.

"It's time to get down to the first floor," Finn called from the doorway. "The grooms are all upfront and getting antsy for the wedding march to start."

Mia stood and grabbed her grandmother's hand. Then she reached for Christina's. "Thanks for making this day special. To many years of wedded bliss for all of us."

"You're going to tax the Goddess's blessing," Grans said, but she was smiling. They walked over to the elevator as the rest of the group went down the stairs.

As they stepped out of the elevator, Finn got everyone situated. Grans would walk with James and go first. Then Christina would walk with Isaac, because her father hadn't come to this wedding. Finally Mia would walk with her dad. Her mom kissed her on the cheek before being sent out to be seated with an usher. Finn had everything in order.

Mia watched through the gym door opening as Grans walked up to the altar. Dorian helped her up the stairs and then kissed her as they separated to wait for the other couples. Three weddings was a lot, but the academy society didn't do anything small.

Just before Christina and Isaac left to walk the aisle, he turned to Mia. "I'm so glad you're happy. This is where you belong. I know that now."

Mia watched them walk out, and her dad leaned into her and asked, "Is it too late for me to punch him at the reception? I wouldn't hit him hard, but he needs to learn to read the room. This day is not about him."

"I love you, Daddy." Mia kissed him on the cheek and waited for Christina to be handed off to Levi at the altar. This day was perfect, and the joint honeymoon in Hawaii would be even better, even if she couldn't partake in fruity hard drinks. She had everything she ever wanted right here.

Buttercup, the library ghost cat, rubbed up against her leg, and Mia saw several of the library ghosts at the back of the gym, watching. They were here to celebrate as well. Mia could see Buddy looking in from a second-floor window, and Cerby was up on the altar with Trent. Mr. Darcy hissed at Buttercup to go back to the library ghosts, then sat next to Mia's large skirt. He'd come to walk her down the aisle as well.

Her world in Magic Springs might not be usual or normal, but it was hers. She loved it and all the people she'd added to her family. The vows she and Trent would take today would just seal the deal in others' eyes. They were already family. And that family would continue to grow as their lives expanded.

A new life was starting for Mia and her family. A new life with new adventures.

"Are you ready, dear?" her father asked as he moved her closer to the gym entrance. "Your new story awaits."

She turned and kissed him on the cheek. "I've never been more ready."

Acknowledgments

Mia Malone and her magical beginnings was one of the first books I wrote. I had this manuscript in the drawer for years, waiting for the right time. And when the publisher picked Mia over several other ideas, I was ecstatic to be able to write about my magical home state of Idaho. I've always felt like the mountains were where the magic started. Where magical creatures lived and watched us. Yes, I read a lot of fairy tales when I was growing up. I loved the way they all ended with the same sentence. *And they lived happily ever after.*

As always, big thanks to the Kensington crew, including Michaela and Cassidy in editorial and Larissa and Sofia in publicity. And as always, thanks to my agent, who always tells me the truth. Even when it hurts.

Recipe

Readers–

One of the first things I learned to bake in Mrs. Higgin's Freshman Home Ec class was muffins. I still love making them. They're an easy way to make a breakfast dessert that can use so many other ingredients. When I found the Costco muffins as a young mother with a career, I brought home a box every week. Especially the chocolate with chocolate chip ones.

I hope these fall muffins send you into a memory of good times or at least a tasty breakfast.

Hugs,

Lynn

Easy Pumpkin Muffins

Preheat oven to 375 degrees.

In a large bowl, combine all the ingredients except the flour. Whisk all the ingredients together until smooth.

1(15-ounce) can pumpkin purée
¾ cup granulated sugar
½ cup vegetable oil
2 large eggs

1 tablespoon pumpkin pie spice
1 teaspoon baking soda
1 teaspoon vanilla extract
½ teaspoon kosher salt

Add flour. Fold the flour into the batter until just combined and no dry streaks remain. DO NOT overmix. Your muffins will be tough.

1¾ cups all-purpose flour

Scoop the batter into the wells of a muffin pan and bake for 25–30 minutes or until a toothpick comes out clean from the middle of a muffin.

Let cool.

Over the moon for Lynn Cahoon? Turn the page for the first chapter of

CONFESSIONS OF AN AMATEUR SLEUTH

A Bainbridge Island Mystery, available now from Kensington Publishing Corp.

Chapter 1

Interviewing is a conversation, not an interrogation. Especially when you don't wear a badge.

Something was missing. Okay, a lot of things were missing. Meg Gates stared at the local authors' shelf as she stood at the front door of Island Books, her mother's bookstore. She'd made the display eye-catching, but the shelves were almost empty. Three weeks ago, her mom had promised she'd get Meg the list of books she'd been curating since she'd opened the shop. Right now, only L.C. Aster's books inhabited the bookcase. Of course, Lilly Aster, Meg's other boss, had been writing for years, so she had a lot of books to showcase.

Meg wanted to highlight other local authors as well. She typed out a text to her mom since her phone calls had gone unanswered that morning.

As she clicked "Send," the bell over the door alerted her to a customer. "Welcome to Island Books, may I help you?"

"Where's Mom?" Stephen "Junior" Gates beelined directly to the counter. "She usually works Tuesday mornings."

"Good morning to you." Meg rolled her eyes as she addressed her brother. Junior dressed like an accountant. Even on days off, he wore a polo shirt and chino shorts. He still worked for their dad at his accounting firm, and the job fit his personality. Junior liked his life orderly. "Why aren't you at work?"

"I take off the second Tuesday of every month to take Mom to Seattle for lunch. I called her when I got on the ferry this morning. But she hasn't answered." Junior tried to peek around Meg. "I guess she must have gotten my message since you're here to cover for her. Is she in the back?"

"One, it's not the second Tuesday, it's the first. And no, she's not here." Meg leaned back on the stool. "Funny, I haven't been able to reach her by phone this morning either. She emailed me on Monday with my hours for the week. She didn't explain, but I'm working the day shift on Tuesday, and then on Thursday I have the entire day from open to close. She said I could close when it got slow Thursday night. Maybe she has appointments this week."

Junior seemed to analyze the information as he read the back of a memoir of an English prime minister that a customer had left unpurchased on the register counter. "But that doesn't explain her not picking up her phone. And why would she have appointments on two different days? You don't think she's sick, do you?"

"I saw her Sunday at church. She looked okay." Meg thought about how her mom had acted that day. She'd eaten her entire lunch at the restaurant and even ordered dessert. Something Mom never did. "She even had a tan."

"So you think it's just a checkup?" Junior set the book down. "I wish she'd called me back so I wouldn't have wasted a ferry ticket."

"You were already heading here when you—" Meg started but then stopped. Explaining to Junior that the world didn't work on his schedule was a waste of breath. She watched as he pulled his phone out and started texting someone. "So why did you come this week and not next week anyway?"

Junior's face turned red.

"Junior?" Now Meg was curious. Her older brother had always been the steady one. Meanwhile, Meg had been a three-time loser—she failed to finish college, then the tech startup she'd joined went bankrupt, and, of course, her wedding was canceled due to her fiancé's lack of understanding of the definition of the word *faithful*. Meg had returned to Bainbridge Island to live in an apartment over her aunt's garage and work at her mom's bookstore. Junior, on the other hand, had finished his degree and gone to work for their father in Bellevue at his accounting firm. She loved her family, but she hated that she was always seen as the needy one.

He kept his gaze on his phone. "I've got plans next week."

"Plans. At work?" Meg noticed he'd turned even

redder. When he didn't answer, she asked again, "What plans?"

"I'm going to a conference in San Francisco if you must know, nosy." He looked up and met her gaze. "Are you happy? Or do you need the rest of my schedule?"

"Why are you blushing about a conference?" Meg searched his face for clues. "Unless you're going with a woman. Don't tell me you're dating someone at Dad's firm. Please don't let it be your secretary."

Now Junior's face turned scarlet. "We don't have secretaries anymore. We have assistants. Besides, I'm not Dad. Anne works in corporate accounts. She's an accountant. We've only been dating for a few weeks. We'll be staying in separate rooms. Now can we stop the third degree?"

Meg felt bad about bringing up their father. His new wife, Elaine, had been his secretary, but they both claimed that the relationship had changed from work friends to something romantic only after the divorce. Meg wanted to believe him, but he'd been the first of her parents to start dating. Mom still hadn't gone out with anyone. At least as far as Meg knew.

She realized Junior was watching her. "I'm sorry. I shouldn't have brought Dad into the conversation. So, Anne, huh? She's an accountant and what else? Is she from Seattle? What does she look like? Is she nice?"

The door to the shop opened and with the bell's announcement, Dalton walked into the shop. "Hey Junior, are you ready?"

"What's going on?" Meg looked from Junior to Dalton. The two men had been friends since middle school.

"Mom's not here so I checked in with Dalton to see if he had time for lunch." He picked up the memoir again. "Put this on my account. Tell Mom I'll call her later. When you see her."

Watson, Meg's tan cocker spaniel, had roused himself from his morning nap and started circling Dalton for attention.

Dalton leaned down and gave the excited pup head rubs. Then Dalton looked up at Meg. "Do you need me to take him out before we leave?"

"Would you?" Meg glanced at her watch. "He's been asleep for almost three hours now. I'm sure he needs a walk."

"Sure. And do you want me to bring you something back from the restaurant for lunch?" Dalton walked over and grabbed Watson's leash from behind the counter.

Junior groaned as he perched on the edge of the couch. "You've been spending too much time here with my sister. Her dog loves you and you know where everything is."

"Maybe you've just been spending too little time here." Dalton stood and headed to the door. "I'll bring him back in a few and you can answer my lunch question."

"No lunch," Meg said as a group of tourists came into the bookstore. "I'm going to a writers' meeting this evening over at Island Diner. I brought a lunch."

"I'll come with you," Junior declared as he followed Dalton out the door. "Just tell Mom I was here."

"When I see her," Meg muttered, then she smiled at a woman walking toward her. "What can I help you with?"

When Dalton brought back Watson, she had a line of customers at the register. He tucked the leash back under the counter as the dog headed to his water dish to refill. "Junior's waiting for me at Island Diner. Do you need me to stay?"

She handed a credit card receipt and a bag to the customer she'd been helping. "No, I'm good, but thanks for taking him out."

"My pleasure," Dalton responded as he made his way out of the shop.

The next customer watched Dalton leave, then handed Meg her card after she'd rung up the book purchase. "Your boyfriend's cute and thoughtful. You need to keep that one."

Meg smiled as she ran the card. She turned the screen toward the customer for her signature. "Dalton's not my boyfriend."

"Oh?" The woman turned and looked out the window where Dalton had disappeared seconds before. "Does he know that?"

Mom hadn't called back by the time Meg needed to close the shop. She could get dinner at the meeting, but she couldn't take Watson inside the restaurant. She needed to take him home and feed him. And turn on his favorite movie.

Yes, her dog was spoiled. But he was also good company and kept Meg from talking to herself. She'd found him on a rescue website one day and had gone down to the shelter the same day to adopt him. She did one thing right—take care of her dog.

By the time she got back into town, the meeting had started. She grabbed a waitress and gave her order, then sat down at the back of the banquet room to wait for food while she listened to the presenter.

A man leaned over and held out his hand. "Hi, I'm Lee Anderson. I'm a freelance food writer."

Meg leaned closer so she could lower her voice. "Meg Gates. I guess I'm a nonfiction crime writer. I'm working on my first book. Who's talking today?"

"That's Crissy Lorde. She writes cozy mysteries and she's talking about her experience self-publishing versus the more traditional route." He held up his notebook to show Meg. The page was empty except for the date that Lee had written on the right corner. "I'd share my notes, but so far, I've got nothing. She's just talking about her own journey in writing. But she promised ten comparisons between the two options sometime tonight. The way she's going, we might be here until midnight by the time she hits number ten."

Meg suppressed a giggle. The speakers at the writers' group ranged from people who were just there to sell their book to professional writers like L. C. Aster, who'd come to talk to the group about her thrillers last month. Meg was Lilly's author assistant and had recently told her boss that she was trying to write a nonfiction book about solving mysteries. Lilly had suggested that Meg join the local writing group to meet other writers and learn about the industry.

Writing a book was harder than Meg had imagined. Sometimes she felt like she had control of the nonfiction book about how to become your own Nancy Drew. Sometimes she thought the book was controlling her. The good part of the process was that it gave her an inside look at what authors like Lilly went through when creating the product. The bad part was she felt like an imposter a lot of the time. Lilly's advice. One page at a time. Don't look back until it's done, then you can see if it works or not.

Meg was beginning to think the "or not" advice was what eventually would happen. But she was going to finish it, mostly because she was tired of changing lanes when things got hard. Whether or not it eventually sold was out of her hands. But she could help it along. Like by attending and learning from the local writers. Which was why she was here tonight.

This presenter may not have been worth the time to attend the meeting, but as her mother always said, "You get what you get and you don't throw a fit." Besides, Meg could probably find at least one tidbit in the talk to get her excited about writing.

Apparently, Lee Anderson hadn't had the same upbringing. He pulled out his phone and started scrolling through his emails. He looked over at Meg when her food was delivered. "Wake me when she's done."

Meg had finished eating when the speaker finished her presentation. Crissy *had* presented them with ten comparisons, and Meg had written them down, wondering if her amateur investigation book would be appropriate for self-publishing. She wanted the book in bookstores. And that meant an agent and a publisher.

Lilly had read the first chapter of Meg's guidebook and told her it was promising, so at least one person thought she might be on the right track. Besides, she wasn't going to worry until she finished the book. She took notes on marketing ideas and wrote down any editors who seemed to be accepting queries in her area. But she was mostly there for the hour of sprint writing and the happy hour afterward. She'd already met several nonfiction writers and they'd been friendly. She just hadn't made any new friends. Yet.

The group transitioned into a quick write-in. Thirty minutes of uninterrupted writing. Meg opened her laptop and got busy.

Lee found her again during the happy hour. "Did you get any words?"

"Four hundred new words and a chapter read and tweaked. I swear, every time I look at a page, I find a typo or something I want to say differently. Does the editing ever stop?" Meg sipped her wine as she scanned the group. Crissy was still holding court over by the bar talking about how she published.

"That's why I write for local papers. I have a deadline, so once it's out of my hands, I'm done. I can't play with it forever. So many people go over the first three chapters of a project and never move on. I'd love to write a book someday. Maybe like Anthony Bourdain, an exposé on the state of restaurants in the Pacific Northwest." Lee shrugged and looked around the room. "Someday, I guess."

"I don't know about Someday," Meg said.

Lee turned toward her, a frown narrowing his eyes. "What?"

"There's Monday, Tuesday, Wednesday . . ." She tapped her fingers as she listed off the days of the week. "And it all ends with Sunday and starts over. But Someday? I've never heard of it."

"Okay, fine. You got me. I need to just shut up and do it. Like in the Nike ads." He grinned and finished his beer. "I've got to catch the ferry, but I like you, Gates. Why don't you come with me to dinner tomorrow night? I'm reviewing a local restaurant. But we can't let them know that's why I'm there. You can be my cover. No one ever expects a food critic to have a sidekick. And we can talk more about writing nonfiction. I've got a few contacts you might want to interview. And my paper will buy your dinner."

"Sounds good." Meg glanced at her watch. She had a new project from Lilly she needed to start tonight. Especially since now she wouldn't be home tomorrow night. "I'll meet you at the restaurant. Which one and what time?"

He opened his phone. "My reservation is for eight at the Local Crab. Do you know it?"

"Yeah, I've met the chef before. Maybe I'm not a good sidekick for this one." Meg hoped Lee didn't have a reputation for trashing restaurants.

"Don't be silly. You're perfect. I'm just a friend from Seattle. He'll never suspect anything, and I can get a clear reading on the meal without them trying to impress me." He snapped a picture of her as she was taking a drink. He laughed at her widened eyes. "I like to remember where I meet people. That way I don't forget their names. Although you seem pretty unforgettable."

Meg shook her head. "No sweet-talking your writing partner. This is just about writing. I'm not looking for a relationship."

"Good, because I'm not either. I just got out of a long-term relationship a few months ago, and my head is still not clear from her games. So we're just friends, right?" He scanned the room as he talked.

"Exactly." Meg finished her wine and set her glass on the counter. "I've got to run. Watson is probably waiting for me."

"Oh, so there's a boyfriend?" Lee called after her.

She shrugged and headed out the door. If Lee was looking for something more, Watson would keep him from misinterpreting her agreeing to go to dinner. She liked Lee, as a possible friend. Besides, one of the rules of investigating was to find out more about others, not give out all your personal information. It was a skill she was still working on.

Meg didn't want to be an open book. Especially when she was working on an investigation, she needed to learn to be more invisible. It said so in her book.

As she left Island Diner, a small blonde waved at her. Meg waved but didn't go back inside.

She'd practice her casual interviewing skills on Lee tomorrow night. Maybe she'd find out more about the food critic. And he could be her second writing friend. Lilly Aster was her first. Even if the famous author didn't know they were friends.

Meg was playing the long game.

She was almost home when she realized who had waved at her as she left the meeting. Irene Olsen. The cruise salesperson who she'd been avoiding since she'd had coffee with her months ago.

The woman was relentless. As Meg hurried up the stairs, her phone buzzed with what was probably the first of many messages she'd get from Irene.

This day wasn't turning out to be one of Meg's favorites.

Visit our website at
KensingtonBooks.com
to sign up for our newsletters, read more from your favorite authors, see books by series, view reading group guides, and more!

BOOK CLUB
BETWEEN THE CHAPTERS

Become a Part of Our
Between the Chapters Book Club
Community and Join the Conversation

Betweenthechapters.net

Submit your book review for a chance to win exclusive Between the Chapters swag you can't get anywhere else!
https://www.kensingtonbooks.com/pages/review/